A LOVE
for All Seasons

BETTYE GRIFFIN

A LOVE
for All Seasons

ARABESQUE®

A LOVE FOR ALL SEASONS

ISBN-13: 978-0-373-83010-7
ISBN-10:   0-373-83010-6

www.kimanipress.com

Printed in U.S.A.

For Anecia, whose life is just beginning.
May it be a long and happy one.

Acknowledgments

Bernard: still crazy after all these years. Even when you bring out homicidal urges in me, I love you madly.

Mom: still kicking at eighty-eight. I want to be just like you if I am fortunate enough to receive the gift of longevity.

Aunt Weenie and Cousin Teddy: still kicking at ninety.

Uncle Chester: still kicking at eighty-five.

Pops and Aunt Micki, because I wish you were still here.

Beverly Griffin Love, Dorothy Clowers Lites, Lillian Morton Walton, sister and cousins.

Kimberly Rowe-Van Allen, you do such a great job pre-editing my books before submission (a service more important now than ever before!). You've got a sharper eye than many professionals. I only wish your schedule had permitted you to look at this entire manuscript. (Be sure to put down your editing pen while your read the finished product.)

LaVerne Caples, Velma Jones, Cheryl Warren, Shaemia Newsome and Karine Smith: thanks for reading my books…and for making Illinois a little less chilly.

The unofficial Dyslipidemia Reading Group at Abbott Labs: Marie Wilson, who actually *read* my book *One on One;* and Maureen Kelly, Noreen Travers and Dawn Carlson for their good intentions/plans to read it.

The Westchester homegirls: Dorothy Hicks-Terry,
Sheila Tyler, Rebecca West Ogiste,
Sharon McDaniel Hollis, Beverly Brown,
Karleen Burke, Barbara Qualls, Lillian Tyee,
Jackie Moore, Carolyn Harmon Crute.
Your ongoing support has been overwhelming,
and I am truly humbled by it.

Terry Clements: it was fab to see you again.
I still can't believe little Monet is married and Lauren
is so grown up! How come *we* don't look eighteen years
older…or do we?

Jacqueline McGuggins of Waldenbooks in Yonkers,
New York: for agreeing to host a signing. I hope we
weren't too raucous.

Glen Hoftetter of the Book Nook in Jacksonville, Florida:
for hosting the virtual signings I used to do when I lived
there and for being an all-around great guy.

Loyal readers everywhere: I can't tell you how much
I appreciate you all.

Since the heroine of this book is named Alicia,
I must mention the Alicias in my life: my niece,
Alisha Griffin Baez, and my second-generation cousin,
Alicia Morton Coates. I've witnessed both of you grow
from pigtailed little girls to women with families of your
own. I'm very proud of both of you.

Bettye Griffin
Gurnee, Illinois
Winter 2006-2007

Chapter 1

I Just Saw a Face

As he left the restaurant Jack held the door open for a woman who entered. Suddenly, his mouth fell open.

Never before had he seen anyone so lovely.

She smiled in that impersonal way people tend to when they really don't notice you. "Thank you," she said in a low-pitched voice he found incredibly sexy. She dashed through the entrance, the memory of her face etched in his mind.

It had been an enjoyable evening, even before he arrived at the restaurant. The warm early June weather made moving about the city a pleasant experience. How kind of his old college roommate, Pete Robinson, and

Pete's wife Rhonda to insist on taking him to dinner after his round of interviews and before his return flight to Birmingham. The human resources department at his prospective employer had kindly honored his request to be put on an evening return flight to Birmingham to give him some time to spend with his friends.

Truth be told, Jack couldn't really pinpoint his exact location in Manhattan, but the low rise apartment buildings with retailers and restaurants on the ground floors told him he had ventured beyond the tall buildings of the business district, or, as they called it in New York, midtown.

Judging by how well things went this afternoon, he expected to be offered the director position he'd interviewed for after a round of phone interviews plus a series of face-to-face meetings with key personnel. Funny how his sixth sense had never failed him in this regard. He'd always correctly predicted whether a job offer was forthcoming. But he wouldn't start packing until the offer had been made and he'd accepted.

Jack's own father had worked in the steel mills of Birmingham, Alabama, for decades. Things had certainly changed in a generation. Jack had changed jobs several times in the nearly fifteen years since college, nor would his contemporaries likely spend their entire careers at the same company until retirement.

If everything worked out, he anticipated easily finding his way around the city before too long once he made the move here. It certainly seemed a lot busier than Birmingham, which, despite several relocations over the years, he still considered home.

"It's really good to see you two again, guys," he said to Pete and Rhonda. Then he laughed as he made a sweeping gesture with his right hand. "And it's nice to meet all of you." Originally he met Pete at his office in midtown after his interviews, and the two of them took the subway up to a Cuban restaurant, where Rhonda met them. She promptly announced that a friend of hers was coming to join them, but not until after they'd had a chance to have a good talk with just the three of them.

While they ate she explained that she'd mentioned her dinner plans to a few other people, who said they might pop in later. The others who came all ordered food, and it amused Jack that an impromptu meal between three old friends could end up with such a large group sharing a table.

That was how it started. Now, nearly an hour after he finished his meal and sat leisurely sipping sangria, no less than seven people sat around a makeshift rectangular table, made up of two tables pushed together.

In the midst of the chatter going on around him, Jack surveyed the restaurant. He supposed that similar scenes took place at restaurants all over Manhattan, as the work crowd left the office and met friends for dinner and drinks.

Fortunately, the restaurant wasn't overly crowded on this spring evening, so they could literally sit there for hours, the sangria flowing as freely and easily as the conversation.

Rhonda laughed. "If you're going to be living here, we want you to meet all our friends," she said. "You won't be lonely, believe me."

"Speaking of friends, Rhonda, where's Alicia?" Pete asked.

"She didn't answer her cell, so I left her a message. I hope she can make it. She hasn't called back, so I don't know."

"Do you suppose she went up to her mother's?"

"She didn't say anything about it. And she wouldn't go on a Wednesday unless something really bad happened." Rhonda twisted her lower lip as she considered this possibility. "I did say we'd only be here until about seven-thirty."

Jack glanced at his watch. "It's ten to seven now. I guess I'd better get going."

"What time is your flight, Jack?" one of Rhonda's friends asked.

"Eight-thirty. We're not that far from LaGuardia, are we?"

The airport was perhaps a twenty-minute taxi ride, said someone sitting next to him.

"Ask the hostess to get you a cab," Pete advised.

Within five minutes the hostess informed Jack that his cab was waiting for him. He rose and said thanks and goodbye to Pete. The two had been best buddies through their college years at Fisk. And although in recent years they barely kept in touch, they'd never completely lost contact.

Since graduation, Jack's career as a graphic artist had taken him first to Galveston and then to Houston before he decided he wanted to return to Alabama. Pete, on the other hand, had headed straight to New York, armed with a degree in chemistry. He'd met Rhonda there, the two fell in love, and four years ago they married in a destination wedding on St. Croix. They seemed so happy, and Jack couldn't help feeling a little envious. His friend had a loving wife to go home to after work…he had no one.

He had managed to rack up a series of failed relationships, their endings all rooted in silly stuff that wouldn't be important enough to do in a relationship of any substance. He'd heard that the older and more set in their ways a person became, the more difficult it was to put someone else first. His mother always reassured him, telling him that when he met Miss Right he would know it. Jack personally didn't put much faith in that scenario. It took more than merely meeting a woman to know she was the one he'd been waiting for.

After giving Rhonda a farewell kiss on the cheek and waving to the rest of his table-mates, he headed for the door and his fateful encounter. He took one last glance at his surroundings. Nothing about the restaurant's decor jumped out as being special, but he liked it, with its flavorful cuisine and no-fuss atmosphere. A real neighborhood restaurant, with many of its tables occupied by people of all sorts of ethnic backgrounds, including Afro-Hispanics speaking fluent Spanish. Now, that was a sight you didn't see much of in Birmingham.

Nor was a woman so exquisitely beautiful as the one who passed him by.

He turned and stared at the woman's back after she passed through the door. The view from that angle was equally appealing. She wore a tailored cotton shirt with a wool tweed blazer and jeans. A small leather shoulder bag hung at her side. Her hair hung in an asymmetrical side-parted bob that grazed her shoulder on one side and was even with her chin on the other.

He longed for another look at her beautiful face, but she didn't turn around. Instead, apparently looking for someone, she moved to her right, her head turning from left to right and her hair bouncing as she searched for her dinner partner. Then a honking horn jerked him back to reality and the taxi double parked outside.

Reluctantly, he let the door close and stepped into the street. He crossed the wide sidewalk and got into the back seat of the yellow taxi. "LaGuardia Airport," he told the driver.

Inside the restaurant, unbeknownst to Jack, the woman, upon spotting a familiar face, rushed up to Rhonda's table and hugged her warmly. "I'm glad you guys are still here. I ran all the way."

"We weren't sure how long we should wait," Rhonda said. "But now that you're here, we aren't going anywhere." She indicated the empty chair opposite her. "You can sit next to Pete. His friend just left."

Pete signaled. "Waiter. Another pitcher of sangria." He turned to the woman. "Will that work for you, Alicia?"

"Sure."

He grinned at her. "Don't want to try a Tequila Sunrise tonight, huh?"

She winked; her ability to nurse one glass of wine for

hours on end was legendary in their circle. "No, not tonight. Maybe next time."

Jack settled into his leather Business Class seat. He accepted a complimentary Scotch and soda and reclined. His thoughts went to the woman at the restaurant. He knew it made no sense for him to waste time thinking about someone he'd never see again, and it surprised him that he kept thinking about her. Again he thought of what his mother always said about him being able to recognize the right woman when he met her.

Except he'd only seen her, not actually met her…and the odds were against him ever seeing her again, much less meeting her.

Chapter 2

I Saw Her Standing There

Alicia nearly gasped when she opened the door and saw him. She felt a jolt rush straight through her chest to her back, immediately followed by a sense of exhilaration, like she'd been pushed out of an airplane and was free falling in the few key seconds before inflating a parachute.

Her friend Rhonda Robinson had asked if it would be okay if she brought someone along to the party, her husband Pete's college roommate who was new in town and didn't know many people. Alicia had said sure, but for some reason she'd expected some nerdy type with glasses. She hadn't expected this tall, well-built man whose navy sports coat seemed tailor-made for him, and who appeared to be fresh from the barber's chair. My, my, my....

The moment she opened the door Jack felt thunderstruck. He could hardly believe it, but it was *her,* the same woman he'd glimpsed in the restaurant last spring, when he came to New York to meet the company brass face-to-face. Four months had passed since then. Spring had long since given way to summer, and now even the last vestige of that season had become a memory to savor until next year, going out with the annual Indian summer of unseasonably warm temperatures in mid-October. The air now held a hint of the cold weather that was to come. Last spring he'd only seen her for a moment, but he'd never forgotten her. He didn't realize she was a friend of Rhonda's, never even thought of the possibility. No new arrivals had joined them in the last hour, and while he had a vague memory of Pete and Rhonda discussing the possibility of another friend of theirs joining them, he didn't think it would happen, not that long after their meal ended.

"Oh, where are my manners?" Rhonda exclaimed. "Alicia Timberlake, Jack Devlin."

Alicia promptly held out her hand. No one must know the effect he had on her. "Hello, Jack. Welcome." She kept her expression impassive as he swallowed her hand with his and shook it firmly.

"Thank you, Alicia," he said. "Glad to be here."

"Jack's new in town," Rhonda explained. "He's from Birmingham."

"Really," Alicia said, falling into step beside him

as they moved into the apartment. "What brings you to New York?"

"Work. I just accepted a new position."

He had a way of looking at her, directly, yet simultaneously roaming over her body, that struck her as almost too sexy to bear. It left her mouth dry, like she had a mouthful of sand. She struggled to keep up her end of the conversation. He'd just stated that he accepted a job here, but she felt it would be too forward to ask what he did. "How do you like it here?" she asked instead.

"I'm still learning my way around," he admitted. "It's different from what I'm used to, but I like it. And it's nice to know at least two people here. Pete and I went to college together. Fisk University." Jack frowned when someone called out to Alicia and she excused herself with a light touch on his forearm. He wished he could escort her into a corner and have her tell him all about herself.

Instead he went to the buffet, which had been set up on top of an attractive painted Bombay chest near the door, and helped himself to barbecued chicken drumettes, cheese puffs, meatballs and potato salad. He quickly joined Pete in a conversation with another man as they munched, keeping an eye on the whereabouts of Alicia all the while.

She mingled with her guests, looking chic in a long-sleeved off-white cable sweater that covered her hips, wool slacks the same color, and brown suede pumps. She'd brushed her hair back and applied a leopard print headband. He admired the way she moved easily between pockets of people, always with a cheerful word. He could barely tear his eyes away from her.

Not wanting anyone to notice him staring at her, Jack forced himself to check out her apartment instead. Rhonda described their destination as "a party at a friend's studio." He knew one-room apartments existed, but never knew anyone who actually lived in one. He always imagined studios as claustrophobic little rooms with perhaps one window, but this *L*-shaped apartment seemed plenty large enough for one person to live in, even with fifteen people milling about. The outside wall—the bottom of the *L*—contained two sets of double windows, one at each end, with a Pullman kitchen neatly tucked into the opposite side. Between the kitchen and the window sat a small oblong cloth-covered table with rounded edges, holding an ice bucket, glasses, cocktail napkins, a large bottle of white Zinfadel, a half-dozen or so seven-ounce bottles of beer, and a tall martini pitcher.

The joint of the *L* had been set up as a sitting area, with a small sofa, coffee table, and two compact rounded back chairs. The apartment seemed to have everything, despite its small size.

Well, almost everything. Jack's eyes narrowed in thought as he realized there didn't appear to be a bed. He decided the sofa must open up.

There might not be a visible bed, but guests had a variety of choices for seating. In addition to the corner sitting area, two matching oval-shaped chairs flanked a small maple wood Parsons table in the corner by the bar. Also, an odd-looking, oversize European-looking couch, reminiscent of the days of King Arthur and Queen Guinivere with its high wooden sides, stood opposite the Bombay chest near the entrance to the apartment.

Jack finished his finger food and moved toward the kitchen, where he tossed the plate in the white plastic trash bin. He turned to see Alicia brush past him, watching with unabashed interest as she lifted a bag of ice from the sink and filled the brass ice bucket.

Possibly feeling his eyes on her, she looked up and smiled at him. "Finding everything all right?"

"Yes, I am, thank you."

"Can I get you a drink?" she offered as she approached where he stood.

"Yes, I'd like that. What do you have?"

"Just the basics. Wine, beer, soda, and the drink of the evening, which, by popular demand, is a Kamikaze. It's in the pitcher." She noted his surprised expression. "I'm afraid I'm a no-fuss hostess. I find that if I fix just one cocktail I can mix it up in advance and not have to worry about constantly replenishing this liquor or that mixer." With a boldness that came from nowhere, she raised her lips toward his ear and lowered her voice. "Confidentially, when the drinks are pre-mixed as opposed to letting guests fix their own, the liquor goes a lot further."

He liked having her stand so close to him. How nice it would be to imagine her whispering something much more intimate than what she'd just shared with him. He felt his arousal form and kept his voice even. "I imagine it would. And I think that's very wise."

She took a deep breath. Somehow—she didn't know why—it mattered that Jack Devlin thought well of her.

"Would you believe I've never had a Kamikaze? I don't even know what's in it."

"It's pretty simple. Vodka, triple sec and lime juice, all in equal parts." She hoped she wasn't talking too much, but he did ask. From the moment she saw Jack Devlin standing outside her door she felt ill at ease, like she didn't belong in her own skin.

All Alicia's friends admired her hostess skills. They said she always knew the right thing to say, even to complete strangers. But something about this particular stranger made her nervous as a flickering flame. What could it be?

Surely not his looks, which were undeniably well above average, but hardly extraordinary in a city where a woman could barely walk down a city block without passing someone who looked like he belonged on the cover of *GQ*. Jack had a nice rugged look about him, which she preferred over the pretty boys, with a medium brown complexion, sturdy build, perhaps four or five inches taller than her own five-seven, and close cropped haircut, brushed forward, framing expressive brown eyes. Unlike many African-American men, he was clean shaven, and she thought she spotted a smattering of gray at his hairline and in his sideburns. He was quite attractive, but she saw good-looking men all the time and conversed with them without her tongue feeling too big for her mouth, so that clearly wasn't the reason for her unease. Her hands with their manicured fingernails felt awkward. As she picked up the tongs that rested on the ice bucket, it relieved her to have something to do.

To her embarrassment, Alicia had difficulty grasping ice with the tongs; the cubes kept falling out. She laughed to cover her nervousness as she tried repeatedly.

"Why don't you let me do that?" he offered.

Finally she managed to hold the cubes long enough to drop them into a highball glass. "No, that's all right. I've got it, Dev." She gasped. Where had *that* come from? She'd just overlooked his first name and shortened his surname, and she hardly knew him well enough to be giving him a nickname.

Or did she? Could that be it? Had she met Jack Devlin at some time in the past? When? And if she had, why didn't she remember?

Jack grinned. No one had ever called him "Dev" before. He didn't know how he would feel if it came from anyone else, but coming from Alicia Timberlake he liked it. It gave the impression that he was special to her. A ridiculous notion for someone he'd just met, to be sure, but an appealing one nonetheless. He'd like to be special to her.

"I'm so sorry," she said. "I don't know what made me say that."

"Don't apologize."

She handed him the glass and managed to get ice cubes into a glass for herself. Maybe if she had a Kamikaze instead of ice water it would help her nerves.

"So," she said, careful not to call him by name lest she use the wrong one, "how does New York compare with Birmingham?"

"Actually, they're not all that different. I mean, Birmingham is a city. We have tall buildings downtown, just like any other city. And every place has the same services. Restaurants, bars, book stores, dry cleaners, McDonald's. I've also lived in Galveston and Houston." He shrugged. "I guess you can say I move around a lot."

"Have you been to New York before? You look familiar to me somehow." If she could just figure out where she'd seen him it would all come back to her, and she could deal with it…whatever it was.

"Uh…I was here the second week of June." He didn't know if he should confess that he remembered seeing her then, not when she so obviously didn't notice him. In an instant he made up his mind. "I did see you during that visit, but just in passing, up at that Cuban restaurant here on the Upper West Side." He now knew enough about Manhattan geography to pinpoint the section of the city he had eaten in that day, which wasn't far from Alicia's apartment. "You came in as I was leaving. I held the door for you and cast you an admiring look, but I really didn't know you were coming to join Pete and Rhonda." Again he chuckled. "Although I don't know why I didn't figure that out, since the size of our little group had already doubled."

She looked embarrassed. "I'm afraid I don't remember. I was in a rush that day, trying to catch Rhonda before she left."

"I didn't expect you to remember me. But that's the only time I saw you. Believe me, I would never forget you."

Warmth spread to her nose and cheeks, and she didn't even try to hide her pleasure. "Well, thank you. But I was thinking in terms of something more than just passing by. I—" She broke off, realizing it wouldn't do to tell him that his presence unnerved her, but it did. She raised the highball glass to her lips and took a sip. Anything to steady her shaking hands.

"Alicia, the pitcher of Kamikaze is running low. Can I help you mix some more?" her friend Jenny offered.

"Oh, no thanks, I'll take care of it." She turned to Jack, glad to have an excuse to get away from him. Being around him was simply too unsettling. Her stomach continued to behave like a contestant in an Olympics gymnastic competition, running and flipping all over the place. She couldn't take much more of this. "Excuse me."

As she hurried toward the kitchen she said a silent prayer of thanks that the Kamikaze drink continued to be so popular among her guests. Mixing up a fresh batch gave her the perfect excuse to get away from Jack Devlin.

She concentrated on his name as she carefully measured the three ingredients. *Jack Devlin, Jack Devlin.* Where had she seen him before? And what had transpired between them? It had to be something major, or else she wouldn't be acting like such a fool. But why couldn't she remember? And why didn't he?

She stirred the liquors and lime juice together in the tall martini pitcher. "Here, I'll take that," Pete Robinson said with a laugh.

"Ready for a refill, are you, Pete?" she said knowingly as she handed him the pitcher. She smiled as he immediately filled his glass.

Alicia's preference would have been to stay away from Jack Devlin until she identified their past history, but she knew that made for a poor hostess. Her friends brought him to her party because he didn't know anyone in town. The least she could do was introduce him around.

She found him standing with his plate near the buffet

table, exchanging a few words of small talk with her old friend Derek Taylor. "Have you two met each other?" she inquired.

"Not really," Jack said. He wiped his right hand on a napkin and held it out. "Jack Devlin."

"Derek Taylor."

"Jack's a good friend of Pete and Rhonda," Alicia explained as the two men shook hands. "He just moved to New York from Alabama."

Derek grinned. "A little faster paced than what you're used to, huh?"

Alicia tried not to glare at him. Derek was one of her closest friends, but she didn't like the smugness in his tone that suggested Jack was some kind of country bumpkin. Birmingham was one of the largest cities in the Deep South, and only New York, L.A., and Chicago boasted of larger populations than Houston.

But Jack didn't seem to mind, nor did he elaborate on his background. "A little too fast for me, actually," he admitted. "I work in midtown, but when it came time to find a place to live I decided to get a place up in Stamford."

Derek nodded. "Nice town." He then turned to someone walking past and began a conversation with them.

Alicia smiled at Jack, thankful for the drink in her hand and the calming effect of the alcohol. She had a nice warm feeling that started in her belly and branched out to the rest of her. "Have you met many people here?"

"Probably not by name, but everyone's very friendly."

"Shame on Pete for leaving you on your own. Here, let me take you around." She slipped her arm through his, telling herself he was just another friend of a friend, and that she had no need to feel nervous as she tried to make him comfortable. And thank heavens for the thick fabric of her sweater and for the blazer he wore. Her gesture seemed less personal with no skin-to-skin contact.

She led him to the nearest person, who stood at the buffet fixing a plate. "Jenny Walters, this is—" she stopped momentarily to make sure she said his name correctly "—Jack Devlin." She stood by as Jack and Jenny greeted each other.

They moved on, and he said, "You know, you really don't have to do this. But I must admit I like having you on my arm."

A wave of pleasure swept over her. Damn her memory for failing her. She felt certain that Jack Devlin was somehow linked to her past, but had absolutely no recollection of any other details. She'd never been to Birmingham, nor had she ever traveled to either of the other two Southern cities he mentioned as former residences. But from the way he affected her, she suspected that whatever happened between them had significance.

She raised her glass to her mouth and took another gulp. Funny, but since she'd started drinking this Kamikaze, the missing link between her and Jack didn't seem to matter as much. If Jack didn't remember her other than that one quick glimpse at the restaurant last spring, maybe she shouldn't worry about not remembering him.

"I want you to find New Yorkers friendly and outgoing," she said warmly. "I can't have you calling home and reporting that we're just as callous as the press makes us out to be."

Eventually they had covered the twenty or so people

now in the apartment, including Pete, who spoke with another couple, and Rhonda, who they encountered in the kitchenette with another female guest, Alicia suspected indulging in gossip.

"I'm so sorry, Jack," Rhonda said. "I guess Pete and I should have taken you through the room instead of leaving it up to Alicia."

"Oh, that's all right," she said graciously. "By now Dev and I are old friends." She gasped, then looked at him in distress. "I did it again. Why do I keep calling you that?"

He shrugged. "Maybe it's because you already know someone named Jack that you don't like very much?"

What is this, Freud? she thought, instantly dismissing his theory. But to scoff at his suggestion would be rude, so she merely said, "Maybe, although no one I can think of. Excuse me."

At the bar Alicia poured herself another Kamikaze. She'd probably spent enough time in the company of Jack Devlin, who seemed to bring out the very worst in her. Instead she'd better relax and enjoy her other friends, some of whom she hadn't seen in many weeks. Her mother's heart disease had worsened in recent months to the point where she was now largely bedridden. Alicia had been spending evenings with her in Connecticut, commuting by train into the city. Now that her mother had stabilized, Alicia felt it safe enough to spend one evening in her apartment. Tomorrow she would grab a train north and spend the remainder of the weekend at her mother's bedside.

The appearance of Jack Devlin—the stranger who somehow didn't seem like a stranger—unnerved her to the point where she couldn't really relax. Maybe if she knew where she'd met him or what suppressed memories she had of him, she could better cope with the situation. But nothing came to her, which she found terribly frustrating, in spite of her attempts not to be concerned about it.

She sipped on her drink. Funny, she'd never been much of a drinker, but tonight she drank like the answer to her questions could be found at the bottom of a bottle of triple sec.

She knew the reason for her atypical behavior stood just a few feet away, talking with her other guests.

Chapter 3

I Don't Want To Spoil the Party

By ten o'clock, when the guests started leaving, Alicia sensed she had put away one Kamikaze too many, courtesy of an odd weightless feeling she knew hadn't come from anything on the buffet table.

"Alicia, dear, it was a lovely party," Rhonda said. "But then again, you always entertain so effortlessly. I don't know how you do it. I'll bet you put in a full day at work today."

"I left at three."

Rhonda turned to Jack. "Can you believe that? She worked practically the whole day and still manages to put on a great party. She ought to write a how-to book.

Whenever Pete and I have people over I'm always still in the kitchen when the guests arrive, even if I've had all day to prepare."

"Nuttin' to it."

Rhonda looked at her strangely. "Alicia, are you all right? You sound a little tipsy."

"Ahm awright." Her voice sounded strange to her own ears, and what the hell happened to her enunciation?

"Whoa!" Pete said. "Since when do you get a buzz on?"

Even through the alcohol-induced fuzziness, Alicia felt Jack's intense gaze. She made a special effort to form her words distinctly. "I'm fine. Really."

"Pete, why don't you and I stick around and help Alicia put the food away?" Rhonda suggested.

Jack turned to look at the buffet, where only a few stray hors d'oeuvres remained. "I don't think it'll take more than a minute or two to put what's left in the fridge. A walk would probably do her the most good."

"Yeah, a nice li'l walk. Iz awfully hot in here." Alicia stuck an index finger inside the top of her sweater and fanned it away from her collarbone.

Rhonda yawned loudly. "Excuse me. I guess we can manage to walk around the block."

"If that yawn is any indication, Rhonda, I think you need to get home," Jack said. "You're both exhausted. I'll make sure Alicia gets some air and gets back home safely."

"Jack, you've got to be just as tired as we are," Pete pointed out. "Didn't you drive in from Stamford?"

"No, when you said it would be an early night I decided to take the train in, so I don't have to drive home."

"Well, I do feel a responsibility for Alicia," Rhonda said. "She's a good friend to us, but you just met her tonight, Jack."

"Don't worry about it. I'll enjoy taking a walk before going to the train station."

"She'll be safe with Jack, Rhonda," Pete said.

Rhonda nodded. "All right. Just give me a minute to clean up a little." She stood on tiptoe and pulled a small container off the top shelf of a kitchen cabinet. "I don't want to leave her with even a little mess. I've got a feeling she's not going to feel so good in the morning."

"I'll help you," Pete said. "But Jack, I see no reason to hold you up. The sooner you get her outside, the better. We'll lock the door behind us when we leave. We can't latch it without a key, but it should be all right for the short time you two will be out walking."

"Sounds good," Jack said. He turned to Alicia. "Get your jacket. We're going to clear your head. And don't forget your keys."

In the end it took Alicia more than a few minutes to locate her keys, and Pete and Rhonda had finished straightening up and were ready to leave at the same time. "I'm worried," Rhonda said as they slowly descended the stairs, Jack holding one of Alicia's arms and Pete the other. "I've never seen her like this before."

"She never drinks," Pete added. "I tease her about it all the time. I don't understand why she overdid it tonight."

"Will you two stop talkin' 'bout me like I'm invithible?" Alicia said with a scowl.

"It's just that we're worried about you, dear," Rhonda said, placing a reassuring hand on her friend's shoulder.

"We want Jack to understand how out of character this is for you."

Alicia closed her eyes. *Jack,* she thought, *is the problem.* Fortunately for her, she had enough control over her faculties not to express that thought aloud.

The entrance to the subway was just a half block from Alicia's front door. They bid goodnight to Pete and Rhonda, with Rhonda extracting a promise from Alicia to call her in the morning. After the Robinsons disappeared into the hole in the ground, Jack gallantly offered Alicia his arm, and by unspoken agreement they headed down Broadway. At this hour the avenue still had heavy southbound traffic. Neon lights of bars shone brightly in the night, and every available parking space was filled by a vehicle.

They walked in companionable silence for a few minutes, Alicia's trench coat billowing in the breeze, before Jack remarked, "The city is nicer at this time of year than it is in the summer, isn't it?"

She laughed. "Oh, iz nice in the summer, too, but it can get awfully hot. Few things are more insuff... insuffra...worse than an un-air conditioned subway train in August."

Her demeanor had improved, he noted, even if her diction hadn't. Good. That meant the fresh air helped. "I'll bet. Have you known Pete and Rhonda long?"

She breathed deeply. The crisp fall air was as fresh as air could be in New York. She felt significantly better now than she had upstairs in her apartment, cooler and less light-headed. "Rhonda and I useta work down the hall from each other. We kep' bumpin' into each other in the ladies' room, and both of us liked to walk at lunchtime. We went from casual acquain…acquaintances to real friends. That was, oh, I don't know how many years ago, but it's been awhile."

"Were you at their wedding?"

"I'd planned to be there, but my mother had to be hospitalized, so I wasn't able to make it. I could have managed if they'd gotten married locally, but they got married in Sssssss…somewhere in the Caribbean," she concluded after giving up on trying to remember the name of the island.

"Saint Croix." That explained why he didn't see her at Pete's wedding. But he'd seen her now, and he would do all he could to ensure he'd see her again. "I was Pete's best man."

"Fortunately, I wasn't Rhonda's maid of honor. I'm afraid my having to cancel at the last minute might have caused them real problems."

"Oh, I don't know. They only had me and Rhonda's sister as attendants. I remember Pete saying they didn't want to saddle their closest friends with the expense of wedding attire after they paid for their trip. We didn't even rehearse. Pete and I wore our own clothes, navy blazers and white slacks; and even Rhonda's cousin wore an ordinary dress to be maid of honor."

"An ordinary dress?"

"You know, not one of those bridesmaid dresses."

She chuckled. "I guess even a man can recoc… knows a bridesmaid dress when he sees one."

"The puffy sleeves usually give it away." He laughed,

then turned serious. "I'm sorry to hear your mother was ill," he said. "Did she recover?"

"She rebounded, but her health hasn't been good for a long time. It's taken a turn for the worse since the spring." She sounded sad, and he could readily understand. She brightened a little with her next words. "That's why I had this little get-together tonight, because I've been spending most of my time with her. I haven't seen any of my friends in weeks, aside from the one I work with every day. And she's not here tonight."

Jack nodded.

"I know it's become cliché to say one's mother is a saint. I get this mental picture of Richard Nixon, looking all pinched and righteous, resigning the prez-i-denzy," she said with a giggle.

His eyes widened with curiosity. "You actually remember when that happened? That was over thirty years ago."

"No, of course not. I'm only thirty-four. I saw the news ar…archives in history class. But I can truly say that my mother is a completely kind person." She shrugged. "Of course, I've only been around maybe half her life, but I've never known her to say a mean thing to or about anyone."

"Is it just the two of you?" He welcomed this opportunity to learn more about the woman who'd so captivated him.

"My father died two years ago. My folks were older than the parents of most of my friends. Late bloomers, they used to say."

"Are you an only child?"

"Nah, I've got a sister."

He looked at her sharply. Alicia spoke of her sister with a dismissive air very different from the loving way she described her mother.

"So whawazit that brought you to New York from Alabama, Dev?" she asked, then stopped and drew in her breath. "Doggone it, I did it again. It just keeps slippin' out."

"It's all right for you to call me that," he said easily. He liked the thought of Alicia having her own name for him that was hers alone. He'd noticed that Derek Taylor kissed her on the mouth when he left the party, and he didn't like it. It made him wonder about the nature of their relationship.

"I doan know why I keep doin' that," Alicia said, sounding frustrated.

"Alicia. Don't worry about it."

"What'd you call me?"

"Alicia. Isn't that your name?"

"You say it differently." He pronounced it A-*lee*-see-a, which sounded more melodic than the usual A-*lee*-sha. "Alicia," she said, saying it the way he had. "Thas pretty. I like it."

"A pretty name for a pretty woman. And in answer to your question," he said, feeling he'd made his point and not wanting to fluster her in her slightly intoxicated state, "I took a job here." He named the pharmaceutical firm that employed him, a name Alicia instantly recognized. "I'm Director of their Creative Network division."

"Ah, good for you. I guess they paid all your relocation expenses."

"They reimbursed me, yes."

"What do you think of our fair city?"

"I think it's an exciting place, but not for the faint of heart. I'm glad I live in Stamford."

They shared a laugh. Jack glanced at the street sign and saw they were approaching Seventy-Ninth Street. They'd walked nearly seven blocks. "How far did you want to walk? Remember, we have to turn around and walk back. But if you're tired I guess we can always flag down a cab."

"Oh, I'm fine. This walk is doin' me good. Lez go another couple o' blocks. Unless, of course, you didden wanna get home too late."

"Not a problem. I'm not driving, so all I have to do is cab it to Grand Central and I'm good to go."

They walked down to Seventy-Second Street before turning around to head back to Alicia's apartment. Their conversation flowed just as easily as the traffic headed down Broadway.

"I'd like to see you to your door," he said when they approached the dismal-looking five-story building of dark brown brick.

She smiled knowingly. "Oh, thas not necess…sary."

Her knowing smile both embarrassed and annoyed him. "I'm sure you've heard that line before, but this is on the level, Alicia. I'm concerned for your safety."

"Once I get in the building I'll be fine. Besides, for all I know you're an ax murderer."

"It would be pretty hard to conceal an ax," he said, looking over his crew neck sweater, sports coat, and slacks.

"Oh, I don't know," she said doubtfully. She stopped

suddenly, placing her hands on her hips. "Iz that an ax in your pocket, or are you jus' happy to see me?" she said in an imitation of Mae West. Then she broke off into a fit of giggles.

Jack managed an uncomfortable smile, resisting the urge to look down. He assumed that his navy slacks gave him a certain amount of discretion. Had she actually noticed....?

He decided to make light of it. "You're a fun person, Alicia. I'd like to see you again, if you haven't noticed."

She hesitated long enough to make him nervous. Had he misread the vibes? She seemed to be as drawn to him as he was to her. How could he be so wrong?

"Call me," she finally said.

He tried not to show his relief. Then again, the excessive liquor she'd consumed could have made her a little slow on the draw.

"I don't have your number."

She recited it.

"I don't have a pen," he said.

She smiled slyly. "Then you'll have to remember it, won't you?"

Jack knew then that her slow response to his suggestion that they see each other again hadn't come from liquor. Alicia's words might be slurred, but her mind remained sharp as a Ginsu knife. Something else had made her hesitate. He wished he knew the reason.

"Are you sure you'll be able to make it up all those stairs?" he asked, genuinely concerned. She had to climb three flights of stairs to her fourth-floor apartment in the building, which had no elevator.

She chuckled. "You know, that man in London they called The Ripper, his first name was Jack, too."

"All right, all right. I get the message." He couldn't fault her for being cautious, even if *he* knew his motives were pure. He just wanted to make sure she got safely inside her apartment. He wouldn't trust himself if she invited him in.

"Let me make sure I've got it," he said before repeating her telephone number. When she nodded he said, "I won't forget it."

"G'night, Dev. And thanks for the walk. I feel a lot better now." She unlocked the front door to the building rather smoothly and slipped inside the vestibule, leaving him to stand and watch her through the glass window as she passed the mailboxes and headed for the stairs. He hoped she'd turn and wave to him, but she didn't. Maybe she thought he'd already gone.

Or, he thought with a sinking heart, maybe she just wasn't interested enough to want to.

Chapter 4

Behind That Locked Door

Somehow Alicia managed to drag herself up the stairs. Her knees felt like they would buckle at any moment, and she panted as she fumbled with her keys. Eventually she managed to turn the key in the Medeco lock on her door and get inside.

She'd rented this fourth-floor walkup apartment for a song four years ago. It had been in deplorable condition then, but after putting considerable work into it, it truly felt like home. And it was cheap.

She did a quick inspection of the studio, suddenly grateful to Rhonda for insisting she help with the cleanup. The leftover food had been put away, the counters wiped down, and as a result nothing imperative had to be done tonight. She could go to sleep without guilt and simply do a quick clean and vacuum in the morning, before she left for her mother's.

Out of habit she carefully hung her clothes up and tossed her undergarments in the hamper inside her large walk-in closet. She pulled on a button-down-front flannel sleep shirt, then removed the oversize pillows that covered her daybed and climbed between the covers. She realized too late that she'd forgotten to get her sleep pillows out of the closet, so she angrily kicked the covers off and got back up again to retrieve them.

The moment she laid down the second time her thoughts immediately went to Jack Devlin. What was it about him that unnerved her so? Usually at social functions she had no more than two drinks, and not particularly strong ones at that, like wine spritzers. On the other hand, tonight she'd consumed so many Kamikazes she'd lost count. She never drank this much, and it didn't take a rocket scientist to figure out that Jack Devlin lay at the root of her behavior.

Clearly, she'd had an effect on him as well, a more traditional one. She hesitated when he asked her out, torn between curiosity and apprehension before the former won out. How could it not? Every time he said her name her body tingled.

Still, she wasn't sure whether or not she should see him again. She certainly had a demanding schedule, between work and her mother's illness. She really didn't need another complication in her life. Surely Jack Devlin, a man she'd never seen in her life but who had an almost haunting familiarity about him, represented an upset to a demanding but manageable life....

Her head felt a little heavy when she awoke at eight the next morning, a fact she became painfully aware of when she tried to sit up. She raised her hands to steady her head, expecting it to be as wide as a football, but surprised to find that it felt like its normal size. Instantly she remembered the events of last night and the tall stranger who made her react so oddly.

Slowly she pushed her body up until she reached a standing position, supporting herself with a hand on the tall headboard. She'd purchased this daybed at an estate sale in Westport after she rented this apartment in a deplorable run-down condition and did enough work in it to make it habitable.

She still remembered the first day she'd come to look at the apartment that had been her home for more than four years. She'd taken one look at its filthy linoleum floors, its walls full of holes, and the flood-damaged kitchen floor and prepared to walk out, cursing the rental agent who told her about this place, but then the landlord named an incredibly low rent figure. That number enticed her to take a closer look. The landlord preferred to rent the apartment in its present condition at a substantially low rent to a tenant willing to work hard to restore it than to make the repairs himself and rent it at market rate.

Alicia decided that the thousand dollars or so it would take to rehab the studio apartment would be well worth it. She'd recently invested in the court ste-

nography business of her childhood friend Shannon
Anderson, and she preferred not to make that long
commute to Connecticut every day. Besides, she
wanted to offer more than financial backing to the
business. That meant she had to attend school to learn
how to do court transcription and how to edit the transcripts, a process called "scoping." If she took classes
in the evening she wouldn't have so far to travel to
get home. Her new field of business couldn't be
learned in a few weeks or even months; it would take
at least two years.

The apartment required long weeks of work, so Alicia
had plenty of time to look for furnishings. She began at-
tending estate sales all along Long Island Sound. When
she saw this bed she knew she had to have it.

One of the reasons she liked it was that the four-foot-
high head and foot boards shut out much of the light, pro-
viding a cocooned environment that felt safe and
welcoming for a person like herself who had no enclosed
bedroom. Its rather odd appearance, with only the high
sides and no back, made it look more like an unusual sofa
rather than a daybed, which were supposed to be low-key
but were generally as easily identifiable as Smokey
Robinson's falsetto. Once covered with an Aztec print
throw and a dozen pillows of different sizes, shapes, and
colors, most guests at her apartment weren't aware this
odd-looking piece of furniture served as her bed.

Alicia stumbled a few feet to the bathroom. Maybe
a cold shower would help clear her head.

She felt better when she emerged, dripping wet. How
could people stand to drink large quantities of alcohol?

She couldn't understand how anyone could function after waking up feeling like this.

She checked the time. Eight-forty. At least she hadn't slept the morning away. If she hurried she could catch the nine-fifteen at One-Hundred-Twenty-Fifth Street.

Chapter 5

Isn't It a Pity

At Alicia's direction, the taxi driver pulled over in front of a stately tan brick Georgian colonial set back from the road. The glistening water of Long Island Sound could be seen in the background. She didn't even have to look at the meter; she knew from having made this ride many times what the fare would be. She handed him the money. "Keep the change."

"Thanks." The cabby looked at the impressive house. "You work here, huh?"

She sighed. She'd heard this many times before. "No, actually, I *live* here."

The cabbie chuckled. "Yeah, and I'm George Dubya."

Having already placed her wallet back securely inside her shoulder bag, Alicia grabbed her nylon duffel bag and opened the cab door, slamming it shut behind her forcefully. She heard these types of remarks all the time, and they never failed to tick her off. No one wanted to believe that an African-American family could reside in the fashionable Green's Farms section of Westport, one of many monied suburbs in Fairfield County. But Fletcher Timberlake, her father, hadn't believed in living small. A successful criminal attorney who served clients of all races at a time when African-Americans were just beginning to rise in the private sector, he'd become only the second person of his race to own a seat on the New York Stock Exchange. He didn't care whose eyebrows went up when he purchased this house over twenty-five years before. Most of the neighbors welcomed them, whether out of honesty or out of a wish not to be viewed as bigots.

Alicia smiled at the memory of her father. He truly had been larger than life, and he enjoyed himself right up until the day he died of a sudden, massive stroke.

She let herself in the front door. She put her bag down in the large foyer with its sweeping staircase. Before she could go into the living room on the left, a full-figured woman clad in a light blue blouse and navy slacks appeared in the doorway. Her concerned expression quickly turned into a smile. "Alicia!" she said happily, arms outstretched. "I'm so glad to see you, dear."

"Hi, Martha!" Alicia warmly embraced the woman who'd worked for her parents since she was in college, probably about fifteen years now. "Didn't Daphne tell you I'd be up today?"

"She sure didn't. But she's been having a hard time of it lately. Your mother's illness has her worried and unhappy."

"She also doesn't think of anyone outside her own little circle," Alicia remarked. She regretted her words when she noticed the uncomfortable expression on Martha's face. After all these years, Daphne still treated Martha like a servant, but Martha simply regarded it as part of the job. She was much too conservative to ever complain about it, nor would she be at ease with anyone else speaking badly of Daphne.

Alicia changed the subject to put Martha at ease. "How's Mom feeling today?"

"About the same. Daphne is up with her. Todd and Fletcher are out somewhere. They took Lucky with them."

Alicia nodded. Daphne's husband and son loved the gentle Irish setter that had been part of the household since the cocker spaniel that had been their childhood pet passed on. "No wonder Lucky didn't come to greet me." Lucky had always been more attached to her than to Daphne, who, it was discovered soon after the arrival of their first pet, had an allergy to dog hair. Unfortunately, Alicia's studio apartment simply didn't have the space a dog of Lucky's size needed. Here in Green's Farms she had plenty of room to run around, plus she was well cared for. Her presence made it seem less like a house of sickness.

"Why don't you go on up, and I'll bring you something to drink," Martha suggested. "What would you like? Coffee? Tea? Hot chocolate with whipped cream?"

"Hot chocolate sounds great. It's a little nippy out this morning. Thanks. Hey, how's Marvin and the kids?"

"Everybody's good. Tyrone is playing varsity this year, and Melody made the honor roll." Martha beamed. "Marvin and I couldn't be prouder."

"And deservedly so. That's wonderful, Martha!" Alicia glanced toward the sweeping staircase. "I'd better get upstairs. We'll talk later, huh?"

"Sure, go ahead."

Alicia picked up her duffel bag and raced up the stairs. The double doors of the master bedroom were open.

Fletcher's desire for the best also included his choice of a spouse. Caroline Pegram was the daughter of a family of undertakers who for generations had served African-American communities in five New England cities: Boston, Springfield, Hartford, New Haven, and Bridgeport. She'd been considered quite a catch, as beautiful as she was nice, with her high cheekbones and dark blue eyes. The up-and-coming Fletcher pursued her with steely determination, and he'd won her hand.

Alicia placed her bag on the floor and tapped on the door as she entered. "Hi, it's me."

Caroline sat not in her bed, but in the love seat near the window of the huge suite, dressed in a coral-colored nightgown and matching peignoir. Despite her too-thin body and almost grotesquely swollen ankles she looked beautiful, Alicia thought.

"Hello there!" Caroline exclaimed. "We saw your cab pull up. What took you so long to get upstairs?"

Alicia bent to kiss the smooth, cool cheek. Her mother's hair had gone completely silvery gray in recent years, and someone—either Martha or Daphne, or even the nurse—had brushed it back neatly and caught it with a coated rubber band at the rear crown, pinning up the ends against the back of her head. Caroline Timberlake had been blessed with remarkable good looks, but weight loss had made her almost gaunt. Her prominent cheekbones kept her facial skin from sagging. When Alicia placed a hand on her mother's upper back she felt a prominent shoulder blade sticking through. It pained her to see her mother waste away before her eyes from heart disease.

"I spent a few minutes chatting with Martha," she explained.

"That figures," Daphne said, speaking for the first time.

"And what's that supposed to mean, sister dear?" Alicia asked, not put off by Daphne's droll tone. Her younger sister always had a complaint about this or that.

"Martha is our employee, Alicia," Daphne said. "It's her job to clean up and look after Mom. It's not up to you to inquire about her family, but it *is* up to her to take care of ours."

Alicia's shoulders squared. Daphne had never warmed up to Martha the way she had, but she wasn't about to be criticized for her good relationship with the woman who had worked for their parents since she was in college. "As far as I'm concerned, Martha is a member of this household who just happens to keep the house clean and organized. She's practically like a sister to me. Besides," she added, "I'm no snob."

"Meaning I am?"

Alicia good-naturedly held up a hand and twisted it at the wrist.

"Say what you want, but I don't think it's wrong

to know one's place," Daphne said defensively. Then she turned to their mother and said, "Don't you think so too, Mom?"

Caroline sighed. "I think you both have valid points. But because Martha has worked for us for so long she's much more than a housekeeper. The nurses who come in, I don't have too much to say to them, or they to me. They're just doing a job, and I'm just another patient. There's no history between us, and besides, the agency keeps sending different ones. But Martha has been a wonderful friend and companion to me, all the while not stepping outside of her role as employee. After all, Daphne, she's here keeping me company when you're at home with your husband and baby."

Daphne looked at her mother through wounded eyes.

"Now, I'm not trying to make you feel guilty," Caroline hastily added. "I just wanted to remind you how things are."

"Personally, I think it's great that her kids are doing so well," Alicia said. "Martha wants them to do better than she and Marvin did, and it looks like they're on their way. I'm glad for her." Their son was a track star who also played basketball, and their daughter a talented gymnast. Both attended the local high school.

"Both of them will probably get scholarships," Caroline observed, adding, "Martha is so proud."

Alicia sat in one of the twin rocking chairs that faced each other, to the sides and slightly in front of the love seat. "It's good to be here."

"How was the party?" Caroline asked.

"It went well."

Daphne grunted. "Same old faces. I don't see the big deal."

"It isn't a big deal." *Unless you want to make it one.* "I don't get bored with my friends. Like Mom just said, it means something to have a history together. And it just so happens there was a new face in attendance. Rhonda Robinson brought along someone new. A college buddy of Pete's."

"And?" Caroline prompted, leaning forward eagerly.

"He seemed very nice, that's all."

"Oh, no dear. That's definitely *not* all."

Alicia felt grateful that Martha appeared at that moment, balancing a tray that held three mugs. "Hot chocolate," she announced.

"How thoughtful of you, Martha," Caroline said.

"Yes, Martha, thank you," Daphne echoed, a little too graciously to be real. Even Martha appeared startled by the praise, which Alicia knew had been motivated by Daphne's desire to please their mother more than any sense of doing the right thing.

Martha set the mugs on coasters on the dark cherry wood coffee table. "Can I get you ladies anything else?" When all three women shook their heads, she took the tray and left the room.

Alicia hoped the conversation wouldn't return to Jack Devlin. She didn't even know why she'd brought him up in the first place.

Probably because you keep thinking about him. Even now, just thinking of him made her want to check her cell phone, make sure it was working properly. Had he forgotten her number? She certainly hoped not. She knew she'd brazenly tempted fate by giving him her number when he had nothing to take it down with. She'd never be so rash if he had no other way to contact her, but all he had to do if he forgot was to call Rhonda and get it from her.

She noticed an anxious look on her mother's face and knew what put it there. That doggone Daphne, always having something negative to say. Commenting that her friendliness with Martha was inappropriate had been uncalled for. Why couldn't she be more considerate? Their mother was dying. She certainly deserved to have her last days filled with peace.

Therein lay part of the problem. While Alicia had accepted the inevitable, Daphne held on to the belief that their mother would recover. But Caroline's fate had been sealed when, at the age of seven, she contracted the rheumatic fever that damaged her heart valves. Alicia felt that Caroline feared the two girls would go their separate ways after she was gone. Six years apart, Alicia and Daphne had bickered their whole lives. Their father Fletcher had already passed on, and with both parents gone there would be nothing to hold Alicia and Daphne together.

Already their lives had gone in different directions. While Alicia still enjoyed her independence in her mid-thirties, Daphne took the traditional route, marrying her college sweetheart, Todd Scott, six months after her graduation. She announced her first pregnancy on her second wedding anniversary. Fletcher Timberlake suffered a fatal stroke shortly afterward, and eight months later Daphne named her infant son Fletcher after the father she adored.

The adoration had been mutual. Alicia had long since accepted that their father's youngest child had been his favorite, probably because Daphne was like a carbon copy of the wife he loved so much, while Alicia, if anything, looked more like Fletcher. But he provided for both his daughters equally in his will, and Alicia had the satisfaction of his telling her on his deathbed that he loved her and was proud of her.

Both Alicia's parents had been older than the parents of her friends. At the time of her birth nearly thirty-five years ago their ages were thirty-six and forty-two, respectively, which put them both past forty when Daphne was born six years later. Caroline told them years later that she had difficulty getting pregnant. It seemed so ironic that they could do everything else with success. "We had everything, but yet we had nothing," she'd said wistfully.

"Mom, how do you feel today?" Alicia asked now.

"Oh, I'm all right. Yesterday the nurse brought me outside, but today it's a little cool for that." A nurse came in nightly and stayed on duty overnight. A small balcony extended from the master bedroom, allowing Caroline to get fresh air without going downstairs. On the occasions when she did need to get down to the first floor, a chair lift had been installed on the wall by the back stairs that led to the kitchen.

"You're doing fine, Mom," Daphne said encouragingly.

Alicia's cell phone began to ring. She quickly reached inside the special compartment in her purse that held her phone. "Hello?" she said, pressing the talk button without even checking the caller's identity.

"Feeling better this morning, I hope."

She tried not to show her disappointment at hearing Rhonda's voice. "Excuse me," she said to her mother and sister, rising and walking outside to the hall so she could talk without disturbing their conversation.

"I'm better, thanks. The walk last night really helped clear my head, although I did have a bit of a headache this morning."

"Alicia, I've never seen you so wasted. It would have been easy for someone to take advantage of you. I trust Jack was the gentleman I've always known him to be."

She smiled at the thought of him. "He was. Tried to see me upstairs, but I said no."

"That might not have been a bad idea. You were a little unsteady going down the stairs when we left."

"Yes, but I felt a lot better by the time we finished walking." Alicia left out the fact that while climbing the stairs she stumbled on the second flight, the quick grab of the banister with her right hand saving her face from meeting the steps head-on.

"How far did you walk?"

"Down to Seventy-Second. And back."

"Wow. Thirteen blocks one way. That made for a heck of a workout. But I'm glad you're okay." Rhonda paused. "You *are* okay, aren't you, Alicia?"

"Yes, I'm better."

"That's not what I mean, and you know it." Rhonda sighed. "But if you want to talk about it, I'm here."

"Thanks." Alicia knew that Rhonda wanted to know why she drank so much last night, but how could she explain to her friend something she didn't understand herself?

"Are you at your mother's?"

"Yes, I got here about a half hour ago."

"How's she doing?"

"Pretty good today, actually."

"Give her my best."

"I will. I'll talk to you tomorrow." Alicia clicked the End button and returned to the sitting area of her mother's bedroom. Her disappointment must have shown on her face.

"Not the young man you told us about?" Caroline asked.

"No," she admitted. "It was Rhonda. She said to tell you hello."

"Don't worry, Alicia. He'll call."

But he didn't, not for the remainder of the day. She felt puzzled and tense. Could she have blown it?

Chapter 6

I Want To Tell You

She slept uneasily that night in her old room, unable to understand her emotions. No man had ever affected her this way before.

Alicia arose early Sunday morning, as was her habit. Lucky slept near her feet. She felt quite at home in the room she'd grown up in, surrounded by furniture she'd had since her high school days.

She slipped out of bed, washed her face in the adjacent private bath and stood at the window as she brushed out her hair. Her room overlooked the quiet street. At this time of year the fall foliage season was at its height, and leaves of yellow, purple, orange and brown covered the trees. The only person in sight was a gardener raking up the leaves that had fallen on the lawn of the large Dutch Colonial across the street. Alicia smiled, remembering how, as children, she and Daphne and other kids from the block went over there to try to grab apples from the tree on the neighbors' property, always getting shooed away by either the lady of the house or the family's maid.

Green's Farms couldn't be more different than the Upper West Side of Manhattan, yet she loved both places. It pleased her to know that this wonderful old house would remain in the family after her mother passed away.

Caroline had sat down with her and Daphne the week after their father's funeral and explained to them the major points of his will. She told them that after her own death the house would be left to both girls. Daphne promptly asked if she would be the one to live in it, "since *I* have a husband and a baby on the way."

Alicia had merely smiled, expecting nothing different from her sister. Caroline replied that leaving the house to both of them meant precisely that. "Which one of you will live here will have to be decided between the two of you. But your daddy left explicit instructions to help keep peace among you two. There's no mortgage on the house. The taxes are steep, but most of it comes from the rent Martha and Marvin pay each month. Any out-of-pocket tax payments, plus the cost of any improvements made, will be reimbursed from the profits if the house is ever sold, although I hope the house will be kept in the family. That baby you're carrying, Daphne, might live here with his or her family thirty years from now. Or maybe one of your children, Alicia."

She tactfully ignored Daphne's eye rolling. "But every future member of this family will own a share in this property. It's all been worked out."

Alicia assured Daphne that she had no desire to live here. As a single woman with no dependents, she would feel terribly lonely living all alone in a five-bedroom house with four-and-a-half baths, even if it meant she could have Lucky. Daphne, with her allergy to pet hair, would probably want to get rid of him, although little Fletch would probably object. He loved Lucky as much as Alicia did.

When a fully dressed Alicia emerged from her bedroom the next morning and went to see her mother, she saw a uniformed nurse taking Caroline's vital signs. She craned her neck for a better look, but she didn't recognize the face. The health care agency rotated their staff of nurses faster than a chicken roasting on a spit. However did her mother manage to keep up with them all?

Caroline's face lit up at the sight of her eldest daughter. "Good morning, Alicia. You might want to buzz Martha. She's making breakfast. Why don't you eat with me? Daphne and Todd aren't up yet, and I like for them to eat with little Fletch, like they would do if they were at home."

"Sure, Mom." She nodded to the nurse, then went to the intercom on the wall. "Good morning, Martha."

"Morning, Alicia. Would you like some breakfast? I'm putting something together for Miss Caroline now."

"Yes, please. A cheese omelet would be nice, with those great home fries you make on the side."

"Coming up."

"Thanks." Alicia removed her finger from the button and turned around. "How is my mother this morning, Nurse?"

"She's doing quite well. Her vitals are strong."

"Do you think she's up to going out for a little while?"

"Nurse Bennett says I can go to church," Caroline said proudly.

"But she should keep her walking to a minimum, and no stairs," the nurse cautioned.

"That's fine. The church has a ramp."

"Make sure she uses her motorized chair to get downstairs and her wheelchair to get in and out, and she'll be fine."

"Thank you." Alicia beamed at Caroline. "I guess we'll have to get you something to wear."

"My gray suit. Don't worry about it now, we have time. I've just been given a sponge bath, and all I have to do is get dressed."

"Mrs. Timberlake, is there anything else you need?" the nurse inquired.

"No, I'm good. I'll see you this evening."

"Enjoy your afternoon. And remember, you mustn't overdo it."

"We'll see to that," Alicia said.

The nurse put on her coat, picked up her bag, and left.

Alicia sat on the opposite side of her mother's bed. "What is Martha making you this morning?"

"A blueberry muffin and yogurt. I didn't feel like eggs—I mean, the egg substitute I'm allowed to have." Caroline smiled. "So tell me, did you receive that call you were waiting for?"

She cast her eyes downward for a second. "No. But I'm not worried."

"Yes, I can tell how not worried you are," Caroline said knowingly. "Alicia, I don't think I've ever seen you this way before."

"What way?"

"You had several calls yesterday on your cell phone. I could see that hopeful look in your eyes and the disappointment that took over when you learned it wasn't the person you wanted to talk to." She paused. "He must have left quite an impression on you."

"I can never fool you, can I, Mom?"

"No one knows you better than I. But I think it's time someone did." Caroline reached out and patted the back of Alicia's hand. "I can't believe that you'll soon be thirty-five years old. I do hope that eventually you'll settle down and have children."

"Maybe one day. There's still time."

"I know you've had your share of boyfriends over the years, but it seems like they never last beyond a few months. What happened to that young man who escorted you to Daphne's wedding?"

"Oh, Derek. He's still around. He came to my party Friday night."

"Do you still see each other?"

"Occasionally. But not lately."

"You mean for sex."

"Mom!"

"Surely I don't need to remind you I was having sex before you were born," Caroline said, unruffled. "Seriously, I worry about you, dear. Your father—"

"Oh, not that again. Mom, Pop was a good man."

"Yes, he was. But he did you a disservice, the way he favored Daphne. He couldn't help it, Alicia. Don't be upset with him."

"But I'm not upset, Mom."

"That's precisely what troubles me. You should be furious, or hurt, or wonder why, or *something*. It's not natural to have no feelings at all. I loved your father, Alicia, but I hated how he behaved. I saw it, remember, I was there. I saw how he'd pick up Daphne and lift her high, and then how he'd rub your shoulder like some kind of postscript at the end of a letter. He'd talk about Daphne so much that people who didn't know him probably didn't realize he had two daughters. We fought about it all the time."

"Mom, I wouldn't want to be the cause—"

"Stop apologizing, Alicia. You haven't done anything wrong."

"Mom, you're getting excited." She could see it in Caroline's face, and in her body language, the way she suddenly straightened up and punched her pillow. Alicia found it alarming. "Calm down, please."

"That's my whole point. Alicia, you never even looked disappointed when your father acted the way he did, but I've watched you look disappointed all day today with every phone call you received. I'm not sure what to make of that, but I am afraid that the way your father treated you might have a negative effect on your relationships with men."

"Mom, don't worry. I know Pop loved me in his own way. He told me so before he passed. He was always there when I needed him, just like you were. He sent me to school, gave me an education…and he provided for me, didn't he?"

"Yes, he did," Caroline admitted.

"So he had a little touch of favoritism when it came to Daphne. I was hardly treated like an ugly stepsister." Alicia refrained from pointing out that in her opinion, at least, she turned out much better than Daphne.

"And I know he was very proud of you, Alicia. But I do worry about you. I don't want you to accept second-class treatment from any man—"

"I never have, Mom. I never will."

"Nor do I want your father's favoritism of Daphne to stop you from loving anyone."

"That's silly, Mom. I love *you.*"

"You know very well what I mean, Alicia." Caroline's expression grew serious. "You're my eldest child. You came along at a time when I thought your daddy and I were destined to be without a family of our own. You brightened our whole lives, and you are dearer to me than I can ever tell you."

Alicia beamed.

"But there's something I have to—"

"Okay, here we are," Martha called out cheerfully. A moment later she entered the room with a large tray holding two plates, orange juice and coffee.

Alicia reached for the rattan weave tray on which Caroline took her meals when in bed, unfolding the legs from each side and placing it over Caroline's lap. Martha transferred the food onto it. "Thanks, Alicia."

"I'll sit at the coffee table, Martha," Alicia said.

"You can stay right there. I brought a tray for you."
She handed Alicia a Formica tray trimmed in pecan
wood. "We have a set of these. Miss Daphne uses one
all the time when she eats in your mother's room."

Alicia found something disconcerting in Martha,
who at forty-two was considerably older than the not-
yet-thirty Daphne, using the courtesy title of "Miss"
when referring to her. She knew Martha did it only to
appease her sister's highfalutin' ways, but it made her
wince nonetheless. Daphne didn't sign Martha's pay-
checks…she just acted like she did.

"Martha, Mom's going to go to church this morning,"
she said proudly. "The nurse said she's up to it."

"That's wonderful, Miss Caroline! I've been telling
you that you're looking wonderful these days."

"I feel pretty good, too. Thanks, Martha."

Chapter 7

Hello, Little Girl
Stamford, Connecticut
Late 1970s

Fletcher Timberlake held his new baby daughter and gestured for Alicia to come to him. "Here she is, Alicia. Your mother and I have named her Daphne. Your mother always said she liked that name."

"Then why did you call me Alicia?" she asked solemnly.

"Uh… We liked that name, too. Now tell me, what do you think of your new little sister?" He peeled the pink blanket back a bit so Alicia could see her clearly.

She looked at the sleeping infant. "Isn't she ever going to do anything but sleep?"

Fletcher laughed. "Sure she will! All babies sleep a lot at first. They sleep, they cry, and they make messes in their diapers. You must have—I mean, you did the same thing yourself."

"I don't remember doing that."

"Of course you wouldn't. No one remembers when they were babies. Even I can't remember being a baby."

Alicia took another look at her new sister. She looked like a big lump of that stuff Mommy mixed up before she rolled it flat and made biscuits, except she had a little bit of hair at the top of her head. "When will she be able to play with me?"

"Oh, not for a while yet, I'm afraid. Babies are very delicate. They have to be handled with care."

"And why can't I play with Mommy?"

"Alicia, I explained that to you. Mommy has to take it easy. She used up a lot of energy having the baby, and she isn't as strong as she should be. She just has to rest for a few weeks, and then she'll be good as new. That's why we hired Sadie. She's going to come in while I'm at work to help Mommy out."

"I can help Mommy out, Pop." Everything was different from how it used to be. Mommy's tummy had gotten so big, and her ankles got all swollen, and she spent all of her time in bed. Then instead of Mommy bringing her to school and picking her up, Sadie started to do it. Alicia liked Sadie, but she missed playing with Mommy. Sadie was kind of old, and she got tired real quick. But Daddy told her that Mommy needed to rest because she was carrying a baby in her tummy. Now that the baby was here, Alicia thought things would go back to the way they used to be, but now instead of Mommy in bed all the time, her new baby sister just laid around, too. And everything had to be so quiet. If she wanted to listen to her *Winnie The Pooh* record, Sadie made it so soft she could barely hear it.

Fletcher reached and rubbed the back of her head. "You're a good girl, Alicia. But you have to go to school, remember? You're a big girl, in the first grade. Remember how you promised you'd make good grades?"

She nodded.

"That's why you can't miss school. Don't you worry. You're going to be a big help to Mommy, though. You'll help her take care of my little princess." He bent and kissed Daphne's forehead.

Alicia's forehead wrinkled. *Princess?* Is that what he would call her baby sister? Why didn't she have a special name, too?

Then he got to his feet and reached for her hand. "Come on, Precious. Let's go see Mommy."

Smiling, she took his hand. So now Pop called her "Precious." She liked it. She started to tell him, but she stopped when she saw his face turned away from her.

He was lovingly gazing at the baby he held in the crook of his other arm.

Chapter 8

Ticket To Ride

Alicia took the four-twenty-eight train back to the city. It had been a pleasant afternoon, but it occurred to her now that after Martha's ill-timed interruption, she never got the chance to resume the conversation with her mother, who'd obviously been about to tell her something.

Daphne, having woken up, soon joined them, sitting to chat while Alicia and Caroline had breakfast. They ended up discussing a completely different subject matter. The moment Daphne learned of their plans to attend church she insisted on going with them. In the end, she stayed at Caroline's as long as Alicia had. Actually, Daphne, Todd and little Fletch dropped Alicia off at the Green's Farms train station on their way home to White Plains.

Alicia massaged her kneecaps. Maybe it was just as well that her conversation with her mother had been interrupted. She probably intended to say more of the same. She'd tried for years to convince Caroline that she had no problems with her father, then or now. Fletcher Timberlake had a soft spot for his youngest child. So what? Nobody said that parents had to be perfect, did they? They were supposed to love their children and care for them…and he had. Martha's appearance at that precise moment had probably cut short another round of exasperating attempts at persuasion. Caroline just couldn't seem to accept the truth. Alicia regretted that her mother would probably go to her grave believing she'd been wronged by her father. She wished she could make Caroline understand that she felt no such thing.

A ringing cell phone interrupted her thoughts. She reached lazily for the silver gizmo that had become her social lifeline since spending so much time away from home. "Hello?"

"Alicia, how are you?"

Her breath caught in her throat. She knew it was Jack simply from the lyrical way he pronounced her name. Finally, after two days, he'd gotten around to calling her.

She decided to play it cool. "Hello, Dev," she said cheerfully. "So you remembered my number, huh?"

"It's tattooed on my brain."

"I figured you just called Pete and got it from him and Rhonda."

"Nah, that would have been too easy. I figured I'd check on you and see how you coped with your hangover."

"Who said I had a hangover?"

"The way you slurred your words Friday night," he said promptly.

She laughed. "All right, I confess. My head did feel abnormally large and heavy when I woke up yesterday morning, but I'm feeling much better now."

She paused as the conductor announced the next stop. "Larchmont!"

"You must have given me your cell number," he said curiously. "You sound like you're out and about."

"My cell is the only phone I have. I don't even have a home phone anymore. I access the Internet through a cable line. Actually, I'm on a train on my way back home. I spent the weekend with my mother."

"How's she doing?"

"I'm happy to say she's gained some strength. I was able to get her out of the house for a few hours this afternoon."

"I'm sure having such a devoted daughter has helped her spirit." He paused. "Alicia, I was hoping you and I would be able to have dinner together this week. Maybe Saturday?"

"I'd love to, Dev, but I'm not sure how I can pull it off." She gave herself an imaginary pat on the back for the breezy way that came out, then went on to explain. "I'm up with my mom in Fairfield County on the weekends and at least twice during the week."

"You have to eat wherever you are, wouldn't you agree?"

"Well, yes...."

"And it'll be easier for me if you're in Connecticut than it would if you were in New York. I live in Stamford, remember?"

"Oh, that's right."

"I'd prefer to pick you up, but I'll understand if you want to keep the house quiet for your mother's sake."

"Yes, why don't we meet?" she quickly agreed.

"I'll be in touch during the week."

"Okay, Dev. Thanks for calling."

"You bet."

Alicia clicked the End button with a smile. Her mother had been right. The call she'd been hoping for had come in after all. And now she had Saturday night with Jack to look forward to. He'd even been considerate enough to offer to meet her, something she planned to take him up on. She didn't want Daphne sizing up Jack and asking him questions; nor did she feel Jack needed to see where her mother lived. She hadn't even mentioned the name of the town, fearing he might get preconceived notions. She seriously doubted he was a gold digger, but sometimes people looked at her differently when she said the word "Westport." It might not be the wealthiest town in Fairfield County—she believed New Canaan held that distinction—but it probably had higher name recognition as a city of privileged residents.

She watched the scenery of the New Haven line pass by as the train moved south. Funny. She found it much easier to speak with Jack on the phone than she did being with him face-to-face. On the phone none of the disquieting feelings existed. She wondered why that was....

* * *

In his Stamford condominium, Jack felt pretty good
about the way the conversation went. He'd forced
himself not to dial her number until now, knowing she
expected to hear from him well before this. A woman
as good-looking as Alicia Timberlake was sure to have
her fair share of admirers, all of whom probably contacted her as soon as they could. He, on the other hand,
wanted to stand out from the pack. Instead he did his
usual weekend errands—the barber, the dry cleaner, the
supermarket. He spent Saturday afternoon playing basketball at the courts near his apartment, where a person
could always get a game going. That night he went to a
local club, but he saw no one who interested him the
way Alicia Timberlake had. Sunday he went for a drive
up U.S. Seven, a particularly scenic route with an abun-
dance of fall foliage, then relaxed with the papers while
watching football on TV.

As the game neared its conclusion he finally reached
for his cell phone and dialed her number. He would
never know for certain if she'd been wondering if he
would call or not, but he nonetheless felt convinced
he'd done the right thing, largely in light of her evasive-
ness. He knew that Alicia's saying her mother lived in
"Fairfield County" had been no more an accident than
when she recited her phone number, knowing he had no
pen and paper. He was a resident of the county himself,
but for some reason she didn't want him to know exactly
where her mother lived. Because of that, he suggested
they meet somewhere. He couldn't imagine her
reasons—he wouldn't care if her mother lived in a cave.

He just wanted Alicia to be comfortable and without reservations about their date.

He had no sooner hung up when the phone rang again. Pete's voice came over the wire. "Hey there."

"What's up?"

"I'm calling at the behest of my wife," he said.

Jack pictured him smiling fondly at Rhonda. He suddenly felt quite alone.

"Both of us wanted to thank you for taking care of Alicia the other night. Rhonda, out of pure concern for your social life, also wants to know if you met any nice girls at the party."

"Actually, yes. I'm having dinner with the hostess herself next weekend."

"Alicia?"

"Yes." Jack picked up on the incredulity in his friend's tone. "Something wrong with that?"

"No, of course not. I'm just kind of surprised, that's all." In the background Jack heard Rhonda say, "I'm surprised, too."

"Why do you say that?"

"I don't think she's your type."

"Why? Because I'm a country boy from Docena, Alabama, and she's a sophisticated city slicker?"

"Please. You're about as much as a hick as Bill Clinton or Condi Rice. You don't even have an accent. Listen, I'm the first one to say that just because a person is from a small town in the South doesn't mean they just fell off a turnip truck. But Alicia's...well, she's different, Jack."

"I didn't notice the antenna growing out of her head."

"Come on, man. I'm not saying she's an alien. It's her personality. I don't think it'll mesh with yours. It's practically impossible to get close to her. We've known her for years, but we still don't know much about her."

"Maybe she doesn't like you very much," he joked.

But Pete remained serious. "I'm not kiddin', man. Alicia's real sweet, outgoing, and considerate, but she's not like most women. I know you've been with women who were clingy and demanding, and so have I, before I met Rhonda. But Alicia can love 'em and leave 'em as good as any man."

Jack's eyes narrowed in suspicion. "And how would you know that?"

"Rhonda shared some things Alicia told her with me. Girl talk kind of things. She probably shouldn't have told me, but I don't think Alicia would feel betrayed if she knew Rhonda repeated a few things she said. After all, I've known her almost as long as Rhonda has."

"What did Rhonda tell you?"

"Apparently, Alicia chafes at feeling fenced in. Nor does she feel that she's got to be in love with a man to sleep with him. I'm not saying she's easy, Jack, she just feels urges like the rest of us and acts on them. Alicia makes no demands on people and can't stand for anyone to make demands of her. She might as well be surrounded by the Great Wall of China. I don't think you'll be able to get through it. And I know you won't be happy if she spends the night with another man just days after being with you. She's the type who'll probably never settle down. But don't say I didn't warn you."

"I'll consider myself warned. But Pete, if you think I won't be able to get next to Alicia, then all I can say is you don't know Jack."

Chapter 9

A Taste of Honey

Jack made sure he arrived at the restaurant fifteen minutes early. He wanted to be there to greet Alicia when she arrived.

"Devlin is the name. I have a reservation for eight o'clock. I'm meeting someone," he told the maître d'.

The middle-aged man nodded knowingly. "Yes, Mr. Devlin. And does the young lady have any distinguishing characteristics?"

"Only that she's stunning," he promptly replied. "Definitely too gorgeous to be entering a restaurant alone."

"I'm sure I'll recognize her. But just to be on the safe side, would you like to give me her name?"

"Miss Timberlake," he said, adding, "I'll wait at the bar."

"Very well, Mr. Devlin. I will bring her to you myself."

"Thanks." He wandered into the separate bar area, where he sat at the end of the counter and ordered a Scotch and water. The maître d' seemed amused by his description, but how else could he describe Alicia? With her high cheekbones, gracefully arched brows, and skin so flawless it looked like it had been painted on, she was a goddess.

Two African-American women entered the bar area and sat nearby, leaving just one stool between them. Jack toyed with his Scotch and entertained himself with thoughts of the pleasant evening that lay ahead. He looked over when he heard a question he believed was directed at him.

"How are you tonight?" a female voice inquired.

He looked over at the women to make sure one of them had addressed him and not some other person. One of them, a striking brown-skinned woman, smiled at him, while the other looked away and appeared uncomfortable. "Good, thanks. You?"

"Not bad. What brings you out tonight?"

"I'm meeting a young lady."

"My friend is a young lady," the woman pointed out. Her friend jabbed her in the ribs and mouthed the words, "Stop it!"

He chuckled as the first one said, "Ouch! That hurt, Charlene!" Both women appeared to be in their early forties. The one doing the talking wore engagement and wedding rings; and Charlene's ring finger was bare. Apparently Charlene's friend wanted to fix her up with someone.

"I'm meeting a *specific* young lady," he clarified, the corners of his eyes crinkling in amusement.

"Oh, that's too bad."

"Will you forget about it already, Andrea?" Charlene hissed.

"Listen, you can't spend your life waiting around for Reggie to get off his butt. Your biological clock isn't just ticking, it's about to blow up."

"Reggie and I are doing just fine."

"So what are you doing out with me on a Saturday night, having Merlot and lobster bisque? You called, all upset because you think Reggie's up to something and you don't know what it is. I say there are plenty of other fish in the sea. You wait and see, this man's date won't look half as good as you do, Charlene. If you wouldn't be so shy you could probably make him forget all about her."

Although they spoke reasonably softly, in trying to be heard over the sound of the television poised over the bar their voices carried, which didn't allow Jack to make out everything they said, but he could follow the gist of their conversation. He found Andrea's comment about his date not looking half as good as Charlene particularly humorous. *I wouldn't bet on it,* he thought. Charlene was certainly attractive, and he'd never shied away from dating women slightly older than himself. Under different circumstances he might take the bait. But make him forget Alicia? Not a chance.

He'd almost finished his drink when his peripheral vision saw movement on the left. He looked up to see the maître d' leading Alicia to where he sat.

He quickly got to his feet. "Miss Timberlake, sir," the maître d' announced with a flourish. "Your table is ready. I'll have someone bring you to it when you're ready." He then bowed stiffly and turned to leave.

Jack had a vague awareness of the maître d' approaching and saying something. As far as he was concerned, the heavyset gent might as well have been both invisible and silent. He had eyes only for the figure behind him.

For a moment all he could do was simply drink her in. She wore an open, belted white wool coat with a berry-colored scarf draped over her neck and a black pantsuit with a tailored double-breasted blazer. The starkness of the black-and-white ensemble was relieved by lips painted the same berry color as her scarf, lips he knew would taste sweet as strawberries in June. He wanted to savor them with his tongue and nibble at their fullness.

Blood rushed to his groin. *No, Jack,* he told himself. *What you need is to forget about what you want, at least for right now.*

She stood silently as his eyes roamed over her with obvious approval. Finally she broke into a shy smile. "Hello, Jack."

He took her hand in both of his, raised it parallel to his mouth and kissed the back of it, his eyes never leaving hers. "I think that's the first time you ever said my real name," he said as he lowered her hand, continuing to hold it.

"My inclination would be to walk in and say, 'Hiya, Dev,' but somehow it didn't suit the mood," she said honestly.

That told him that she, too, felt the sparks in the air

between them. He stroked the back of her hand with the pad of his thumb. "I'm glad you could make it."

"I hope you weren't waiting long."

He loved the sound of her voice, all husky and low. Much as he hated to, he let go of her hand. "Not long," he said easily. In his heart he knew he would have sat there for hours, just to get a glimpse of her. "We should get our table." He noticed the eyes of Andrea and Charlene fixed on them. Neither woman moved to try to make their staring more subtle. If anything, he thought their mouths might drop into their soup bowls.

"Ladies," he said, "this is my dinner partner. Alicia, this is Andrea and her friend Charlene."

Alicia nodded pleasantly, if a bit uncertainly. "Ladies."

The women's shocked expressions at Jack's use of their names told Jack they realized he'd overheard their conversation. "A pleasant evening to you," he said jauntily. He removed a single from his wallet and laid it by his highball glass, then took Alicia's elbow and escorted her out of the bar.

"Friends of yours?" she asked, sounding mildly curious.

"No. It appears one of them is trying to console the other over an issue involving a man."

"What other kind of issues are there?" she said with a throaty chuckle.

As they left the bar area a hostess offered to take Alicia's coat. He stood behind her and removed it, stepping back as he handed it to the hostess just in time to see her turn around slowly. "Wow," he said under his breath, too softly for her to hear. He'd only glimpsed her at the restaurant, of course, and at the party her loose-fitting sweater, at nearly tunic length, did much to conceal her figure, but the black pantsuit left little to be guessed at. Alicia might possess an imposing height, but she was no toothpick thin high fashion model. The short tailored jacket—she wore no blouse beneath—accentuated a cinched waist, rounded bust and lush, full hips. He liked his women curvy.

When the maître d' held out her chair, Jack wanted to push him aside and do it himself. "If I may say so, Mr. Devlin," the maître d' said, "you were absolutely correct in your description of Miss Timberlake."

"I'm glad you agree."

She waited until he departed, then turned a curious gaze on him. "Your description was correct, huh? Tell me, Jack, how did you describe me?"

"I said you would be the most astoundingly beautiful woman to ever enter this establishment."

"What a sweet embellishment!" she exclaimed, obviously flattered.

He leaned forward, his eyes captivated by the black onyx oval overlaid with ivory and gold that tantalizingly teased her cleavage. Her hair looked fuller than he remembered. He pictured her reclining in bed, her dark hair fanned out against a pastel pillowcase, waiting for him....

A lump momentarily became stuck in his throat at that mental vision. Eventually he managed to say, "It was no embellishment, Alicia."

She tried to be cool from the moment she stepped inside the famed steakhouse, but his special way of pronouncing her name took her breath away. She inadvertently rolled her head back and shivered, her shoulders momentarily rising around her neck, her chest rising. "You're very kind," she managed to say. In truth, she'd gone through special pains with her appearance, having driven into Stamford this afternoon to have her hair washed and set. Laverne, her longtime hairdresser, made her tresses look beautifully thick, like a lion's mane. She'd even bought new shoes, black slingbacks with a two-inch heel, to go with her suit.

"How's your mother today?" he asked, graciously not commenting on her reaction.

"She's good, thanks." She opened her menu.

As they enjoyed an appetizer of bacon-wrapped broiled sea scallops and sipped on Pinot Noir, Alicia companionably said, "Tell me about Jack Devlin."

"Hey, I'm an open book, and probably not all that exciting, either. I'm originally from a small town outside Birmingham called Docena. I went to Fisk for my Bachelor's and started working in Galveston, Texas. I stayed there seven years, then went to Houston—which is like an hour away from Galveston—for three, then back to Birmingham."

"Does your family still live in your hometown?"

"Most of them, yes. One of my sisters lives in Memphis, and I have a brother in Houston."

"Do you have a large family?"

"We were seven. I've got two sisters and two brothers. I'm the second oldest child and the oldest boy. My father was a postman, and my mother worked for the Jefferson County School Board. They managed to give all five of us college educations."

"Quite a feat."

"We all think so."

His handsome face reflected the pride he felt in his parents' accomplishments. "They've been married over forty years."

"That's a long time."

"It sure is. I can't imagine being married to someone for that long. That's more than my entire lifetime." He smiled at her. "I suppose you've never been married." From what Pete told him Jack already knew she hadn't, but it might be interesting if she gave any views on the subject.

"No. I don't think I'm the marrying type."

"Oh? Why's that?"

"Living with the same person, year after year...I'm afraid I'd get bored."

Jack didn't know what to say. Alicia made marriage sound no more meaningful than a marathon session of bid whist. If that was how she felt he couldn't say he hoped to one day find the right woman without sounding like a sap. "I think there's something to be said for having a life partner," he finally said. "For me it's infinitely more preferable than going through life with a series of, uh, significant others, drifting from one affair to the next." He didn't see how she could feel otherwise, but then he thought of Derek Taylor and how he kissed Alicia's lips when he left her party, and suddenly his shoulders went taut.

"What about you, Jack? Ever been married?"

"I was engaged once."

"What happened?"

"She broke it off. An old lover came back into her life, and she realized she wasn't ready to commit to me." He shrugged. "The way I see it, it was for the best. Better to find out sooner than later."

After dinner they shared a raspberry soufflé, laughing and talking about a variety of topics, including their respective professions. "I enjoyed this, Jack," Alicia said as she delicately patted around her mouth with her napkin. "Thank you."

"It sounds like you've been under a lot of stress lately, with your mother being ill. I'm glad you were able to get away for a few hours." He hadn't exaggerated. His watch read ten-twenty p.m., which meant they'd been sitting here for nearly two-and-a-half hours. For him it wasn't nearly enough time.

"Time has been passing so quickly. Can you believe that in another few weeks it'll be Thanksgiving?"

"Fortunately, I made my reservations the moment I accepted the job here."

"You must be going home to Alabama."

"Yes, for a long weekend. I leave Tuesday afternoon and come back Saturday."

"I'm surprised you're not staying until Sunday."

"The Sunday after Thanksgiving is a mob scene. Everybody's going back home that day. I think the only day that's worse is the Wednesday before. I figured I'd travel on Saturday and avoid some of the insanity."

"That makes sense. Will you be spending Christmas with your family, too?"

"No. I've got a huge project pending with a deadline just after the holiday. DVD, titles, the whole nine yards.

I won't be able to take any time off until after the first of the year."

Their waiter appeared just then. "You can bring me the check," Jack requested. Then he turned his attention back to the lovely woman sitting opposite him. "I'm not accustomed to that. Usually I take off the last week of the year. You see, my birthday is Christmas Eve."

She drew in her breath. "No!"

"Yes. People do get born on Christmas Eve, you know."

"I know. I'm one of them."

His head jerked. "Really? I don't think I've met three people my whole life who shared my birthday."

"I only knew one person, someone from school. How old will you be?"

"Thirty-seven."

"I'll be thirty-five." Her face brightened. "Have you made any plans for that day?"

"Not yet. It's still early."

"Why don't we plan on spending it together?"

He broke into a grin. "It's a date."

He opened the door for her as they left, then linked his arm with hers. "Now I'm thinking that I should have insisted on picking you up instead of having you meet me," he said. "I don't like the thought of you going home alone." She seemed steady on her feet, and she spoke clearly and distinctly, but that didn't change the fact that she'd had at least three glasses of wine. He didn't want her going out and getting into an accident.

"I'll be fine, Jack. I only have to drive maybe ten miles."

"I'd like you to call me when you get back to your mother's."

"I will. This is me." They stopped in front of a red Solara convertible. Alicia clicked her remote control, and the lights flashed for a second, indicating unlocking doors.

"Nice ride." Jack began to feel a little nervous. When he suggested she might want to meet him he didn't consider the awkwardness of saying good night in a public parking lot. He'd been so anxious for her to agree to go out with him, he hadn't wanted to provide her with any outs. Fortunately, like him she self-parked instead of using the valet. The last thing he wanted now was an audience.

"I've been happy with it. I keep it at the house so I don't have to deal with the hassle of parking in the city." She turned to him and grasped his forearm through his suit coat. "I had a nice time, Jack."

In an instant he moved in, placing his hands on her shoulders and pulling her to him. He couldn't kiss her the way he wanted to, not here where other patrons might see them, but he just had to get even a quick taste of those luscious berry red lips. He raised his right hand to cup her jaw and raised her face to his, then quickly pressed his lips to hers, running his tongue over them for an instant before pulling away. Her skin felt soft and warm to his fingertips. He could caress it infinitely.

Reluctantly he let his hand fall to his sides. "So did I, but next time I'll definitely call for you." That meant he could bring her home…and kiss her properly.

He held the car door open while she seated herself behind the wheel. She started the engine and lowered the window. "I promise I'll call you when I get in. I've got your number on my caller ID. But you should really get to your car and out of this cold."

"All right. Drive carefully."

He returned the wave she gave him before driving away, then stood watching as the Solara went out to the main road before turning to walk toward his own vehicle.

He'd just eaten a full meal, but he was still hungry.

Just not for food.

the window. "Know it's Christmas Eve and all. I'll
put your number on my schedule," she said, more than a
little unsure of what to say next.

"I really didn't expect—"

Devlin had drawn in a breath, and turned to face
her. "I'm sorry, you have me at a disadvantage. You
mentioned being from a wire service. Do I recognize—"

"Is there someplace we could go before we talk?" she
asked, not sure.

Chapter 10

Something

Alicia's hands trembled on the steering wheel. She
flicked on the heat, but her jitteriness didn't come from
being cold, and she turned it off.

It came from the feel of Jack Devlin's strong hands
on her shoulders, drawing her close to him. It came
from his long fingers on the side of her face, warming
her cheek and making contact with that sensitive spot
behind her earlobe…and it came from his insistent lips
and moist tongue against her mouth.

No doubt about it. The man was dangerous. She
knew all about sexual exhilaration, but Jack represented
something else, something deeper, exactly what she still

hadn't identified. At least she had begun to feel more comfortable with him. The feelings of unease didn't hit until he kissed her in the parking lot.

She considered staying away from him until she had a better handle on her feelings. Maybe something would jog her memory and she would finally understand her reactions to him.

But even as she had the thought of staying away from Jack she knew she wouldn't do it.

Because she could no more ignore the pull she felt toward him than she could defy gravity.

Alicia returned to a quiet house. She'd hoped her mother would be asleep. She wasn't ready to answer any questions about Jack, and she knew her mother would ask.

She went to her room and removed her coat, all the while remembering her promise to Jack. She'd call him, but now she felt the old uneasiness returning. She needed to do something first....

She quickly undressed and washed her face, patting it dry. The tartan plaid flannel pajamas she packed weren't very feminine—actually, they were hideous—but at least they didn't require a bathrobe in case she ran into her brother-in-law, Todd, on the stairs. She plodded down the back stairs to the kitchen. She and Jack had shared a bottle of Pinot Noir with their meal, but she wanted something to bolster her when she called him, just in case she got that nervous feeling. Talking to him on the telephone usually didn't make her unstrung, but this would be the first time they talked since that kiss less than an hour ago.

She found a half-empty bottle of Cabernet Sauvignon in the liquor cabinet, and she carried it upstairs with her, along with a glass.

She poured herself a glass and took a generous swallow before sitting down and reaching for her cell phone. She looked up his number on her list of incoming calls, then pressed the Send button to autodial. As the connection went through she took another swallow of wine, her fingers wrapped around the stem of the glass.

He answered on the first ring. "Are you home?"

"Yes." He'd obviously glanced at the caller ID before answering. "I'm fine, Jack."

"Yes, you are."

She smiled and began to relax. Talking to him on the telephone after that kiss outside the restaurant didn't perturb her like she thought it might. Still, she held on to her glass. "Thank you for tonight, Jack. I had a nice time."

"We'll have to do it again. Soon."

Her eyebrows shot up. Tonight had gone rather well, but she didn't know about doing it again soon—the key word being *soon*.

"Of course," she said lightly. She felt reasonably certain that he wouldn't try to pin her down to specifics; he'd been astute enough to give her the option of meeting him. "I gather you're home."

"Yes, I got in about a half hour ago. I worried about you out driving alone. I really do feel bad about not picking you up, Alicia."

"It's all right. When I got here everyone had gone to bed."

"Everyone?"

"My sister and her husband are here, and so is my nephew. They spend weekends here, too."

"Sounds like you've got a house full."

"Fortunately, the house is large enough. I think that spending every weekend here is a little trying for both of us, especially my sister because she has a family, but we truly do want to be with Mom."

"It's good that she has two loving daughters. Everyone doesn't have that luxury." Jack yawned. "Excuse me."

"I know how you feel. I'm a little sleepy myself."

"Why don't we say good night? We'll talk tomorrow."

"All right. Good night, Jack."

"Alicia?"

"Yes?"

"I'm glad you called. And I hope you'll think about tonight as you fall asleep."

"I'm sure I will," she said honestly. That now-familiar disconcerting feeling came over her again. She felt a tingling from her chest down to her toes. Time to end the call. She disconnected, drained her glass in one last gulp and stretched lazily with the glass still in her hand. Then she shivered, although the heat kept the house comfortably warm on the chilly autumn night.

Alicia placed the glass down, but she couldn't stop trembling. She rushed to her bed, turned it down, and slipped between the sheets, which felt cool to her already chilled skin. She pulled the covers up to her chin and curled into a fetal position, remaining that way until she finally felt warm again.

She turned off her bedside light. The incident of shivering combined with the late hour had left her drained, and she had no difficulty falling asleep.

Chapter 11

I've Got A Feeling

Alicia breezed into her office on Lower Broadway on Monday morning. "Good morning," she greeted her business partner, Shannon Anderson. Five years ago Shannon had an opportunity to purchase an established court reporting service from the retiring owners, and she came to Alicia for financial assistance. At the time Alicia was laboring as a cost accountant and not liking it very much. She jumped at the chance to join her longtime friend.

"Hey there. We've got—"

She looked up expectantly, curious to learn the reason Shannon stopped speaking mid-sentence. To her surprise, her friend simply stared at her, a knowing smile on her face. Alicia lowered her chin and demanded, "What?"

"You met a man. A special one."

Instantly she reached inside her handbag and pulled out her compact. She looked at her reflection, half expecting to see a confession written across her face.

She saw nothing unusual. "Okay, I give up," she said. "How did you know?"

"I'm not sure. You just look different to me today. Happy. I've waited to see that look on your face for years now."

Alicia had to agree with her friend, but she didn't like the idea of being so transparent. Then again, she and Shannon had known each other since fourth grade at Hurlbutt Elementary School, so Shannon could read her better than most people.

"I had a date Saturday," she said lightly.

Shannon smiled knowingly. "And how."

Alicia pointedly cleared her throat. "You were about to tell me something?"

"Oh, yes. I filled an order for a medical malpractice case Friday afternoon after you left. I assigned it to Frances, but we're running short on stenographers who know medical terminology. The others are tied up doing depositions. I'm thinking we should get someone in to give them a quick course."

"Not a bad idea," Alicia said thoughtfully. "We're okay with our technical and financial stenographers, but so many cases are related to medical matters."

"That's my concern, that we'll have to start turning down orders because we're short on staff with technical knowledge. I'll make some inquiries, see how much it'll run to have an instructor do maybe five hour-long sessions to cover the basics."

"Why don't we see how many contractors would be interested first," Alicia suggested.

"All right. I'll phrase it so that it's optional but not optional, if you know what I mean." Shannon smiled at Alicia as she backed her five-foot-nine-inch slim frame toward her office. "I know you don't want to talk about him, so I won't pry. But I'd love to hear all about him when you're ready to share."

Jack reached for the receiver of the ringing phone. "Hello?"

"Guess what?" a female voice half-shrieked. "I'm pregnant!"

He lowered his chin to his chest and frowned. "Uh…who *is* this?"

His response met with another shriek, then a quick word to someone in the background. "Can you believe it? He just asked me who this is." She dissolved in laughter, and Jack heard the receiver being passed.

The next voice he heard belonged to a laughing male. "Rhonda just told me what you said. I guess that wasn't the best way to break it to you."

"Oh, man. Pete. I didn't recognize Rhonda's voice. She scared the bejeezus out of me."

Pete chuckled. "Made you think of that old flame you left behind in Birmingham, huh?"

"Yeah, the one who flew up in September to break it off with me in person, but not before we, uh…."

"I get the picture. We just got the news this afternoon. My wife is already driving me nuts. First she gave me the speech about not telling anyone outside of our parents and siblings until she's through her first trimester, and now she's calling everybody."

Jack didn't buy the aggravated bit for a minute. The pride with which Pete said, "my wife" suggested he felt nothing but joy and good humor. "I'm happy for you both," he said. "I know you've wanted this for a while now."

"Yeah, I guess it's time to stop living like carefree young marrieds and do that whole settle-down thing. House in the suburbs, minivan, the whole shebang." Pete paused a beat. "So, how was dinner with Alicia?"

"It went very well. I took her to Morton's."

"Morton's, huh? That must have set you back a couple of bills."

Jack grinned. "You offering to reimburse me?"

"Not a chance. I'm about to become a family man with a stay-at-home wife. The best I'll be able to do is take-out Chinese. But that was an excellent choice for someone like Alicia. Those rich girls from Westport are used to livin' large."

Jack spoke without thinking. "Westport. Is that where she's from?"

"Yeah. Didn't she tell you?"

"No. I got the feeling she was being cagey about where her mother lived, so I suggested she meet me at the restaurant if she felt my picking her up would disrupt the household."

"That's Alicia for you," Pete said knowingly. "I'll bet she had you thinking her mother lives in a tiny apartment. The truth is that she's got a house with something like fifteen rooms. And Long Island Sound is just beyond their back yard."

Jack whistled. "Sounds impressive."

"Yeah. I was there once, when her sister got married. They had the reception right there on the grounds. Westport probably never saw so many brown faces as it did that day." He chuckled. "Alicia joked that their family and that musician Nile Rodgers are probably the only black residents of the town. And that's probably more than you'll find in Greenwich."

Jack was silent. At least Alicia freely admitted that the house had no shortage of bedrooms, but why had Alicia felt she had to hide her family's wealth from him? He made no bones about his lower middle class background, but he'd become a director for a pharmaceutical giant, overseeing an annual budget in the millions. Did she think he was some poor little nobody after her for her money?

"So I gather she didn't mention much about her personal life," Pete said gently.

"Well, she told me about the business she and her friend started."

"Yeah, Shannon. Another rich Westport girl. I guess her family should be added to the short list of African-Americans living there. Anyway, that's what I mean about Alicia, Jack. She's so charming and so personable that you don't realize you're doing all the talking."

Jack grew quiet with sudden embarrassment. They'd had such a nice conversation that went on for so long, but now he felt almost duped. Sure, he knew about the interesting work she did—"scoping," she called it—in her capacity as partner in a court transcription service. She talked a bit about her college days at U. Conn, but that was virtually the only personal information she'd divulged. Instead he'd rambled on about growing up in Docena and his family, plus a few fond memories of his high jinks at Fisk with Pete. Everything else they discussed had been more of a general topic. How could he pat himself on the back at a job well done when she hadn't even seen fit to even mention the name of the town in which she'd grown up and where her mother still lived?

His mouth set in a determined line. The next time he asked her out—provided there *was* a next time—he would insist he pick her up. And if she refused, he'd just cut his losses and move on.

Chapter 12

All Those Years Ago

Alicia whirled around. "How do I look?"

"You're breathtakingly beautiful," Caroline proclaimed, her hands clasped at the level of her chest.

"Thank you." Alicia made a playful mini-curtsy. She had dressed casually in jeans, suitable for their plans to see a movie.

"I want to meet your young man when he comes," Caroline stated firmly.

"Mom, don't you think going downstairs will be a bit much for you?" Daphne said quickly.

"No, I don't. That's why I have a motorized stair

climber, so I can go up and down without over-exerting myself. I'll go downstairs and sit in the living room."

"But Mom, it's late. You've been up all day. You really should be getting to bed." Daphne turned to Alicia, mouthing the words, "Help me!" with panic in her eyes.

"Daphne, stop over-reacting," Alicia said with undisguised annoyance. "Going downstairs for a few minutes is hardly the same as going out and dancing until dawn. Mom'll be safely in bed before nine o'clock." Sometimes she believed her sister made it a point to disagree with everything she said just to be difficult.

Daphne crossed her arms over her chest. "You just want her to meet your date."

"Yes, I do." Alicia was eager for her mother's impressions of Jack. She started to say, "Just like you wanted Mom to meet Todd when you first started seeing him," but quickly thought better of it. She didn't want to give the wrong idea, like that she expected, or even hoped, to marry Jack, a man she barely knew. But Caroline's instincts had always been dead on where she was concerned. No one knew her better. Maybe she could provide some insight on why he affected her the way he did. Her eagerness for her mother to meet Jack outdid any qualms about Daphne getting in the way. Besides, Jack sounded awfully determined when he asked what time he should pick her up. A sixth sense told her that if she told him she'd meet him again, he would withdraw the invitation. This would be the last time she'd see him before he went home to spend Thanksgiving with his family.

"Well, that's settled. I'd better get downstairs." Caroline placed her palms down on the sofa in her sitting area and pushed herself up. "Help me," she commanded of Daphne, who promptly rose and offered her arm.

"I'll answer the door," Daphne said.

"Gee, thanks," Alicia replied dryly. She would have preferred for Martha to get the door, even if it meant her coming over from the guest house over the three-car garage where she lived with her husband and two high school-age children. She felt Martha would be glad to do it, since she'd expressed curiosity about the first man she'd allowed to pick her up at her mother's home.

Jack pulled into the driveway of the impressive beige brick two-story house. No, make that mansion. From lights in the back of the house he could catch a glimpse of the dark waters of Long Island Sound. He'd love to see it by the light of day. He'd bet it was fabulous. Certainly far removed from his parents' modest home in Docena, which started with two bedrooms, with bedrooms and an additional bath added on in rather haphazard fashion over the years as their family grew.

He rang the doorbell, and after about a minute or so the door opened and he stood face-to-face with a striking young woman whose long reddish-brown hair framed a face highlighted by light blue eyes. This must be the sister Alicia mentioned so off-handedly. "Hello, I'm Jack Devlin, a friend of Alicia's."

"Hi, Jack. I'm Daphne Scott, Alicia's sister. Please come in." She made a sweeping gesture with her hand.

"Alicia will be down in a minute," Daphne said as she closed the door behind them. "I was just sitting with my mother. Come and join us."

"Thank you." He fell into step beside her, forcing himself to look away from the grand winding staircase in the foyer. Not only was this house impressive, such grandeur was a little bit intimidating as well. They went into a living room furnished with red flowered print sofas and matching drapes, solid red easy chairs and red-and-white striped Queen Anne chairs, all with pillows upholstered in one of the opposing prints. The effect was homey, especially with the fire that snapped and crackled in the fireplace, but so coordinated he felt certain a decorator had done it.

A small gray-haired figure sat upright in one of the Queen Anne chairs, most of her body concealed by a tiger print throw.

He walked up to her as Daphne performed introductions. "Jack, may I present my mother, Caroline Timberlake. Mom, this is Jack Devlin, Alicia's date."

He held out his hand. "I'm very glad to know you, Mrs. Timberlake."

She took his hand in her thin one. Her heart-shaped face had lines around her mouth and under her prominent cheekbones. In spite of ill health, Caroline Timberlake was nonetheless a stunningly beautiful woman.

He stiffened as an expression he could only describe as shock formed across her face. "Mr.... Mr. Devlin," she said, making a quick regain of her composure.

Jack had never seen anyone look at him with that expression before. Mrs. Timberlake, a woman he'd never seen in his life, looked like she recognized him as someone repugnant. He felt like he'd suddenly sprouted a third eye.

"Welcome to our home," she said warmly.

Her demeanor was so friendly, he could hardly believe that just seconds ago she recoiled like he was the Ghost of Christmas Past. "Thank you very much. And please call me Jack."

"Please, sit down."

He did as instructed, lowering himself into a comfortable-looking easy chair opposite Caroline's maple rocker. Daphne sat on one of the sofas, a tan leather with a tufted back.

"Did you have any difficulty locating us, Jack?" Caroline asked. "I know that we can be hard to find, especially being so close to the water."

"I'm happy to say I had no problem at all. Alicia provided me with excellent directions." He paused, not sure if he should elaborate before continuing. "I drove up from Stamford."

"Ah, Stamford. I used to live there when Alicia and Daphne were small. We lived in Strawberry Hill."

"Yes, I think my real estate agent showed me a condo in that development. Nice place."

"Are you from Connecticut, Jack?" Daphne asked.

"No, I'm from Alabama. I relocated here to accept a job offer." He realized Alicia's mother and sister were merely making conversation, but he wished they'd stop asking so many questions. Couldn't they just talk about the weather?

"Oh, how quaint." This from Daphne. He was beginning to understand why there seemed to be no love lost between the sisters. She wouldn't have made that remark if he'd said he came from a city north of the

Mason-Dixon line. Next thing she'd be asking how they managed to drive on dirt roads when it rained.

The sound of footsteps rushing down the steps quieted them all. "This must be Alicia," Caroline said expectantly.

Jack rose when she entered the room. He broke into a smile at the mere sight of her. Even in jeans, a blue chambray collared shirt and a red pullover sweater, she looked gorgeous.

"Hi, Dev," she said to him. "I hope I didn't keep you waiting too long."

"I think I could have held off running amuck for another minute or two," he said with a smile.

"Well, the movie starts in twenty minutes, so we'd better get going." She removed her coat from over her arm, and Jack quickly moved behind her to help her into it. He noticed her hair was twisted in a single French braid down the back of her head.

"Mrs. Timberlake, Daphne, it was a pleasure," he said politely.

"Same here, Jack," Caroline said warmly. No traces remained of her quickly concealed but obvious disconcertment of just a few moments before, but Jack knew he'd never forget her reaction. "Come and see us again."

"Thank you, ma'am." He placed a hand on Alicia's elbow.

She stepped forward to Caroline's side and bent to kiss her cheek. "Good night, Mom. I'll see you in the morning. 'Bye, Daphne."

"I'll get the door," Daphne offered.

The moment the latch clicked into place Daphne

returned to the living room, where Caroline sat staring out the window. "Mom, when you got a good look at Jack you had a look on your face like you'd just seen a poltergeist. What was that all about?"

Caroline sighed. "I couldn't help it. He just looked so much like—"

"Like who?"

She bowed her head. "All those years ago. It was like a photograph come to life."

"Mom, what are you talking about?" an exasperated Daphne asked.

Caroline looked up again, but she appeared to be speaking to an unseen person rather than Daphne. "It's all come together. No wonder Alicia said he gave her an unsettling feeling. I was going to tell her, I swear I was. And I will. I want her to know the truth before I go. I'll tell her first chance I get. Praise God, there's still time."

"Mom, you're confusing me something awful, so whatever it is, why don't you tell me *now?*"

Chapter 13

Maybe I'm Amazed

"Your mother has a beautiful home," Jack remarked as he drove out of the semi-circular driveway. "Is that where you grew up?"

"Yes. My father bought the house in Nineteen Eighty. It had been built forty years earlier and was still in the hands of the original family. I was nine years old and in the fourth grade when we moved here from Stamford. My sister and her husband had their wedding reception out back."

"If you don't mind my asking, what did your father do for a living?"

She grinned at him. "I hope you're not wondering if he did anything illegal."

"No, of course not."

"He was a criminal attorney, one of the best. He represented a lot of well-to-do folks in New York when they were charged with crimes like embezzlement or fraud. He also represented their children when they got into serious trouble. Plus, he took a few pro bono cases here and there, if it was a case he believed in."

"A good field, law. How did he feel about your getting into court stenography?"

"He didn't like it. He felt it was beneath me, that I should have gone to law school if I wanted a legal career." Alicia sighed. "Sometimes my father could be hard to please."

"You miss him, don't you?"

"Of course. But my fondest memories of him are from when I was small, before Daphne was born. I remember him carrying me up on his shoulders. He was very tall, and I'd wrap my arms around his neck tightly because it seemed like I was so high up. I'm amazed I didn't choke him to death." She chuckled at the memory. "As he got older he started getting a little crochety and *very* opinionated, as if his way was the only way."

"Some people get that way as they age. Alicia...."

She shivered. She wasn't cold, she just reacted to the way he said her name. It left her breathless. She'd never responded to any man the way she did to Jack Devlin. It amazed her. "Yes?" she managed to say.

He covered her palm with his. "I'm glad you didn't object to my picking you up tonight."

She chuckled. "It almost feels like I'm seventeen

again, with my date coming to pick me up and meeting my parents."

"I'm glad I got the opportunity to meet your mother. She's a beautiful woman." He tactfully refrained from mentioning the strange look Caroline Timberlake gave him. At best, it could be described as shock; at worst, horror.

"She is, isn't she?"

"Daphne looks a lot like her."

"I know. I look more like my father, other than inheriting my mother's cheekbones."

"Maybe next time you'll show me a photograph of him."

"I'll do that."

After the movie they stopped at a restaurant and ordered a light meal. As they walked back to his SUV he captured her soft hand in his and held it, not tightly, so she could pull away if she wanted. To his joy, she didn't.

They'd seen one of those thought-provoking films that spurred conversation long after the final fade-out. The plot had taken twists and turns that neither of them anticipated. They talked about it all the way back to the Timberlake home.

Jack steered the Aviator into the circular drive, carefully passing the three vehicles parked on the right border. He quickly got out and went around to her side and opened the door for her, extending his hand to help her down from the high-sitting vehicle. He moved in to close the passenger door and found himself standing just inches from her. He could smell her perfume, and a little bit of the vinaigrette she'd had with her salad.

Later, he couldn't even remember how it started. He only knew that she was in his arms, and he was kissing her with the pent-up fervor that he'd harbored since meeting her. Better yet, she kissed him back. Her arms went around his neck and then to the back of his head, holding him in place.

He broke away from her lips to nibble on her earlobe, and as he did so his fingers smoothly unbuttoned the large buttons that held her jacket closed and slipped beneath it, desperate to feel feminine curves rather than a shapeless mass of wool.

That accomplished, he found her lips once more. He felt her body tremble. As he felt her passion rising, his own grew stronger. He'd waited for this moment for weeks.

Alicia tried to hold steady, but she couldn't control her reaction to him. She moaned into his mouth, her body quaking unstoppably. Whether his voice saying her name in his special way, or his mouth ravaging hers, she had never experienced these feelings with any man. Her emotions whirled and skidded like an out-of-control vehicle on an icy road.

When they parted at last she held the front of her jacket together with her hands. The mercury had dipped since they set out hours earlier. "It's cold," she said, steam arising from her warm mouth.

He slipped his arm through hers. "Come on, let's get you inside."

He guided her the few feet to the front door, waiting behind her as she retrieved her keys from her purse and unlocked the door, aided by the lights that flanked the doorway.

She pushed the heavy oak door open and gestured for him to follow her inside. He shut the door behind him to keep out the cold. A night light shone dimly in the foyer, another illuminated the stairs.

"I'm not going to stay, Alicia," he said. "I just wanted to see you inside."

She didn't seem surprised at his statement. "I had a nice time tonight, Jack. We'll do it again, huh?"

"You bet." He leaned in and kissed her again, briefly this time.

Jack jauntily walked back to the Aviator. Alicia Timberlake was one amazing woman.

If he had his way, she would be *his* woman.

Chapter 14

Hello Goodbye

"It was so nice of you to invite us to dinner, Alicia," Florence Scott said. She had just given her coat to her husband, Henry, to hang up in the closet and prepared to sit down in the living room. The large room was warm and inviting, courtesy of the fire Todd had going in the fireplace and the scent of roasting turkey that wafted out through the kitchen. "We would have had you over to our home, but Todd said he didn't feel Caroline was up to riding to New Rochelle."

Alicia had always been fond of her brother-in-law's parents. "No, Mrs. Scott, I'm afraid she isn't."

"I know it's been hard on all of you, spending your

weekends up here all these months. I'm proud of you
girls, and my son as well, for being so understanding.
A lesser man would have put his foot down after all
this time."

"Yes, Todd's been wonderful, coming up here on the
weekends and taking over most of Fletch's care so
Daphne can tend to Mom." Todd worked as assistant
prosecutor in the Westchester County jurisdiction, while
Daphne's career as an elementary school teacher was on
hold as she raised little Fletch. "A rambunctious toddler
is a bit much for Mom to take, even if he's her only
grandchild and she's crazy about him."

"Again, I think it's just wonderful how devoted you two
girls are to your mother. It's like you never leave her side."

Alicia nodded politely with a secretive smile. Mrs.
Scott's statement was more accurate than she knew.
Ever since Sunday morning Daphne had become an
extra appendage to Caroline, virtually never leaving her
alone. She'd been right there that morning when Alicia
went to her mother's room to find out what she thought
of Jack. Alicia would have preferred it if she and her
mother could speak privately, but since Daphne made
no move to leave she had no choice. Part of her couldn't
blame her sister. After a short-lived rally, Caroline had
become visibly weaker. Her cardiologist had told Alicia
that she might not live to the end of the year.

"He's handsome, isn't he?" Caroline had remarked.

"Yes, he certainly is. But it's the strangest thing,
Mom. The minute I saw him I felt all shaky and nervous,
like I knew him from someplace. I tried and tried to
remember, but I couldn't. And from what I've learned

about him, he and I have never even been in the same state at the same time."

"Do you still get that feeling?"

"Not as often." Alicia didn't want to admit that she usually bolstered herself with three or four glasses of wine before seeing Jack, and that in spite of that she still felt flustered when she knew he was about to kiss her, almost like there was something forbidden about it.

He'd kissed her senseless when he brought her home Saturday night after a movie and a late meal, a deep, tantalizing, openmouthed kiss with her back blissfully up against the wall. She wouldn't have a problem discussing it with her mother if the two of them were alone, but she felt it too personal a matter to discuss in front of Daphne. It pleased her that Caroline, despite rapidly failing health, appeared genuinely interested in knowing all about Jack.

"You're probably thinking of someone else," Caroline said. "I wouldn't let it bother me if I were you. He seems like a well-mannered, well-educated, well-spoken young man." She shrugged her shoulders. "What else could any mother hope for her daughter?"

"He probably just reminds you of someone, Alicia," Daphne said in a dismissive tone.

Alicia found herself annoyed at her sister's breezy attitude toward her inexplicable emotions regarding Jack. On one hand, she was glad to know that Daphne had finally accepted the inevitable, but at the same time she resented Daphne's attaching herself to Caroline's bedside, thus robbing her of any opportunity to have a private conversation with her mother.

At this point, it would be hard for anyone to convince themselves that a recovery was possible. Caroline's longtime cardiologist, during a house call, advised her to try not to leave the house, and LPNs now alternated around the clock seven days a week, each working twelve-hour shifts.

Alicia and Daphne arranged for a catered meal for the family, including Daphne's in-laws, the Scotts, plus Martha, Marvin and their children. Daphne initially balked at sitting down to dinner with the family housekeeper, but Alicia held her ground and Caroline backed her. "You remember what Mom said?" Alicia said. "Martha is almost like another daughter to her. There's no reason why they shouldn't eat with us. They've done it before, when it was just Mom and Pop and me and you were with Todd's family. If anything, it's more befitting now than ever before," she said meaningfully.

From the way Daphne's face wrinkled like she was about to cry, Alicia knew she understood. This would be their mother's last Thanksgiving.

After a leisurely dinner that ran two hours from the carving of the turkey until dessert and coffee, Todd and Daphne slowly walked Caroline to the motorized stair climber and got her upstairs. Alicia helped Martha and Martha's daughter, Melody, clean the kitchen. Daphne, returning from upstairs, simply joined her in-laws in the rec room in the basement. She didn't even offer to help, which surprised neither Alicia nor Martha.

Martha loaded the dishwasher while Melody put away the last of the leftovers. Alicia had put the place mats away and was wiping down the dining room table when her cell phone began vibrating in her pocket.

She pulled it out and sank into an upholstered French Provincial chair. She wondered if it could be Jack. She hadn't talked to him since Sunday, when he called to tell her how much he enjoyed himself Saturday night. The very thought of him calling her from Alabama made her tingle. She took a moment to calm herself, then unfolded the cell and uttered a collected-sounding, "Hello."

"Happy Thanksgiving, Alicia!"

She broke into a smile at the sound of his voice. "Dev! What a wonderful surprise!" Although she'd been hoping he would call, she really didn't expect he would. This was his time to enjoy his parents and siblings. She'd been a bit disappointed when she didn't hear from him in the days before he flew home for the holiday, even though she knew he was immersed in a major project at work. She didn't understand it. She usually despised it when a man called her every five minutes. It made her feel like someone had placed a pillow over her face while she slept, not tightly, but just enough to cause impairment in her breathing.

When it came to Jack, everything seemed different. It delighted her that he had thought of her during his vacation. "Are you enjoying your holiday?"

"Absolutely. It's always refreshing to be around my family. Nieces and nephews running all over the place, my parents glowing, everybody patting their bellies and saying they ate too much. The usual."

She laughed. "Here, too. But it's been a wonderful day. Mom came downstairs for dinner." She paused, then spoke in a near-whisper. "The doctor doesn't think she'll be here for next Thanksgiving."

His heart ached at the sorrow she clearly felt. "I'm sorry to hear that."

"I know you are."

"I thought of you today, off and on all day. I decided to call you after I was certain you were done with dinner."

"I'm glad you did, Jack."

He noticed that she called him "Dev" during casual conversation and banter, but when she felt serious she called him by his given name. He wondered if she was aware of making the distinction. Not that he was about to fill her in. It gave him a clear advantage to figuring her out.

"And I'm glad to hear you're having such a good time with your family. I know you miss them."

"Right now I'm missing you. Will you be spending the rest of the weekend at your mother's?"

"Definitely. And I'd love to see you when you get back Saturday."

He broke into a grin. He liked it when a woman took the initiative, and even more when that woman was Alicia Timberlake. "Great. My flight gets into LaGuardia at one o'clock. I'm not sure how long it'll take me to get home from there, but why don't you reserve Saturday night for me?"

"Let's make it earlier," she heard herself saying. "It won't take you an hour to drive to Connecticut. You parked at the airport, didn't you?"

"No, I went to work Tuesday morning and took a cab to the airport from midtown that afternoon. I know they have transport services, or else I'll just get a bus to One Twenty-Fifth Street and I'll catch the train from there. All I have is a duffel bag."

"You'll do no such thing. I'll come down and pick you up."

"No, Alicia. It's too far. I can't have you drive all the way from Westport."

"Give me your flight information."

He chuckled. "I see there's no stopping you once you've made up your mind."

"That's right."

He recited the flight and the arrival time.

She repeated it. "I'll go write it down right now so I don't forget. See you Saturday, Dev. Enjoy the rest of your time with your family. And—" She broke off, suddenly shy.

"What?" he asked curiously.

After a moment's hesitation, she said with the shyness of honesty, "I'm glad you called."

Jack hung up the phone with a satisfied smile on his face. Alicia wanted to pick him up on Saturday. Could it be that she missed him?

"So, Jack, who were you talking to that gave you that smile on your face? Is that the girlfriend?"

"Oh, please." He kept his tone droll, determined not to let his sister see how pleased he really felt.

Everyone knew that the woman he had a fledgling relationship with in Birmingham dumped him after he relocated, not seeing any future in a long-distance love affair. Most of his siblings and their spouses, and especially his parents, wanted to know if he'd met anyone special. Jack, the middle child, was the only one who hadn't yet married. He told them he'd met someone, but fibbed and said they were still getting to know each other, that it was too soon to know if anything would come of it. Even that morsel of information spurred a barrage of questions. "What does she look like?" "How old is she?" "What kind of work does she do?" "When will we meet her?" "Are you bringing her on the cruise?"

The last question referred to the trip the family took together every three years. With Jack's recent move to the Northeast, only two of Clarence and Melba Devlin's five children remained in greater Birmingham. They decided it was imperative that their children stay in touch and their grandchildren know each other, so six years before they implemented a family reunion. The entire family met in Orlando for a week of socializing, relaxation, fun, and worship. It went so well that Jack and his siblings vowed to get together every third year. They opted for that particular timing to give everyone a chance to budget and to take other vacations on intervening years. They insisted that every member of the family attend, no matter how young. It was as much an obligation as paying one's mortgage. Missing out simply wasn't an option.

Three years before they all went to Phoenix, and this year they booked a five-night cruise to Key West, Mexico, and the Cayman Islands for February.

He good-naturedly answered all the questions. "She's very pretty… She's thirty-four, and she has the same birthday as me… She owns a court stenography service… I don't know when you'll meet her… I'm not sure she's ready to meet all you guys. You might make a bad impression and then she'll quit me."

That remark met with affable protests, and his mother said, "Seriously, Jack. Have you thought about asking your young lady to join us on the cruise?"

"Mom, I haven't even thought about it," he said truthfully, managing to keep a straight face. The thought of Alicia at his—or anyone else's, for that matter—family reunion was enough to make him burst out laughing. He could hardly tell his mother that Alicia simply wasn't the type to attend such a function. Melba Devlin would be indignant that Alicia wouldn't jump at the chance to accompany him. Worse, she'd probably comment that she didn't sound very family oriented.

Which, of course, she wasn't.

Right now he looked forward to seeing her on Saturday. He didn't get a chance to say goodbye to her before he left, but when he saw her again he'd certainly give her an ardent hello.

Chapter 15

Drive My Car

The moment Jack heard the bell that signified the turning off of the Fasten Seat Belt sign he shot out of his aisle seat and removed his duffel from the overhead rack. He sat in the first row of Coach, springing for business class only on flights longer than three hours. Usually he sat reading while his fellow passengers lined up to disembark, even those folks way in the back who clearly weren't going anywhere anytime soon. This time it was different. In about five minutes he'd see Alicia.

Soon off the plane, he moved with long strides toward the escalators leading to the baggage claim area and the exits. He pulled his cell phone out of his pocket.

He probably had time to tell Alicia not to bother to park, that he had no luggage to retrieve at the carousel and was all ready to go.

He held the phone to his ear and said the command, "Call Alicia," which prompted the voice-activated gadget to dial Alicia's cell number. She'd mentioned to him previously that she had a cell mount in her car so she could take incoming calls without violating New York law.

"Hello," she said in the low-pitched voice that made his pulse race.

"Alicia, it's Jack. Just wanted to let you know I'm on my way down to the exit, so you don't have to worry about parking when you get here."

"Already? Your plane must have had good tailwind to get in so early."

"Actually, we landed on time, but I was near the front and I didn't check my bag."

"Okay. I'm on the Grand Central Parkway now, probably one exit away. I'll be there in a few minutes."

Her voice sounded soothing to his ears as an incoming surf. He pictured her zooming down the highway in her red Solara. "I'll be waiting."

Less than five minutes later he flagged her down as she slowed by the terminal doors of his airline. But she was not alone. A large Irish setter sat perched on the arm rest.

"Hey!" he greeted as he opened the passenger door and tossed his duffel carelessly in the back. He wished her eyes weren't covered by sunglasses, but her broad smile and warm greeting suggested she was happy to see him. "I didn't know you had a dog." He reached out to gently rub behind the setter's ears. "Hiya, boy. You *are* a boy, aren't you?"

"Yes," Alicia said. "Jack, this is Lucky. Lucky, this is Jack."

Lucky barked, a quick bark that suggested a "Hi!"

"You must have practiced that," he said in disbelief.

"No. We're in tune, Lucky and I. Always have been." She leaned toward the animal and sang the first few bars of "Luck Be a Lady Tonight," and the dog made a whimpering sound, as if to say, "I like it!"

"Lucky is actually my parents' dog," Alicia explained. "He stays in Green's Farms, but he usually comes with me when I go out in the car. He likes to ride. And he doesn't get car sick."

"Glad to hear it." He knew she wondered why he still knelt on the passenger seat instead of sitting down. "Um…I don't mind taking the wheel for the ride back, since you drove all the way down here." He still felt a little guilty about her coming down from Westport. At least if he drove back it wouldn't seem so much like she was serving as his chauffeur.

"Sure, why not?" She clicked her seat belt open. "Sit tight, Lucky. I'm just going to change places with Jack." She opened the door and stepped out, and Lucky didn't as much as blink. It was as if he understood what she said.

He met her halfway as they walked around the front of the Solara. She smiled up at him, and he took a lingering glance over her figure, dressed in jeans, flats and a pea jacket, before impulsively bending to kiss her mouth briefly. "Thanks for driving down to pick me up." Then he jauntily stepped aside to let her pass.

"We're leaving right now," he said pleasantly to the security officer who approached, before he could tell them to move on.

Inside the Solara, he slid the seat back a few inches to give him more leg room. Lucky practically jumped in his lap to start sniffing him. "Uh...Lucky, why don't you move back a little, let me drive, and we can get acquainted later," he suggested.

Alicia patted the center console. "Come on, Lucky. Get back."

The setter obediently obeyed.

Jack looked on in amazement. "You've really got that animal trained, don't you?"

He guided the car through the airport export and onto the parkway, into typically heavy but moving traffic. Jack felt that people exaggerated the skill needed to drive in New York City. Unfortunately, motorists cut in front of other vehicles on highways all over the country, even in greater Birmingham. Driving on I-65 might even be more dangerous than any roadway in New York. He'd read that a startlingly high percentage of drivers on the interstate in Alabama packed pistols in their glove compartments, and more than one incident of cutting off a fellow motorist had ended in road rage tragedy.

As he drove Jack heard music, what sounded like an untalented male singer warbling a ballad. "I don't know who that is, but he sure sounds awful. Whoever told him he could sing?"

"Oh, that's my cell ringing," Alicia said easily. She removed it from its holder. "Hello."

Jack's fingers clenched the steering wheel as he

recalled what Pete told him about Alicia's easygoing nature. He didn't want to share her with anyone, especially another man.

His being behind the wheel allowed her to hold the phone to her ear, rather than using the speaker. He might not be able to hear the caller, but he couldn't help overhearing her end of the conversation due to their close proximity. "Hi!" she greeted sincerely.

She certainly sounded happy to hear from whomever was on the other side of the line, he thought suspiciously. He listened as the conversation continued.

"That sounds great, but I'm afraid I won't make it. I just picked up Jack—you remember Jack Devlin, he was at my apartment last month—from LaGuardia, and we're headed back up to Connecticut."

That dude Derek Taylor would remember him, Jack thought with annoyance. Could she be talking to him? His grip on the steering wheel tightened.

"I don't expect to get back to the city before tomorrow night," Alicia continued. "But you guys have a good time. Maybe we'll be able to join you next time. Okay. 'Bye, Jenny."

Jack felt like he'd just been sprayed with fairy dust. Alicia hadn't been speaking with a man, she'd talked with her friend Jenny, whom he remembered from her party. And, better yet, she'd said that "we" might be able to join them another time. He wondered if she realized that she'd referred to them as a couple.

Alicia disconnected the call and replaced her phone in the holder. "That was Jenny Walters. You met her at that little get-together at my place, even if you don't remember her. She said a group is getting together to check out some new place on Columbus Avenue tonight and asked if I wanted to come along. I told her maybe next time."

Secretly he liked her response, but he felt he ought to say something modest. "I hope I'm not putting you out."

"No, not at all. I planned to stay at my mother's until tomorrow anyway."

"Hey, that's some ring tone you've got. I'm thinking I've heard it before, but I can't place it."

She laughed. "I downloaded it from the Internet. It came from that old Eddie Murphy movie, *Coming to America.*"

He snapped his fingers. "That's it! Now I remember." He now had a clear memory of the heavyset employee of Eddie Murphy's royal family presenting Eddie with the bride chosen for him by his father, the king. How could he have forgotten the way the man's voice cracked as he strained to hit the high notes? It had been a laugh riot.

"I can always tell when it's my phone ringing because no one else has that ring tone," Alicia said.

As if on cue, the cell phone began ringing again. "Oh, who is this now," she said, sounding slightly annoyed.

"It better not be any of your male admirers," Jack said. The moment the words came out he regretted it. He sounded like a jealous, possessive old poop, and this after he'd vowed to give her space. He'd just put distance between them.

To his surprise, Alicia didn't seem to mind. "Well, if it is I'm giving them the boot," she said. "This afternoon belongs to us."

He fixed his eyes on the road ahead of him. Could that mean she'd missed him? He'd had some weak moments on Monday and Tuesday, when he desperately wanted to pick up the phone and call her. He managed to stick to his guns, knowing that he would fare better if he kept her at the same distance she wished to keep him. If he called her daily she never would have said that the afternoon would belong to them. Instead she would have dropped him off at his condo with a kiss and driven away.

Part of him, especially when looking at her lips, which this time were a luscious red, wanted to ask, *What about the evening?* The only thing stopping him was the suspicion that she might accept. He'd rather keep their relationship chaste before becoming just another man she fell into bed with when the mood struck. He wanted intimacy between them to mean as much to her as it would to him.

Once again he listened to her end of the conversation. It really couldn't be called eavesdropping; in the close confines of the vehicle she could have no secrets from him.

"Yes, I'm on my way to Stamford," she was saying.

Jack became alarmed when he saw her expression change to one of distress. "Oh, no!"

"Alicia, what is it?" he hissed.

"Just a minute, Martha." She spoke away from the receiver. "It's Mom. Daphne was sitting with her when she suddenly went limp. Martha—she's the live-in housekeeper—got her revived, and Daphne's husband called the paramedics. They should be there any minute."

Jack immediately sped up. This was no longer a

pleasant Saturday afternoon drive, but a mission. "I'll
drive as fast as I can without getting pulled over for
speeding." That might be difficult in a red convertible,
for even with the top up; the sleek lines of the car practically screamed out, "Arrest me!"

Alicia put the cell phone back to her ear. "Sorry. I
needed to fill Jack in on what's going on." She paused,
and Jack could hear Martha's voice, although he
couldn't make out what she said.

"Well, I don't know," Alicia said. "We just left the
airport maybe ten minutes ago. We haven't even gotten
to the bridge yet. By the time I bring Jack home and then
drive up there—"

By the time she brought him home! "Give me the
phone, Alicia," he commanded.

Surprisingly, she didn't object, ask his intentions, or
remind him that talking on a cell phone while driving
was illegal in New York. She merely handed him the
phone without another word to Martha.

"Hello, Martha," he said. "This is Jack Devlin. I'm
a friend of Alicia's. You and I haven't met, but I want
you to know that we won't be making any stops or
taking any detours from the straightest route to
Westport. I'll get Alicia there as soon as I can." It
shocked him that, under the circumstances, Alicia would
even consider bringing him home before going to her
mother's home.

"Thank you, Jack. I'd hoped you'd be driving. I was
afraid of upsetting Alicia while she was behind the
wheel, but she had to be told. I couldn't take the chance
of her stopping off someplace for an early dinner."

"I understand." Jack glanced over at Alicia, who met his gaze with gratitude in her eyes. "Now I'd better give this phone back to Alicia before I get arrested for violating the law." He calmly handed the phone back to her.

Six hours later he returned her to her mother's front door. Martha called back to inform Alicia that Caroline had been brought to the hospital in Norwalk, and they went directly there. They spent the next two hours waiting, finally learning that Caroline's condition had stabilized. It took another two hours to get her into a room.

Jack met the entire group: Daphne's husband, Todd Scott; the longtime housekeeper Martha Lewis and her husband Marvin, and even Caroline's personal physician, Dr. Ivan Jordan, who had driven up from Stamford. Daphne and Todd's toddler son, Fletch, had been left in the care of Martha and Marvin's teenage children at home.

He'd been surprised to see that Martha appeared to be only in her early forties. She'd sounded relatively young on the telephone, but his own mother also sounded much younger than her actual age. He felt that her retaining a youthful, higher-pitched speaking voice had something to do with her having never been a smoker.

Martha's old-fashioned name had given him the impression she was a woman in her sixties. He liked her immediately, and Marvin, too. They seemed more like family than employees, genuinely worried about Caroline.

He did what he could to comfort Alicia, and she seemed to respond to him, at one point resting her head on his chest. Waiting together gave him the opportunity to observe the family dynamics. At first they seemed like a typical family, united in concern for their hospitalized member, but then he noticed the limited interaction between Daphne and Alicia and a total lack of contact between Daphne and Martha and wondered what it was all about.

Jack waited in the reception area while Alicia and Daphne, having received clearance, went into the emergency bay to visit with their mother, followed by Martha and Todd. Dr. Jordan had been allowed back even before the family, and Marvin Lewis opted to stay with and chat with Jack, saying he would see Caroline later.

"Miss Caroline's a good lady," he said, his stocky brown face anxious. "She and Mr. Fletcher have been real good to us."

"Do you work for Mrs. Timberlake, too?"

"No. I'm an Operations Supervisor for McDonald's. But fifteen years ago the apartment house where we lived in Bridgeport burned down, and Martha and I lost everything. Our son was two and our daughter just a baby. The Timberlakes heard about us through the church network—theirs was an upper echelon church in Stamford—and offered Martha a job as their housekeeper. She'd never done that type of work before, but their old housekeeper retired and they needed the help, and taking the job meant she could keep our kids with her.

"Best of all, in those early days they didn't charge us any rent to live over their garage. They didn't pay her a whole lot, but that free rent and no day care really helped us get back on our feet. At the time I'd just gotten into the Management Trainee program at McDonald's and wasn't making much money. To this day they still don't charge us anywhere near the full market rate for the apartment."

"That's awfully nice of them," Jack said.

"Good people, the Timberlakes." Marvin looked at Jack curiously. "You know, I've never known Alicia to bring anyone home. She's pretty much kept her social life confined to New York."

"I met her in the city. But I live in Stamford. She'd just picked me up from the airport when Martha called. We rushed right over."

"Yeah, I hope they get Miss Caroline to her room soon. I'm startin' to get hungry."

"You and me both, man."

After Caroline had been transported to a private room, Jack prepared to wait in a different reception area. He was exhausted and hungry as well, but wanted to stick it out for Alicia's sake.

It caught him by surprise when Alicia asked him to come along with her to Caroline's room. "Shouldn't it be family only?" he asked hesitantly.

"No, anyone can visit, and it won't matter if we're all in there at once, since she has a private room. I just want to sit with her for a few minutes. Then I guess we'll all leave so she can get some rest." She took his arm, an affectionate move that surprised him. "Then you and I can go get something to eat."

* * *

They went to a small Italian restaurant in the village. The end of the meal found Alicia yawning uncontrollably. He realized how stressful the afternoon had been for her. "I honestly don't think you're up to driving me to Stamford."

"I think you're right. I hate to ask you this, but would you mind terribly staying at the house tonight?"

He shrugged. He'd expected her to tell him to take her car and return it in the morning, but staying at the house would work, too. At least he'd still be close to her. "I've slept on sofas before."

"You can stay in my nephew Fletch's room...or, I should say, the room where Fletch usually stays."

"He'll probably freak out at having a stranger sleep in the same room."

"Oh, he won't be there. Daphne and Todd are going home tonight."

Her words hit him like a sock in the stomach. "So it'll just be you and me?"

"Yes. And Lucky, of course. But there's no need for Daphne and Todd to stay at the house if Mom's in the hospital, and the nurses aren't needed, either." She smiled at him, amusement in her dark eyes. "You're not afraid to be alone with me, are you?"

"Of course not," he said, too quickly.

He did the driving when they set out for the Timberlake home, Alicia directing him. Inside, he followed her up the curved staircase, duffel bag hanging from his shoulder.

The room he would sleep in was at the end of the hall,

near the back stairs. He wondered where she would sleep, but didn't ask. Maybe it was best he *didn't* know....

The temperature in the house was warm, almost too much so. Lucky wandered into the room as Jack dug out a pair of flannel drawstring pants from his duffel bag. "Looks like you're trapped in here with me, fella," he said to the dog as he rubbed his back.

Jack closed the bedroom door and put on the drawstring pants, taking off everything else, even his T-shirt. He took a few minutes to call his parents to let them know he'd arrived safely. His father didn't ask why it had taken so long for him to call, and Jack didn't volunteer any information about Alicia or her family emergency. Feeling restless, he reclined in bed channel surfing with the remote control when she knocked on the door. Lucky curled up on the floor beside his bed, looking content.

"Come in," he said.

The door opened, and he gazed at her in awe. Her hair had been brushed back away from her face and pinned up, looking almost like she was going out for the evening. She wore a belted tan print bathrobe of some kind of slinky material, over what appeared to be a matching nightgown. She looked absolutely ravishing. He moved into a sitting position, quickly tossing a pillow lengthwise on his lap to hide both his bare chest and his pulsating erection.

"I hope I'm not interrupting anything," she said.

"No. I just got off the phone with my parents, wanted to call and let them know I'd made it back, even though I'm sure she figured out hours ago that I'd landed safely. I was just watching some TV."

She took a step closer, light glistening on sections of

her gown and robe. "I just wanted to thank you for being such a good sport about this afternoon, coming with me to the hospital and all, and staying." After the ER physician's pronouncement that Caroline was stable and resting comfortably, a statement backed up by Dr. Jordan, Alicia suggested to Jack that she bring him home while they waited for Caroline's transport to her room, but he refused. To cut out then struck him as abandonment. He was determined to see it through.

"I know I said the day would be ours," she continued. "It didn't exactly work out that way, did it?"

"Like they say, it's the thought that counts," he said, not taking his eyes off her.

"I'm sorry I couldn't get you home tonight."

"My place will still be there tomorrow."

"You're very understanding."

"I wouldn't say that." His voice suddenly went hoarse. "Don't you know it's dangerous to come into a man's room looking as good as you do?"

She took a step backward, the fabric of her robe swirling around her ankles. "I just wanted to tell you I appreciated your being there," she said shyly. "And I also wanted to make sure you were comfortable."

"I'm good."

"In that case I'll say good night. I'll see you in the morning."

"Good night, Alicia." He caught one last glimpse of her as she backed out of the room. Lucky suddenly jumped up and squeezed through as she closed the door, apparently deciding he'd rather sleep in her room. Jack didn't blame him. So would he.

He threw the pillow off him and sank back into a reclining position. His eyes closed, but instantly he saw
a vision of her as she'd just appeared. He imagined
going over to her, untying the sash around her waist and
pushing the robe off her shoulders, taking the pins out
of her hair....

And he knew it would be a very long time before he
got to sleep.

Chapter 16

Act Naturally

Snow began to fall lightly after the morning rush hour. The TV weather folks had predicted flurries, not unusual for mid-December and giving a nice seasonal touch to the holiday season. Alicia looked out of the window of her office in mid-morning and noticed that the precipitation had become steadier. She instantly became suspicious. It didn't look like mere flurries to *her*.

By lunchtime the ground was covered with a blanket of white. She pulled out the old pair of nylon lambskin-lined boots she kept in the top drawer of the file cabinet in her office, along with other personal rainy day—in this case *snowy* day—supplies.

"This is incredible," Shannon complained upon returning with lunch from the deli on the ground floor of the building. "It's covering my feet already. I've never seen such a snowfall this early in the season. We usually don't get slammed with anything more than flurries before January."

"I told you to let me pick up your salad when I bring back my calzone." Shannon, tall and slim, perpetually watched what she ate, consuming salads two or three times a week. "Of course, if those size eleven clodhoppers of yours could fit into my boots, you'd be welcome to them."

"We can't all wear a size eight," Shannon muttered as she pulled off her Bass Weejuns and massaged her sock-clad feet. "If this keeps up court will let out early and we'll be able to get out of here. Hopefully I can get home without breaking my neck."

"Maybe you should go buy a pair of boots," Alicia suggested. "It's a cinch you won't be able to get a cab." Shannon lived in a basement apartment in Greenwich Village.

"The hell I won't. And any man who tries to cut in will find his butt sitting in the snow." Shannon had enrolled in a self-defense course at the local Y, and Alicia knew she couldn't wait for an opportunity to kick some butt.

Alicia felt that today would present an excellent chance to demonstrate the defensive skills her partner had learned. Bad weather often brought out the worst in people as taxis became scarce and mass transit less reliable.

She left Shannon munching on her crunchy salad, venturing outside where the snow already measured two or three inches. Pedestrians stepped with care on the slippery sidewalks, practically taking baby steps, to prevent loss of balance. Most of them wore regular street shoes, with a few women clad in cold weather boots—not the same thing as snow boots, since most had high heels. The vendors who usually sold hot dogs from pushcarts hadn't shown up today.

An unusually light number of patrons came to the pizzeria around the corner from Alicia's office, but she soon noticed that most people had sizeable take-out orders, like they'd taken lunch orders for their entire departments. One enterprising young man brought along a thick plastic carton on wheels, the kind usually used to transport documents. He placed numerous food orders into the carton and left the pizzeria, pulling it behind him.

Alicia returned to the office with the steak-and-cheese calzone she'd gone out to get. Shannon waited in her office grimly. "They've revised the forecast, Alicia. Apparently, the storm system stalled somewhere over the entire metro area. They say this could be one for the record books."

"Oh, fine," she said with a groan. "It couldn't have waited another ten days or so, when everybody's home for Christmas?"

"I sent Amy home," Shannon said, referring to their administrative assistant. "Word from the courthouse is that they're adjourning at two."

"Why don't you go on home?" Alicia suggested. "I have to eat lunch anyway. I'll take any calls that come in and forward the phones to you before I leave." The partners usually took turns taking after-hours calls, but since Caroline Timberlake's decline in health, Shannon suggested she do it exclusively so Alicia would have one less thing to worry about.

"Alicia, I live much closer than you do."

"But I'm wearing boots and you aren't. Now, scat!"

After Shannon left Alicia sat in the break room with her calzone. She poured some water from the cooler bottle into her personal cup. Impulsively she reached for the wall-mounted telephone. She knew Jack had been busy working on his big project while overseeing multiple others. She'd barely gotten to see him since the day he slept over at her mother's house. She wondered if he even knew it was snowing outside.

"Hi," she said when he answered the direct line. "It's Alicia calling with your latest weather report."

"Well, hello, weather girl," he said amiably. "What's the latest?"

"Snow, snow, and more snow. They're predicting twelve to fifteen inches. I wanted to warn you not to work too long, or else you might not get a train out. They often can't keep the tracks clear when it snows this heavy."

"So I'm told. Now that you mention it, it seems a lot quieter around here than it did an hour ago. I think my co-workers might be leaving for lunch and not coming back."

"I can see that, especially those who don't sit near windows. What's on the ground now is a far cry from the flurries they predicted on TV. I'll be heading out of here soon, and I'll be the last to leave."

"Will you be going home or up to your mom's?"

"Home, I think. I want to see what we end up with before I try to get all the way to Green's Farms. Mom's okay. If there was a problem with her nurses Martha would have called me."

"Does she receive round-the-clock care?"

"Now she does, yes. My father thought it might come to this because of her heart condition, so he bought a policy years ago that would provide for LPNs so she could be cared for at home instead of having to go into a nursing home." She paused. "Do you have any plans to leave for home anytime soon?"

"Not really. I'm working on a portion of the project that I can't do from home."

She decided not to press the issue, despite knowing he wasn't familiar with how a massive snowfall could paralyze the city. It generally didn't snow in Birmingham and Houston, at least not in any great quantities.

"Well, just remember this…if you find you can't get home, you can always come to my place." She recited the address for him.

"I'll remember that, Alicia. Thanks. I'll catch up with you later, huh?"

The familiar shiver ran through her when he said her name. He sounded so immersed in his work, in spite of the genuine enthusiasm with which he greeted her. But whenever he said her name somehow she knew she had his full attention.

It reminded her of the way he'd said good night to her the first night of her mother's most recent hospitalization. He'd just told her she'd tempted him by coming to his room in her nightclothes. She'd been fairly tempted herself. She hadn't expected him to be shirtless. It was all she could do to not stare at the expanse of brown skin, the muscular chest and wash-board abs. Her instinct told her he would be a marvel-ous lover.

Under other circumstances she probably would have wanted to find out, but the timing was all off. He'd done a tremendous job of putting her mind at ease, but she was still worried about her mother. For all Alicia knew, Caroline might not ever come home again. That thought disturbed her even more than her reaction to Jack Devlin.

But it was the latter that unsettled her to the point where she needed three more glasses of wine before she could sleep with him just a few doors down the hall.

Alicia finished her lunch, took a few calls from contrac-tors reporting an abbreviated workday. No one from the courthouse called for coverage, indicating that tomorrow's activities were still uncertain. It would have to stop snowing before the plows could get out, and the revised forecast now called for snowfall until late in the evening.

She left the office at twenty minutes after two, her shoulder case stuffed with documents needing editing, and the office phones forwarded to Shannon's cell phone.

The narrow streets of lower Manhattan were filled with slow-moving vehicles. The snow fell thickly, creating poor visibility, and the air was filled with the sound of honking horns, squealing brakes, and noisy engines as they worked overtime to get through the ac-cumulation on the roads. She slipped into the subway, grasping the banister for balance as she descended and headed uptown.

* * *

By five o'clock the snow had been falling steadily for over six hours, and the city was rapidly approaching whiteout status. Alicia stopped at a neighborhood deli— the only restaurants still open tended to be family-run establishments where the families lived upstairs—and bought three foot-long hero sandwiches, since all she had at home were some frozen entrees.

Three submarine sandwiches were more than she could eat in the day or two it would take before the restoration of any lost services and the re-opening of most businesses, but she wanted to be prepared in case Jack came over.

She was chatting on the phone with Shannon, comparing their experiences getting home in the storm, when she heard the beep signaling call waiting. A quick look at her cell phone window revealed Jack's cell number. "Shannon, can I call you back? I've got another call."

She clicked over and wasn't at all surprised when Jack said, "Alicia, I'm having trouble getting a train. My feet are soaked and getting numb. I guess I should have heeded your warning to get out while I could." He paused. "Does your offer still stand?"

"Of course. I'm in for the evening. Possibly longer than that," she joked.

"Okay. It'll probably take me a little while to get up there. I hope the subways are running better than Metro-North. They're anticipating delays of about two hours."

"I believe the subways are running okay, at least the portions that run underground. Then they'll run into the same problems Metro-North is having with snow on the tracks. This storm took everybody off guard."

"Hope to see you soon. And, Alicia…"

"Yes?"

"Thanks. Thanks a lot."

She smiled as she ended the connection. Jack made it sound like she'd saved him from sleeping on a park bench. Of course, that was far from the case—he could always call Pete and Rhonda and stay at their apartment on Convent Avenue in Harlem—but he'd called on her.

She couldn't begin to describe how good that made her feel.

Thirty-five minutes later her buzzer rang. She let him in, did a quick inspection of both the apartment and her appearance and then waited for him in the doorway.

She heard his footsteps before he came into view. His large frame seemed stooped and his steps clumsy.

"My feet," he said apologetically, seeing her shocked expression.

"You come right here," she said, taking his arm. She led him inside the apartment, kicking the door shut behind them.

She helped him out of his overcoat and took his wool golf cap off his head. "Sit down," she ordered. "We've got to get the circulation going in your feet, or else it could be serious."

He obeyed, sitting down and carefully removing his dress shoes, which would need a good polishing to get rid of the moisture on them, which she knew would dry as white streaks.

Jack slowly peeled off his socks. "This must be how it was in Birmingham the year they got hit with about a foot of snow, around 'Ninety-Three, 'Ninety-Four. I was in Houston at the time, but my parents told me about it. We don't get much snow there as a rule. Tell me, have you spoken to your mother?"

"Yes. She sounds about the same. The nurse is there with her." She inspected his feet, which had no visible discoloration, but that didn't mean he was out of danger. Only a severe frostbite would be apparent on darker skin tones like theirs. Judging from the way he winced as he massaged one foot, it was painful. She knew he wasn't accustomed to snow.

"I've got just the thing," she said, snapping her fingers. She ran to her closet and pulled a white plastic box from the top shelf. "It's a foot massager," she said in response to his wide-eyed curiosity. "I use it to give myself pedicures. It has a heat feature. Ten minutes in this and your feet will be good as new. I'll get some water in it." She carried it to the sink and filled it to the line with warm water, then carefully brought it to where he sat and placed it on the floor.

After plugging it in and setting it to the heat massage, she sat on a floor pillow near his feet. She noticed that the bottom three or four inches of his suit pants were dark with moisture.

"You'll need to take those off."

"What, my pants?"

"They're soaked, Jack. And you'll have to soak your feet."

"I'll roll them up," he said, bending forward to begin the process. "No way am I going to take off my pants and sit on your couch in my underwear."

She rolled her eyes. "I can see you're going to be a

problem patient. Do you refuse to take your clothes off in the doctor's office, too?"

"You're not a doctor, Alicia."

"Yeah, like you'd even consider having a woman doctor."

"I have nothing against women, Alicia. In fact, they're my favorite species."

"Well, just don't blame me when you get rheumatism in your legs. And don't ask me to iron your pants when they dry and get all wrinkled, either. The iron is hanging on the back of the pantry door."

"Okay, I promise I'll live uncomplainingly with the consequences of my stubbornness." He lifted his feet and then lowered them into the warm water of the massage tub. "Ahhh, that feels good."

"That'll get your blood rushing again," she said confidently.

His hand rested on her shoulder. "Thanks again, Alicia." He wanted to tell her she'd make a good wife to some lucky man one day, but his gut told him not to say it.

"Hey, what are friends for?"

Her statement startled him. While he saw nothing wrong with starting off as friends, he wanted so much more than that from her. He couldn't resist asking, "So is that what we are? Friends?" Unconsciously he increased the pressure in the hand that rested on her shoulder.

"I hope so, Jack. I like you. I like being with you, and I hope you like spending time with me. But I can't stand being hemmed in. I can't abide being asked to give up my friends because someone wants exclusive rights to me, like I'm…song lyrics or something."

At that moment Jack became aware of his hand pressing into her shoulder and immediately removed it. "Oh, I agree," he said loftily. "In my time a number of women have suggested that I burn my address book." He chuckled at the memory, but nonetheless Alicia's words stung a little. He wanted more than mere friendship from her, damn it! But he couldn't ask if she saw anything more developing between them without coming off sounding like a simpering idiot, no better than the women who'd tried to fence him in like he was a pet cocker spaniel.

Then he had an idea of how to get a feel for her thoughts without it looking like he was out to pin her down.

"You sound like you've never been in love, Alicia," he said. "Like you've never met someone you couldn't get enough of. Someone you wanted to be with night and day."

She didn't reply right away. He watched as she lithely raised her body off the floor pillow and moved to sit next to him, wondering if it was an attempt to stall.

"No, I haven't," she finally said. "What I've seen of love is stifling. Like Rhonda saying she has to hurry home to fix Pete's dinner. You'd think he never ate before they got married." Her eyes met his, and she flashed a devilish grin. "On the other hand, I *have* had intervals where I felt I couldn't get enough of someone, but it always passes."

"You're talking about sex," he said roughly. "I'm talking about something completely different."

She pretended to look confused, not fooling him for an instant. "What's wrong with sex?" she asked innocently.

"Not a thing. Sex is good." He kept up the banter, but privately he marveled at her obvious comfort with what was, in his experience, a subject broached by the man of the species and usually avoided by the female like a credit card bill after a spending spree.

He decided to steer the conversation back to her views on love. "I'm surprised to hear you say you've never been in love," he remarked.

"Does that make me a freak or something?"

She sounded playful, he noted, not insulted. "No, of course not. Just unusual. After all, you're not a kid. But you're not even particularly close to anyone, are you?"

She thought for a moment. "I guess that's true. I'm really rather self-sufficient. But there are a lot of folks I care about. My mother, of course. And my friends."

Like me, he thought. "You've got a lot of friends, don't you?"

"It's rather a small circle. A lot of people merely pass through a person's life. People you see every day at work, for example. Then they move on and you don't see them anymore. And old boyfriends, or in your case, girlfriends. Although I've remained friendly with many of mine."

Jack immediately thought of Derek Taylor.

"I've even been invited to some of their weddings," Alicia continued.

"You must have parted on good terms." He liked this conversation; it gave him important insight into Alicia's psyche. If he expected to get anywhere with her he had to first understand how her mind worked. While Pete's offerings had been helpful, he wanted more. She'd been uncharacteristically open this afternoon.

Suddenly he became aware of the increasing temperature of the water his feet soaked in. "Whoa! This has gotten awfully hot." He raised his legs, resting his feet on the edge of the tub.

"I'll get you a towel."

He watched as she hurried toward a closet in the front of the apartment near the bathroom. Her rear end rotated nicely in the gray sweat pants she wore. Then he realized something else.

Alicia's apartment only had one bed.

Where would he sleep tonight?

"I picked up some sandwiches from the deli," she said after she handed him the towel. "Hot subs, with melted cheese and sautéed onion, with fixings that stay cold on the side, like lettuce and pickle. I can heat one up for you if you're hungry. I'm ready for dinner, and it'll take a good fifteen minutes to heat them up."

"It'll be quicker if you put them in the microwave," he commented as he dried his feet, which once more felt like a part of his body. He imagined that people throughout the metro area who had gone to work unprepared to tread through deep snow would be soaking their feet tonight. All the shoe repair businesses in the area would probably have a spike in business as well.

She wrinkled her nose. "Microwaves make the bread get all chewy. I'd rather do it the old-fashioned way."

"I guess I should have thought to pick up some food before I got here. To be honest, all I thought about was getting out of the damned snow and drying off my feet."

"How are they?"

"Much better, thanks. The circulation is going again.

My toes aren't numb anymore." He smiled at her. "Thanks for taking care of me."

"Don't worry about it. We're buddies, remember?"

The second time she'd made that point. Next thing she'd be saying another well-used, and in his opinion, equally asinine phrase like "Love means never having to say you're sorry."

No, he decided. Alicia would never say anything like that.

Because she hadn't the faintest idea what love was.

Chapter 17

Nowhere Man

After they ate she offered to fix him a drink, but he said he'd wait. He pulled out his laptop to do a little work after asking if that was all right with her, and she got on the phone, explaining she'd promised to call her business partner back. "Then I plan to do some work myself," she said.

He noticed the glass of Zinfandel in her hand. Pete and Rhonda maintained that Alicia didn't drink, but from what he'd seen she imbibed on a regular basis. He considered it might be her way of coping with the stress of Caroline's worsening condition.

Bits and pieces of Alicia's end of the conversation penetrated his deep concentration, and he couldn't help imagining coming home to a scene like this every day: Spending time talking with his wife, having her massage his feet, perhaps him massaging her back and shoulders, having dinner together while watching the news of the day.

Pete gets to enjoy this every day. He could get used to this himself. Maybe not the part about him sleeping on the sofa....

"You're sweet, Derek."

His head jerked. *Derek!* What happened to her business partner...her *female* business partner named Shannon something or other?

He answered his own question. *Call waiting.* He'd been too busy entertaining happy thoughts of domesticity to notice her saying goodbye to Shannon and hello to Derek. That and the fact that he didn't want to eavesdrop. But hey, a studio apartment didn't give many options for a private conversation.

Now he listened closely, wanting to know what she and Derek said to each other.

"Now, you should know I'm not going to stick around to wait until subway service starts getting disrupted and all that," she said. "I was out of there by two." Pause. "I doubt there'll be any court tomorrow, no. It'll be too hard for anyone to get in. Attorneys, judges, bailiffs, and of course our contractors. I've done some scoping myself to make sure transcripts are available on time." Another silence. "I'm glad you're all right, too. Keep in touch, and stay dry." Another silence. "No, I wouldn't say that at all. 'Bye, Derek."

From the corner of his eye he watched as she disconnected. "I'm sorry about that. A lot of my friends are calling to make sure I made it home okay, usually while I'm on with someone else." That moment her cell began its distinctive ring. "See what I mean?"

He managed a half-hearted smile, but the ringing of his own cell phone distracted him. Glad to have something that would force his attentions away from wondering who was calling Alicia now, he said a no-nonsense, "Hello."

He quickly broke into a smile at the sound of his mother's voice. "Jack, your daddy and I are seeing footage of the storm on TV. Are you all right? Did you make it home?"

He spent a few minutes reassuring her all was well. When he hung up he heard Alicia say, "Here he is."

He took the phone she handed him and heard Rhonda's voice chiding him. "The next time you decide not to go home in a blizzard, would you at least have the courtesy to call someone and let them know?"

He chuckled deep in his throat. "I'm sorry, Rhonda. I got so into the project I'm working on I forgot to check in with you guys. Not just to tell you I was okay, but to see how y'all are making out."

"We're fine. I left work at lunchtime, Pete left after lunch. But my doctor says I'm not supposed to get excited, and we've been worried about you. Here's Pete."

Jack's friend came on the line and good-naturedly blasted Jack for upsetting his expectant wife by making her wonder where he was. Jack dutifully apologized. Pete added, "I thought you would have called us if you couldn't get home. We always have a place for you, Jack."

"I appreciate that." Jack felt grateful to have such good friends, friends who cared about his welfare. Pete and Rhonda had worried about his safety, since he hadn't answered his home phone. Alicia, of course, had called his office to tell him he was welcome at her apartment if he was unable to get to Stamford.

After he hung up he got up and poured some rum into a highball glass, then added some Coca-Cola to it. He'd barely replaced the container of ice back in the freezer when that annoying cell phone ring began again.

He leaned against the sink, making no secret of the fact that he was listening. Alicia spoke to someone named "Bobby."

Enough already.

He went in the bathroom and put on his still-wet socks. When Alicia saw him putting on his shoes, she said, "Hold on a minute, Bobby," and covered the bottom half of the receiver. "Are you going out?"

He slipped on his coat. "I just thought I'd see what's going on outside. I'll be back."

She looked troubled by his explanation, although she nodded.

When he closed the door behind him he heard her continue to talk. Obviously she'd resumed her conversation.

Jack knew it wasn't fair for him to blame Alicia for how he felt. He'd been the one to say how much work he had to do, and she said she would make a few phone calls while he worked. Had she intended to contact the men who ended up calling her first? He would never know. All he knew was that he couldn't bear listening to her talk to other men on the phone, no matter how innocent the conversation.

The streets were practically deserted. He stood outside the building, his shoulder inches away from the row of buzzers, and estimated the accumulation to be at least six inches, maybe eight. He saw a man coming down the street clad in jeans, gym shoes, and a waist-length leather jacket, his hair covered by a wool cap and a scarf knotted around his throat. "Lovely evening, isn't it?" he said in a voice tinged with sarcasm.

"Sure, in Miami Beach." Something just occurred to Jack. "Hey, did you just come out of the subway?"

"Yeah."

"Trains running?"

"For now, yeah, although I had to wait an awfully long time."

"Thanks, man." At that instant Jack made up his mind. He carefully stepped out into the snow and made his way toward the corner subway stop.

Chapter 18

I Just Don't Understand

He called Pete when he emerged at One Hundred Thirty-Seventh Street. "You'll have to tell me how to get to your place from the subway. Everything looks distorted to me in this damn snow."

"Jack? You're up here? I don't get it. An hour ago you were at Alicia's."

"I went for a walk. Next thing I knew I was riding uptown on the subway."

"Something happened," Pete guessed.

"It's not a big deal."

"Does she know you came up here?"

"No. I just said I was going out to see what was happening on the street. Coming here was an impulse, once I found out the trains were still running."

"Don't you think you at least owe her a phone call? She's likely to think you wandered off somewhere and got lost and are somewhere freezing to death."

"Yeah, you're right. I'll call her." *If I can get through, that is.*

Alicia frowned as she disconnected the call. She didn't know what to make of it. What would induce Jack to venture outside in a snowstorm, much less walk half a block to the subway, in wet socks and wet pants? On top of that, he had to walk several blocks from the subway to get to the Robinson's apartment. He'd seemed perfectly content at home with her, and she felt reasonably comfortable herself, but all that talk about love and marriage combined with having him here in her apartment with its one bed made her uneasy. They had a nice dinner, good conversation...she practically felt domesticated. He even fixed himself a drink afterward, a sign that he felt relaxed.

Then it occurred to her that he might have been annoyed at her talking to male friends like Derek and Bobby. She unconsciously stuck out her chest. It was happening again. Once more a man in her life tried to exert control over her. Well, no one would ever tell her who she could talk to.

She went to the table and powered off his laptop, holding the stem of a half empty wine glass in one hand. If he wanted to stay with Pete and Rhonda, let him.

While she felt angry at Jack, she felt a sense of confusion regarding her own behavior. He treated her just the way she wanted, with respect and consideration, not getting into her business, not making demands for exclusivity, not telling her not to see this one or that one. He was the first man to do that. Even longtime friends like Derek and Bobby had tried to claim her as their property. They eventually understood how she felt, and they reached the comfortable friendship they had now. Other men, unable to accept her terms, simply stopped calling her.

But Jack Devlin persisted, calling her infrequently but always sounding glad to hear her voice. He'd proven himself to be her perfect match.

But after all these months she hadn't been able to figure out why she felt so dazed whenever she was close to him. Her stomach fluttered all afternoon yesterday at the mere thought of his spending the night at her apartment. He'd slept at her parents' house a few weeks ago, but that house had hundreds of square feet more than her studio. Genuine concern for his numbed feet had made her temporarily put aside her unnerved state, but it soon returned with their discussion about love and marriage. She expressed her honest opinion, told him how she hated to feel like she was being fenced in, and what did he do? He stalked out into eight inches of snow in a snit.

Well, maybe not exactly a snit. He left with little fanfare, just a quiet announcement of his intent to go downstairs for a closer look at the accumulation on the street. She saw nothing odd about that. He came from a region of the country where deep snow accumulation was almost unheard of, and it could be better seen up close than from a fourth-floor window. But the next thing she knew, he called from Harlem, saying he'd taken a subway to Pete's. When she asked why, he said it was just an impulse, and he didn't really understand it himself. What kind of half-assed explanation was *that?*

A question nagged at her subconscious that she tried to shoo away but became too strong to ignore. Might she have subconsciously contributed to his ire by making sure he knew she was speaking to men friends on the phone? Did she really have to use Derek's and Bobby's names so much on her end of the conversation? Wasn't that like rubbing her friendships with them in Jack's face?

Jack probably had every right to feel miffed, and he'd be even more so if he could have heard the actual conversation she'd had with Derek Taylor. Derek, with typical candor, had come out and asked if she felt lonely, hinting that he would brave the elements to get to her apartment. If Jack hadn't been with her she might have told him yes, but she'd merely said "no," not even telling him about Jack's presence at her apartment.

Alicia made a face. Who was she kidding?

Part of her longed for an uncomplicated relationship like the one she had with Derek, simply because it presented no qualms, gave her no palpitations or nerve attacks; but in her heart she knew she had no interest in being with anyone else. Not since Jack entered her life.

So why did she behave so recklessly? Why had she tested Jack's patience to see how he would react to over-hearing her conversations with Derek and Bobby? Did her ego hurt so much at his take-her-or-leave-her non-pursuit that she felt she had to raise his hackles?

And, most puzzling of all, why would she push away an ideal man like Jack Devlin in the first place?

She'd taken a gamble, all right. And from the looks of it, she'd lost.

Alicia sighed, her heart feeling heavy in her chest. This was more serious than reciting her telephone number and not caring that he had nothing on which to take it down. Jack had an easy solution if he couldn't remember it; namely calling Pete. This time Pete couldn't help him.

She tried to see the bright side. At least she no longer had to worry about those butterflies in her stomach she always got from him that she chased away with increasing amounts of alcohol. She'd seen her last day of waking up with a headache.

Jack tossed on the sofabed in the Robinson's living room. He couldn't stop thinking about what happened earlier tonight, and none of it made the slightest amount of sense.

The whole thing was nuts. This had to be the strangest relationship he'd ever been involved in. Six months and two seasons had passed since that spring evening when he first laid eyes on Alicia Timberlake at that Upper West Side restaurant not far from her apartment. Since that time he'd seen her perhaps the same number of times, six. Then there was the crazy way her mother looked at him that night he picked her up. If she hadn't been in frail health he would have asked her if something was wrong, but given her deteriorating condition he didn't feel it would be right. Besides, she recovered almost instantly. But what had caused that look of shock to cross Caroline Timberlake's lovely face?

He was crazy about Alicia, but instead of losing himself in the joy of exploring his feelings he had to play this crazy game to keep from alienating her. Today she'd practically come out and admitted that she would bolt from any man who stuck too close.

Jack had no interest in playing games. He wanted a woman to share his life with, and his heart told him Alicia Timberlake was that woman. He did agree with Pete that she'd built an invisible wall around her emotions, but he refused to believe it was impenetrable. He'd seen part of it that day two weeks ago at the hospital, when she allowed herself to lean on him and, he hoped, take solace and strength from him.

His forehead wrinkled as he considered a possible connection between her attempts to hide her emotions and the almost excessive drinking he'd witnessed.

Satisfied that he'd hit upon something worth exploring, Jack closed his eyes and finally fell asleep out of sheer exhaustion.

Chapter 19

Magical Mystery Tour
Orlando, Florida,
Early 1980s

Alicia stood off to the side as Fletcher snapped the picture of Daphne and her favorite Disney character, Minnie Mouse.

"What a great shot!" he exclaimed.

Caroline turned to Alicia. "Did you want to get your picture taken with Minnie, Alicia?"

"No, Mom. I'm not really into the characters." Daphne was still young enough to feel that she was really hugging Minnie Mouse, but to her they just looked like adults wearing costumes. "What I'd really like to do is ride Space Mountain."

Caroline nodded. "It's hard for parents when their children are spaced as far apart as you and Daphne. Now that she's old enough to spend a day at Disney, you've outgrown it."

"I'm fine, Mom." Alicia had first asked to go to Disney World when she was about six, the age Daphne was now, but her mother was pregnant and told her that her doctor didn't think that flying and all that walking would be a good idea. She'd asked every year since, and the answer was always the same, regardless of which parent it came from: "Maybe next year." It had taken six years to get here. She had to be the only kid in middle school who hadn't been to the Magic Kingdom yet.

She felt her mother's palm on her shoulder. "You're going to have a great time on the cruise. There'll be lots of kids your age there."

"I'm looking forward to it." Alicia decided her mother could read her mind. There were plenty of kids her age here at Disney World, but the great majority of them were younger, from toddlers to maybe ten. She'd been so busy thinking that maybe it would have been better if they'd just gone to Martha's Vineyard like they usually did, that she'd forgotten about the three-day cruise they were taking to the Bahamas tomorrow.

"They have special counselors on board who set up age-appropriate activities for all the children. You'll be in one group, and Daphne will be in another," Caroline said brightly.

Alicia felt renewed hope. "Pop, can we ride Space Mountain now?" she asked after Daphne said goodbye to Minnie Mouse and she ran back to Fletcher's arms.

"I want to see the little people's village," Daphne announced.

Without hesitation, Fletcher said, "Precious, why don't we go to the It's a Small World exhibit and get it over with, and then you and I can ride Space Mountain while Mom keeps Daphne."

"I wanna ride Space Mountain," Daphne said.

"I'm afraid you're too small, Princess. Maybe next time."

Alicia felt as if she would scream for her life if she heard that annoying theme song, "It's a Small World," one more time. After about an hour the family finally left the exhibit. First they stood by patiently as Daphne tried to open every single door of the little people's village. Then she, Daphne, and their father squeezed into a teacup ride, Fletcher's feet stretched out on either side of Daphne's small body. Caroline, who Alicia knew didn't ride because of her heart condition, waved to them as they spun past.

"That was fun," Daphne said when they got off, her hand in Fletcher's as Alicia walked beside them. "Can we go to the boat now?"

"You must mean Twenty Thousand Leagues Under The Sea," Fletcher replied. "Sure, why not?"

Alicia didn't point out that her father promised her that their next stop would be Space Mountain.

"Where are we going, Fletcher?" Caroline inquired as they headed toward the boat ride and away from Space Mountain.

"We're all going to ride on the boat."

Caroline stopped in her tracks. "What about Space Mountain? Alicia wanted to go on that, remember?"

"We'll get there, Caroline. But I don't want you standing by waiting for us to go through the line and watching us ride. You can go on this. It's a boat, not a ride. You feel the same way, don't you, Precious?"

"Yes, Pop." Alicia realized her father had a point. It couldn't be much fun for her mother to merely watch them having fun; she deserved to enjoy herself as well. She probably needed to stop thinking about herself. This was a vacation for all four of them.

After the boat ride, which featured fish and other sea life that even six-year-old Daphne recognized as fake, they returned to the Contemporary Resort Hotel on the Disney grounds to eat lunch and rest a little before going back to the park for the rest of the day.

Almost immediately, Daphne began saying what she wanted to see, and Fletcher agreed. Caroline intervened. "Fletcher, you know Alicia has been asking all morning to ride Space Mountain. We should do that before we do anything else."

"Of course. Come on, Precious, let's you and I ride."

Caroline and Daphne got on line with them. Like all Disney features, the walls were decorated with interesting exhibits to make the long lines snaking back and forth seem less tedious. When it came time to board the indoor roller coaster Daphne cried. "I wanta go."

"Daphne, you don't meet the minimum height requirement for this ride," Caroline explained.

"I want Daddy to stay with me. I'm scared."

Alicia looked at the people waiting in line. Maybe

one of them could get in with her when her father got out so she wouldn't have to ride alone.

"Princess, there's nothing to be afraid of," Fletcher said. "Mommy will take care of you. You ride the escalator downstairs, and Alicia and I will be out in two shakes."

Daphne cried harder.

"You know, I'm not too keen on riding this, anyway. There's hardly any leg room," Fletcher remarked.

Alicia didn't point out that he'd squeezed the legs of his six-three frame into a tiny teacup ride.

Fletcher rose. "Wait a second," he said to the employees who were checking passengers' seat belts. "Can we get someone to ride with my daughter?"

A youngster riding alone quickly raised his hand, and once the ride operators waved him on he climbed into the seat Fletcher had just vacated.

"Precious, you enjoy your ride," Fletcher said. "I'll be waiting for you when you come out."

As the ride pulled away Alicia looked at her parents, her father holding a calmed-down Daphne, and her mother's stern look his way, which softened to allow her to smile and wave to Alicia as she passed. Alicia waved back, a strange feeling passing through her.

By the time the exciting ride braked to a stop she knew she would never again be bothered by her father yielding to her sister's wishes.

Chapter 20

With a Little Help from My Friends

The next morning the snowplows came out in force to clear the streets of Manhattan. The storm hadn't broken any records, as had first been feared, but was recognized for being rather early in the season, causing many to predict a difficult, snow-filled winter.

Alicia rose at her usual time and took a Tylenol for the mild throbbing in her head. A look at the wine bottle revealed she'd consumed three-quarters of it. She'd never drank so much as she had since that night in October when she saw Jack standing on her doorstep.

By now she felt reasonably certain that she'd never met him before. She'd probably never know why he affected her the way he did. But it looked like it no longer mattered, not now, after she drove him away.

Her phone rang as she was stuffing her feet into snow boots. She reached for it inside her purse. "Hello."

"Good morning, Alicia."

Her back went rigid at the sound of the voice that said her name like no other. "Good morning," she said stiffly.

He paused. "I called to apologize for last night."

She said nothing.

"It wasn't right for me to wander off like I did."

"It seemed more like a walk out than wandering off to me," she said.

"I didn't walk out on you, Alicia. I can't explain it. I don't understand it myself. One minute I was doing a mental measurement of the snow on the ground, and the next I was walking toward the subway."

"It didn't have anything to do with my talking to my friends, particularly the ones who happen to be male?"

She heard him take a deep breath. "All right," he said. "I have to be honest. I didn't like it. When the second dude called I felt like I needed to get some air. But I didn't leave your apartment with the intention of going up to Pete's for the night. It was a last-minute impulse."

"All because I had some phone conversations with a couple of friends."

"Yes," he said with a vehemence that surprised even him. "Because you consider them your friends, and you consider *me* your friend. You classify us all the same way. I might not understand everything, but I do under-stand that much. That's what's so hard for me to accept."

His attempt at a chuckle came out more like a grunt. "For someone who opens up so little, I'm surprised you even have so many friends."

"Maybe 'friends' is too strong a word," she said breezily. "I should probably call them something else, like 'playmates.'"

The double entendre irked Jack. He hardly expected Alicia, a mature woman in her mid-thirties, to be without sexual experience. On the other hand he found it unbearable to hear her refer so cavalierly to having had affairs with other men, especially when he put his own desires on the back burner and held off trying to get her into bed, hoping her feelings for him would grow. He wanted more than just sex from Alicia.

At that moment he knew he loved her. That was why he couldn't stay away from her, why he put up with having to play the game of pretending he could take her or leave her.

Behind her self-imposed isolation, he knew that she, like everyone else, needed someone. He wanted to be that someone.

"I wanted to know if I could pick up my laptop. I'm going to get a train home so I can change, then get to work."

"I was about to leave for work myself."

"Would you mind terribly bringing it with you? I can come by your office and pick it up."

"I don't mind, but Jack, I work way downtown by the courthouse. You work up in midtown. It's a little bit out of your way, don't you think? Besides, that part of the city is a lot more difficult to navigate than midtown."

"I don't see where it can be helped. I'll call you if I get lost." He already had his strategy planned.

He intended to invite her to lunch when he showed up, and he wouldn't leave until he'd smoothed things over.

Chapter 21

Ask Me Why

Jack watched carefully as Alicia prepared her hamburger for consumption. She worked almost methodically, first sprinkling pepper on the meat, then adding mustard and Heinz 57 sauce, then using a steak knife to cut the bun and meat in half. She raised it to her mouth and took a lusty bite. "It's not Luger's, but it's not bad," she said with a smile.

"Glad you like it." It still amazed him how much more expensive everything was in New York than in Alabama. He didn't object to the amount of a check at a truly nice restaurant like Morton's Steak House, but this simple lunch of hamburgers, French fries and root beers in a dimly lit pub in the court district would probably run him thirty bucks after he calculated the tip. He couldn't really object—he'd negotiated a handsome salary from his new employer as a condition of accepting the job—but the very idea of paying that much for two hamburger platters boggled his mind.

He felt relieved that she'd accepted his invitation.

"So," Alicia said as after she swallowed, "was there anything you wanted to say to me?"

"Was there anything you wanted to say to *me?*"

"I asked you first."

He hesitated, trying to gather his thoughts. "All right," he said. "I admit it. It got to me last night, hearing you talk to your playmates on the phone last night. I figured the best thing for me to do was to go and check out the snowfall. I planned on staying down there long enough so that by the time I got back upstairs you'd be finished talking. I had this cozy little picture in my mind of you and I sitting side by side on the sofa, balancing our laptops, working away. That picture didn't include listening to you talk to Derek and Tom and Dick and Harry." He shrugged. "Maybe I handled it poorly. But I feel this way, Alicia. I have no right to tell you who your friends should be. But it's like anything else I don't like. I'm a grown man, Alicia. I don't have to sit and watch something that I don't want to see."

"So that's why you left." It came out as a statement, not a question.

"Yes. I don't want to box you in, Alicia. But I care about you, and no man wants to feel like he's sharing a woman he cares about with other men, even if they're 'just friends.'" Jack curved his index fingers into invisible quote marks.

"I saw a guy come around the corner, and I asked him if he'd just come from the subway. He told me the trains were still running. I don't know what induced me to walk to the corner and down those steps. Maybe I was afraid that you'd still be talking on the phone. The next thing I knew, I was getting off at One Hundred and Thirty-Seventh Street and calling Pete from my cell."

"You left your laptop at my place and everything. What would you have done if I refused to take your calls? I easily could have screened you out just by checking the ID window."

"I like to think that even if you were furious with me, you wouldn't have carried a grudge that far. Not when you know I need the files on that laptop for my work."

She stared at him defiantly. "I can carry a grudge clear to California if I want to." Then she softened. She couldn't stay upset with Jack for very long. She'd been so happy when he showed up at her office to pick up his laptop. *I'm impressed, too.* Lower Manhattan could be a real maze, even to people who'd lived there all their lives, but Jack managed to find her. When he invited her to lunch "to see if we could work this out," she wanted to grab him and kiss him. She hadn't, of course. Instead she calmly accepted, showing much less enthusiasm than she felt. Regardless of the uncertainty and flustered feeling she got when he was near, she still wanted him in her life. "But you're right. I wouldn't have withheld your laptop from you." The corners of her mouth turned up, and she said, "I can't imagine saying something like, 'Give me ten thousand dollars if you ever want to see that laptop alive again.'"

"It didn't sound like something you'd do."

"So what happens now?" she asked brightly.

He looked at her through eyes that suddenly felt heavy. A tiny drop of ketchup dotted the right corner of her mouth, and her lips appeared to have salt crystals on it, probably from her fries. He knew what he'd *like* to have happen now....

He shrugged, chasing away the thought. Considering Alicia had to get back to work and he hadn't even been to his office yet, it was hardly appropriate. "Back to where we were, I guess."

"Friends?"

"Friends."

They tapped their root beer mugs and drank. "Uh, Alicia."

"Yes?"

"You've got a bit of ketchup outside your mouth, and if you don't get rid of it, I might lose control."

He expected her to hastily wipe the red dot away, but instead she leaned back, a challenge in her eyes. "Go ahead. I'd like to see what you do when you lose control."

Chapter 22

Birthday

Jack listened as Alicia sang the Happy Birthday song, changing "you" to "us."

They strolled along the beach of Long Island Sound, walking off the heavy lunch Martha prepared for them. "That was a great meal," Jack said. "I don't know what kind of sauce Martha put over that catfish, but it's just as good as any I've tasted in New Orleans."

"She's a fabulous cook. The funny thing is, she learned to make a lot of those sauces after she started working for my parents because that's what they liked to eat. Before that she just made basic meals, meat, vegetable, starch. She swears by Emeril Lagresse."

"I intend to have some more of that bread pudding."

"Martha always makes me a special lunch for my birthday," Alicia explained. "If there's one bad thing about being born on Christmas Eve, it's that you can't really go out to dinner because just about everyplace closes early."

"Morton's is open 'til ten."

She looked at him curiously. "And you know that how?"

"Because I made a reservation for seven-thirty."

"Oh, Jack! You didn't!"

"I wasn't sure if you had anything in particular you wanted to do."

She reached for his hand. "I can't think of anyplace else I'd rather do on my birthday than have dinner with you at Morton's."

At ten-fifteen they left the restaurant, arm in arm. The remnants of the snowfall of ten days before still lay in dirty clumps on the ground. A handful of cars remained in the parking lot, and Jack felt sure that others still sat in the valet lot on the other side. He felt a little sorry for the staff, who surely wanted to go home and get to bed.

He wanted to do the same, but with a twist. He didn't want to go to sleep.

Once Jack starting entertaining the notion of making love to Alicia, he couldn't get it out of his mind. He unlocked the doors to his Aviator SUV with the remote a few yards before they reached it and helped her into it.

"Do you live far from here?" she asked as they drove away.

He blinked. Did she have ESP or something? "No, not at all." He turned his head. "Would you like to see where I live?"

"I'd love to."

He had them there in ten minutes, helped by the lack of traffic at ten-thirty p.m. on Christmas Eve.

"Nice," she said, taking in the redbrick garden-style condo buildings.

"It's old—it was built in Nineteen Fifty-Two—but I didn't want to live in a high rise. I never have."

She thought of his upbringing in a small Southern town. "No, I wouldn't imagine you would have. But I spent the first nine years of my life in a high-rise condominium. We lived on the twelfth floor. I remember my mother always telling us to stay away from the windows. She was so afraid one of us would fall out."

"I wouldn't want to raise children in a high rise, even if it's someplace luxurious, like the Trump Tower. To me they don't mix." He pointed with his right hand. "This works for me, too, because the Metro-North station is right over there, and it was reasonably priced, considering the outrageous cost of real estate in this area," he continued. "Fortunately, someone rented my house in Birmingham last month, so I only had to pay two mortgages for two months."

"Holding on to the old pad, huh?"

He unlocked the door to his unit and pushed it open, flicking on a light for her. He waved a hand for emphasis as he showed her around. "Living room."

She took in the sparsely furnished but neat room, with its eclectic mix of plaid sofa and leather rocker, and its plasma TV hanging above a console table that held a compact stereo.

"Dining area."

A round Colonial style cherry wood table and four matching chairs.

"Kitchen."

Square in shape, with a microwave over the stove, a window over the sink, and a narrow counter between the refrigerator and a stackable washer and dryer.

"Bathroom."

She glimpsed a tub with glass doors.

"Bedroom."

The room she'd been most anxious to see. Jack slept in a king-sized bed that dominated the room. An easy chair was positioned at an angle to make for comfortable TV viewing. A six-drawer highboy in the same stained pine as the TV cabinet completed the ensemble.

"I like it," she said. "You don't like clutter any more than I do."

"For every piece of furniture there is a purpose," he said with a smile.

"How about trying to finish our cake?" she suggested.

He put some music on while she heated the small, round chocolate cake with hot fudge that was a Morton's specialty in the microwave. "Let's have it out here," he called. He lifted the convertible coffee table into the upright position, where it often doubled as a desk and an eating area.

"Isn't that convenient?" she said when she saw the table. "Uh…do you have any wine?"

"I think I've got some Korbel, if you're in the mood for champagne. I'll get it," he said at her nod.

He returned with a bottle of champagne to find her leaning back on the sofa, her hand on her stomach. "Good thing birthdays come just once a year. My goodness. If I ate like this every day I'd be wide as this couch."

"There's no place like Morton's for a good prime rib."

"Do they have locations in Birmingham?"

"Unfortunately, no. I went there when I went to Dallas or Houston on business. In Birmingham the nicest steak house among the chains would probably be Ruth Chris."

She nodded thoughtfully. She wondered whom he'd brought to dine with him. It had to be somebody special. The tongue-twisting titled Ruth's Chris' Steak House was nearly as expensive as Morton's.

"Something on your mind?"

"Oh, I was just wondering who the special lady was that you brought to eat at Ruth Chris."

"Are you jealous?"

He obviously found that scenario enjoyable, judging by his smile. She grinned back at him. "To quote a friend, 'I don't like it.'"

Jack raised his eyebrows. She liked the way he expressed himself with his brows. Not in that exaggerated Groucho Marx sort of way, but they did tend to shoot upward when something surprised him.

"But I won't go out for a walk and end up in Green's Farms."

They laughed together, and Jack liked the fact that they could make fun of his rather childish behavior of less than two weeks ago. He still felt ashamed of what he viewed as no better than a temper tantrum. In hindsight, he felt he could have handled the situation in a much more mature manner.

He opened the champagne with a loud pop, then poured two glasses' worth. He raised his glass to her. "Happy birthday, Alicia."

"Happy birthday, Jack."

They clicked glasses and sipped, their eyes never leaving each other's face. "Funny," she whispered. "All of a sudden I'm not hungry anymore."

"I am, but not for chocolate cake." He leaned in close, and she closed her eyes expectantly, only to be surprised when he pressed his lips to her forehead.

He pulled back, looked into her eyes, and leaned forward again, this time diverting at the last minute and kissing her chin. She held her breath as he pulled back twice more, pressing his lips to each of her cheeks. Excitement built up in her like a rapid snowfall. She wanted to scream at him to kiss her.

At last he touched his lips to hers. Her arms went around his neck, and she felt his hands on her back.

He increased the pressure, and suddenly she felt herself moving. Jack smoothly slid her onto his lap. Just moments later Alicia felt herself falling backward. Jack didn't miss a beat as he lowered her to a supine position. He tore his mouth away from hers and began nibbling on her neck and up to the side of her jaw. With one hand he grasped and gently squeezed her breast. Her nipples had hardened through the fabric of her sweater.

Music played at a low volume, but it became secondary to their pleasured moans.

"It's too cramped on this couch," Jack said between breaths. "Let's go to the bedroom."

She nodded her consent. He rose first, then held out a hand to help her. The moment she was on her feet he took her in his arms and kissed her again, grasping her hips and pressing them into his groin. "Feel what you do to me," he whispered.

He moved his hands to her sides, running them up and down from just above her waist to her thighs, over the indentation of her waist and the curve of her hips. Alicia stood close to him, having no desire to back out of his embrace.

At last they reluctantly parted a few inches. His large hand cupped her jaw as he gazed at her with an unreadable expression in his dark eyes. "I want you to be sure, Alicia." He pressed his index finger against her lips when she opened them to speak. "There's no going back, no pretending this never happened. This isn't just you and one of your playmates falling into the sack for a good time. A man who cares about you very much wants to make love to you…very much. If you can't, or don't want to, handle that, I'll understand." Only then did he remove his finger. God help him if she decided he was asking too much of her. As far as he was concerned they'd already crossed a line that couldn't be backtracked.

But she held his gaze and quietly said, "I'm sure, Jack."

He kissed her once more, removing the pins that held her French roll in place and threading his fingers through the strands of her hair that fell around them.

* * *

Jack felt like he'd been living for this moment as he watched Alicia disrobe in his bedroom. He hadn't made love in months, and then it had been little more than sexual release. The woman he'd dated in Birmingham had flown up to Connecticut shortly after his move to make their break official. There'd been mutual fondness, but no real emotional connection for either of them. It couldn't begin to compare to a man making love to the woman he loved.

Under Alicia's sweater and pantsuit she wore a silky navy teddy set trimmed in lace, the tight-fitting top hugging her torso and letting her breasts stand naturally. He thought it the sexiest thing he'd ever seen. They lay in the center of the bed, him wearing nothing but undershorts. His erection jutted out from his body, but he felt freed from the burden of trying to conceal it. He moved atop her, but she pushed him away, murmuring, "Wait."

He watched, propped on one elbow and breathing hard, as she raised her body, crossed her arms and pulled the top of her fitted camisole over her head, then slid the bottom half over her hips. His breath caught in his throat. She wore no bra, and even in the darkness he could see how beautifully she was formed, the round thighs, the belly with the tiniest pouch just above her groin, the smallish breasts with round areolas and nubs at their centers. As many times as he had mentally undressed her, he never imagined she would be this lovely. She wasn't voluptuous, but nor was she skinny. And, as he so desperately wanted to believe, she was all his.

He ran a hand over her naked flesh, knowing the

time had come to explore the rest of her as intimately as he had her mouth. He proceeded to do just that, taking his time and savoring every second. When she fell back trembling and moaning, he knew he'd pleased her.

He nuzzled her earlobe and licked the skin behind it, loving how she twitched with delight at the sensation. "I've got protection in my wallet. I'll be right back."

He went to his slacks, removed the condom and applied it. He turned to see Alicia lying down but looking at him intently, her hair fanned out against the pillow like he'd visualized so many times before. He knelt beside her on the bed and held out a hand. When she took it he pulled her into a sitting position. His arms went around to her back, his hands bracing her gently. They leaned toward each other, and her eyes fluttered shut....

Alicia moaned softly as Jack kissed her senseless. She laid her palms on his chest and ran her fingertips over his sparse chest hair, knowing he supported her back and wouldn't let her fall. She sucked and nibbled at his lips. When at last he eased her back toward the mattress she felt weightless. She had felt this way many times, but this time it was special. She knew it was because of Jack. He affected her like no other man ever had.

Her lower body shuddered as she accepted his flesh into her own. For a few moments they simply lay still. She heard him gasp, felt his breath on her neck, could hear his tattered inhalations. "Alicia," he said softly in his special way. She felt his male muscle twitch inside her. Never had anything felt so utterly delicious.

Slowly Jack began the familiar push-pull rhythm. She began to move underneath him, feeling like she was floating. They loved each other slowly and deeply, each resisting the urge to join together furiously like scissor blades. When she could stand no more pleasure she held him tightly and cried out, her back arching and her legs contracting around his back. His escalating grunts told her that he, too, had reached a climactic moment.

Even when he collapsed he was careful to fall to her side, pulling her to him like he was afraid to let her go, even for a second.

"Jack?"

"Hmm?"

"Merry Christmas."

"It must be after midnight," he mumbled.

"Just a little."

He stretched an arm across her middle, then raised it to rub her breasts. "Mmm. I've got a Christmas gift for you, if you'd like to have it now."

She reached out, her hand clamping on his arousal. "I'd love to. And I might have a little something for you as well." She threw the covers back and rolled on top of him, one hand stroking him tantalizingly until he gripped her hips and brought her down, turning the smile on her face into an expression of the exquisite sensation she felt.

She awoke Christmas morning with his arm draped around her waist. She lightly rested her hand on his, and he stirred in his sleep and shifted position, moving closer. She thought he was still asleep until he mumbled something she could barely understand.

"Whatcha gonna do today?"

"Just a quiet Christmas at home. We'll make the most of it, although it'll be difficult. Mom doesn't even have the energy to go downstairs anymore." She rolled over onto her stomach. Something occurred to her just then, and she turned her head to face him. "Wait a minute. Aren't you coming with me?"

"Well, I don't want to intrude…."

"Of course you'll come with me. I know that Pete and Rhonda are with her family out in Hollis. What were you going to do, just stay home alone?"

He broke into a smile. "I'd rather be with you."

"Then that's exactly where you'll be."

Chapter 23

Wonderful Christmastime

It turned out to be a thoroughly enjoyable day. If anyone thought it strange that Alicia hadn't come home the night before they didn't comment on it. Coffee cake and a baked dish with eggs, cheese and sausage had been placed on the coffee table. A massive Christmas tree had been set up by one of the front windows, and Todd had just gotten a fire going in the fireplace. The mantel and surrounding stone wall behind it were covered with holiday greeting cards. A CD of diverse Christmas carols played on the compact Bose wave player. Jack decided it had to be downloaded; the selections were too far removed from each other for it to be commercial. One minute Johnny Mathis sang the religious hymn, "O Holy Night" and the next Eartha Kitt purred, "Santa Baby."

The Timberlake living room brimmed with holiday spirit. Jack glanced around with admiration. How sad that Caroline was confined to her bed upstairs and couldn't join her family in this lovely room.

Alicia, who excused herself shortly after they arrived, returning a half hour later wearing jeans and a sweater, gifted Jack with a snazzy tie and hanky set, and he surprised her with a bottle of her favorite scent, having learned its name from Rhonda. He'd removed it from the inside pocket of his leather jacket and slipped it under the tree while she was upstairs.

To his surprise, Daphne handed him a small flat square package, saying, "Merry Christmas, Jack, from Todd, Fletcher, and myself."

He didn't have to be a nuclear physicist to know the cheerful red-and-white wrapping paper contained a CD, but was delighted to see the latest by Peter White. He'd been a longtime fan of the jazz guitarist. "Thank you so much, Daphne, Todd. That was very thoughtful of you."

Alicia handed him another gift. "It's from Martha and Marvin," she said in response to his puzzled expression, her fingernail tapping the label.

"Oh, they shouldn't have." He laughed at the dubious expression on Alicia's face. "Okay, so people always say that. But they really *shouldn't* have."

"I think it's entirely appropriate. Martha and Marvin and their kids are like family."

Neither Jack nor Alicia saw Daphne turn to Todd and make a face like she smelled something unpleasant.

"Well, in that case…." He tore off the wrapping, revealing a DVD of an old black-and-white Alfred Hitchcock movie that starred two legendary Hollywood actors. "This was an interesting choice," he said, bewildered.

Alicia read the description. "I know why she picked this."

"Why?"

"Look at the names of the main characters."

He read the description. Sure enough, the female lead character's first name was Alicia, the male lead was named Devlin. "That was very astute of her."

"That's Martha for you."

"I suppose Martha is in the guest house with her family?"

"She's in the kitchen. I stopped to say hello to her on my way downstairs after seeing Mom and taking my shower."

"I'd like to go in and thank her."

"It's right through there."

He crossed the large living room and stepped into the kitchen, where Martha stood at the sink rinsing cooked macaroni noodles in a large metal colander. "Merry Christmas, Martha!"

"Jack! Merry Christmas to you." She hugged him warmly.

"I got your gift. Thanks for thinking of me."

"Don't mention it. Had you seen that particular movie before?"

"Actually, I haven't. I think the only Hitchcock films I've seen are the later ones, like *The Birds* and *Psycho*." He paused. "I was a little puzzled as to why you chose that one, but Alicia pointed out that the lead characters have our names."

"That's exactly it. Also, it happens to be a very good movie. The most romantic film Hitchcock ever made, I think."

"I'll be sure to watch it." He looked around the kitchen. Before Martha had gotten up to drain the macaroni, she'd been snapping green beans. "It looks like you're cooking."

"Yes. We're going to have a wonderful Christmas dinner."

"Don't you ever get a day off?"

She laughed. "Sure I do, but just like I clean my own bathroom on my day off, I take care of the ones here as well. I suppose I've been spending more time here since Miss Caroline has been failing, but for me it's worth it." She smiled at him. "You know, Jack, I'm so glad you're in Alicia's life. She's never brought anyone home before, you know."

Marvin had said something similar that night at the hospital last month, but Martha's words surprised him nonetheless. "Not even for the holidays?"

"Never. Miss Caroline was so worried about her. I saw how you comforted her at the hospital last month. She's going to need you more than ever when…." She trailed off.

Jack saw the distress on Martha's face and quickly deduced she referred to Caroline passing away. "I'll do whatever I can to help."

"Funny. When Mr. Fletcher died it was so sudden. Miss Caroline tried to be strong, but she was devastated. She told me later she always expected she would be the first to go and he would have to bury her. Daphne, well, she didn't even try to hold it together. She cried for days. We were all so worried about her because she was pregnant at the time.

"But Alicia, she was the glue that held everyone together. Funny," Martha said with a baffled shake of her head. "Caroline's passing was as expected as Fletcher's was sudden, but Alicia seems to be taking it much harder."

"Maybe she felt closer to her mother," Jack suggested. "Girls often are, aren't they?"

"Alicia's always been an independent young lady," Martha replied. "I've never known her to be all that close to anyone."

Jack nodded knowingly. He had come to the same conclusion in his brief period of knowing her.

"Anyway, Jack, I'm very glad to see you here today. Alicia is going to need a shoulder to lean on while she copes with Caroline's loss. I hope you're up to it."

He grinned confidently. He liked the way the housekeeper looked out for her like an older sibling. Alicia and Martha seemed much more like sisters than Alicia and Daphne.

Alicia, Daphne and Martha went upstairs every so often to sit with Caroline, who also had an LPN stationed in her room. With keen observation, he noticed that whenever Alicia went up Daphne followed. That seemed strange to him, since the sisters didn't seem to have much contact with each other under normal circumstances. He decided that Daphne wanted to give Caroline the feeling that her two girls were united. He certainly couldn't fault her for that. It would give her mother some peace.

Martha was in and out of the kitchen, checking on the turkey. When she wasn't in the kitchen or sitting with Caroline she was in the guest house with her family. Initially Jack missed Marvin's presence, but then Todd invited him to watch the football game with him. The Timberlake living room did not include a television set, so Jack followed Todd downstairs to the comfortably furnished basement.

He looked around in awe. The basement contained every fun activity he could think of. One corner featured both pool and ping-pong tables. A few feet away was an eight-sided game table with leather chairs on casters. The U-shaped bar sat eight and was attached to a full kitchen. An extra refrigerator stood in a far corner. A sectional reclining sofa was positioned opposite a wide plasma TV. Shelves mounted on the wall held DVDs and a big binder with spines marked "Karaoke CDs." The basement also featured a jukebox and a pinball machine. It was truly a leisure lover's dream. The entire house had a comfortable lived-in look while being both stylish and spotless. How did Martha manage to keep the multiple rooms of the house so clean?

"Wow," he said. "Now, *this* is a basement."

"It's great, isn't it? My father-in-law believed in playing just as hard as he worked. Many a Friday night we played bid whist or Pokeno at that table—" Todd pointed to the game table "—until well past midnight. And I understand that Daphne and Alicia had all their teenage parties down here. Fletcher and Caroline did a lot of entertaining here as well."

Jack wondered what would happen to the property after Caroline's death. If it was sold it would likely bring in millions. The grounds didn't cover a particularly large area, maybe two acres, but it was right on the Sound, plus it had a guest house over the three-car garage where the Lewis family currently lived.

Alicia came downstairs at four. "We'll be eating in about half an hour," she said. "Jack, why don't you come up with me to see Mom?"

"Sure." He went upstairs with her, first to the main floor and then to the second. The basement stairs emerged near the kitchen, and upon emerging through the door his nostrils filled with the contrasting but pleasant scents of roasting turkey and baking ham. He followed Alicia through the kitchen and up the back stairs. Martha stood in front of the stove, stirring gravy.

"Smells good, Martha," he said, flashing her a thumbs up.

"Thanks, Jack!"

The first thing Jack noticed about Caroline Timberlake was that she'd gotten even frailer than she looked when he first met her. Her beauty was unmistakable, but he knew she couldn't last much longer. He wondered if Alicia suspected.

He liked the way Caroline smiled at the sight of the two of them. "You two make a handsome couple," she said warmly. "Did you have a nice birthday?"

"Very nice, Mrs. Timberlake," Jack said.

"After lunch yesterday we took a walk and then went

to the movies, and then we had dinner together in Stamford," Alicia explained.

"Sounds wonderful. Did you have dinner yet today?"

"Martha says it's almost ready."

"Make sure your sister behaves herself. I don't want her saying anything that will make it awkward for Martha and Marvin. This time she doesn't have Florence and Henry around to keep her in line." Todd's parents were spending Christmas with their married daughter and her family in Westchester.

"It'll be fine, Mom. Don't worry."

The nurse appeared from the hall, where she'd discreetly stepped to allow them some privacy. "Miss Timberlake, Mr. Devlin, I'm afraid I have to ask you to leave," she said gently. "Mrs. Timberlake is under strict orders not to talk much."

"I want you to come see me after dinner, Alicia," Caroline said. "You and I must talk about something."

Alicia walked to her mother's bedside and bent to kiss her cheek. "I'll be back, Mom. I promise."

"Make it about eight," the nurse suggested. "I'd like get her to eat a little, and then she should really nap for a while."

Alicia nodded. "Eight it is."

As they walked toward the back stairs, Jack said softly, "I take it there's no love lost between Daphne and Martha?"

Alicia gestured for him to stop walking. "My sister is an unbelievable snob," she said in a stage whisper. "You should have heard her Thanksgiving, saying how she didn't think it fitting for the Lewises to join us at the table." She turned sharply at the sound of rapidly approaching footsteps on the stairs on the other end of the hall. "Shh!"

Daphne's slim form appeared at the top of the front stairs, moving with the speed of someone trying to rescue a child from a burning building. She slowed down when she spotted Alicia and Jack in the hallway. "Have you been in to see Mom yet?" she asked.

"Yes. We're just going back down."

"Did she say anything?"

Jack's brows knitted in confusion. Had Caroline been nonverbal earlier in the day?

"Say anything like what?" Alicia asked.

Daphne's entire demeanor changed, like someone had just run a veil over her face. Now she looked relaxed instead of anxious. "I mean, is she able to talk much?"

"Daphne, she's not going to get better," Alicia said gently. "The nurse still only lets her talk for a few minutes at a time."

"I guess I keep hoping for a miracle," she said sadly.

Jack felt his heartstrings being pulled at like the rope in a tug-of-war. He had to try to comfort both sisters.

Holding Alicia's hand, he took a few steps toward Daphne and rested his hand on her shoulder. "Let's go downstairs," he said quietly. "We'll be sitting down to dinner in about fifteen minutes."

After dinner, they all returned to the basement, including the Lewis family. Melody Lewis brought various pies downstairs and placed them on the cloth-covered folding tables that lined a wall near the bar.

"I'm glad to see you sitting down for a change, Martha," Jack said. "It amazes me that you do everything around here all by yourself."

"Oh, I don't do it by myself," she said with a laugh. "I have a helper who comes in every Tuesday. She gives most of the rooms a good cleaning. Since most of them aren't used often, that's usually all it takes to keep them up."

"I was wondering how you did it."

"Don't let her modesty fool you," Marvin said proudly. "My wife is really Superwoman in disguise."

After dessert Melody Lewis and her brother Tyrone went to the movies, while the adults and little Fletcher ordered a movie on Pay-Per-View. Jack sat next to Alicia on the large sofa, his arm draped around her shoulder. He turned when he felt her shifting position. With her lips perhaps an inch from his ear, she whispered, "I'm going to try to slip upstairs at eight without Daphne noticing. I haven't been able to spend two minutes alone with Mom for weeks now, and Mom didn't say anything about bringing Daphne with me."

He nodded. He, too, had gotten the distinct impression that Caroline wanted to speak to Alicia alone. His voice was too deep to reply without someone overhearing him, so he accompanied his nod with a squeeze of her shoulder to convey he understood.

Caroline, awakening after a nap, gestured to the nurse to come to her bedside. "Toni, I know you don't want me to do a lot of talking, but there's something I must tell my daughter," she pleaded.

"Mrs. Timberlake, I'm under strict orders from both Dr. Jordan and Dr. Gertz not to allow you to overexert yourself, and you certainly mustn't get over-excited."

"I know you don't want anything happening to me on your watch," Caroline said, "but Alicia will back you that it was my decision in case there's any finger-pointing." The LPN hedged, and Caroline added, "This is my wish, and I'm the patient."

Nurse Antoinette Livingston finally nodded. "All right, Mrs. Timberlake. I'll be right outside if you need me."

At a minute before eight Jack felt a squeeze on his hand. He smiled at her, and she stood up and crossed in front of him to slip out the side of the sectional.

Immediately Daphne said, "Should we pause the movie, Alicia?"

"No, go ahead. I've seen it before, anyway." She headed for the stairs.

"Where're you going?"

"I just decided I'm in the mood for some popcorn."

Jack knew she'd had the excuse ready. The powder room off the kitchen and bar area shot holes in the most obvious reason for excusing oneself.

"There's popcorn in the cabinet down here," Daphne called, but Alicia had already begun ascending the stairs.

Jack had inadvertently leaned forward during Daphne's questions, hoping Alicia would get away alone. Now, watching Daphne shrug and return her attention to the movie, he leaned back again, relieved.

"Here I am, Mom," Alicia said cheerfully. "Did you feel up to talking?"

"Yes." Caroline looked over at her nurse, who promptly rose and left the room. "She worries about me," she said with a weak smile.

"Mom, I got the impression you wanted to tell me something important."

"Yes, dear. Sit down."

Jack found himself keeping a closer eye on Daphne than he did on the movie. He tensed as Daphne checked her watch repeatedly. Finally she whispered something to Todd, who, engrossed in the film and holding his now-sleeping son on his lap, simply nodded. Then she got up and ran to the stairs, no doubt to go looking for Alicia in their mother's room.

Damn, he thought. Why was Daphne so determined to keep her sister and mother apart unless she was present? It looked like relations between the sisters were about to become even less amiable, for he sensed that Alicia would not hesitate to inform Daphne that the current conversation was just between the two of them.

Then again, maybe that's what it would take to cure Daphne of her possessiveness. How could he forget how she'd raced up those stairs like a cannonball this afternoon the moment she suspected Alicia was visiting Caroline. He wondered what her problem could be.

Chapter 24

Do You Want To Know a Secret?

Alicia sat at Caroline's bedside, holding her hand. She wished her mother hadn't spent so much time telling her not to hold Toni Livingston responsible for allowing her to talk more than she should if anything should happen, that she'd been the one to insist on talking at length, no matter what the consequences. At last she'd begun speaking about the matter at hand. Alicia couldn't deny that all through dinner, dessert, and the movie she'd been curious about what her mother wanted to tell her.

"Alicia, you're my oldest child," Caroline said. "You came along at a time when I feared Fletcher and I were destined to be childless, in spite of how well our lives were going otherwise. You can't possibly know how much you mean to me."

"I love you too, Mom."

"I'm afraid your father and I weren't honest with you. We meant to, but we never got around to telling you that—"

"There you are!"

Alicia frowned at the sight of Daphne.

"What's going on?" Daphne inquired.

"What does it look like?" Alicia snapped impatiently. "I'm saying good night to Mom."

"Daphne, I asked Alicia to come up tonight so I could talk to her."

Alicia studied her mother, caught the meaningful look she gave to Daphne. Clearly something strange was going on. Did Daphne already know what their mother prepared to tell her now? "What's happening here?" she demanded. "I know *something's* going on." She stood and faced her sister. "Daphne, for the last couple of weeks you've made very sure I never had a moment alone with Mom. This morning when I got here you parked your butt right here in Mom's room. You were here when I came in to wish her Merry Christmas, and you waited until I'd showered, changed, and stopped in one more time before going back downstairs before you came down yourself. This afternoon, when you thought I might be up with Mom, you damn near broke your neck getting up here. I want to know why."

Daphne's hands went to rest on her hips as she glared at her sister. "Alicia, you need to shut up. What the hell do you think you're doing, raising all this ruckus when you know Mom's not supposed to have any excitement?" She turned toward the hallway. "Toni!"

The nurse promptly entered the room. "What is it?"

"My sister is making a fuss, even though she knows how much it will upset my mother. Will you please ask her to leave?"

Toni looked at Caroline for instructions.

"No, Toni," Caroline said. "Daphne means well, but unfortunately, *she's* creating all the fuss, not Alicia. I need to speak with Alicia in private. Would you please escort Daphne out?"

"Mrs. Scott, you heard what your mother said," Toni said softly.

Daphne stared at Caroline incredulously. "Mom, no!"

Caroline used precious strength to lean forward. "Daphne, I may be on my deathbed, but I know what you're trying to do. I'm ordering you to leave this room right now."

"But, Mom—"

Alicia had enough of Daphne's tantrum and approached her. "You heard what she said, Daphne. Please excuse us."

Daphne's eyes narrowed into slits. "You think you're so damn special. Wait 'til you—"

The rest of her words were lost as Caroline suddenly slumped forward.

"Oh, my God!" Alicia whispered as Toni immediately went into action, lifting Caroline's torso and pushing her back against the pillows. "Call the paramedics," she ordered over her shoulder.

"Mom!" Daphne wailed.

Alicia dashed for the phone on the other side of the bed, practically knocking over her sobbing sister in the process. Quickly she punched out 9-1-1. "I need an ambulance right away. My mother just collapsed. She's a heart patient. Please hurry!" She gave the address.

Toni, calm but quick, searched for Caroline's pulse. She then began massaging her heart muscles.

"Toni, what can I do?" Alicia pleaded.

"There's nothing you can do right now. You might want to tell Martha and the others what's happened. And someone should stand watch at the door for the paramedics so they can let them in right away. Every second counts."

Daphne still stood motionless at the foot of Caroline's bed, tears running down her cheeks. Alicia knew she wouldn't be of much use. "I'm on it," she said.

She ran down the two flights. Someone, having heard her frantic footsteps, paused the movie, and all eyes were upon her. "It's Mom," she said breathlessly. "She's just collapsed. I called the paramedics, and Toni is working on her."

Everyone jumped to their feet. Jack was at her side in an instant.

"Where's Daphne?" Todd wanted to know.

"Still up in Mom's room. I think she's in shock."

"Here, let me have him," Martha offered, meaning little Fletch. Todd handed the roused but still sleepy boy over to her and promptly bounded up the stairs.

"I think I should put him in bed before anyone gets here," she said.

"Come on, I'll go with you," Marvin said, taking her arm and guiding her toward the stairs.

"Someone needs to be by the front door when the paramedics arrive," Alicia said to Jack.

"Let's go."

While they waited in the foyer Jack said, "Alicia, what happened?"

"It was all Daphne's fault. She busted in and started carrying on that I was making Mom talk when she's not supposed to and asked the nurse to escort me out. Mom summoned up all her strength to tell Toni—that's the nurse on duty—that Daphne was the one making all the fuss, and that she wanted her to escort Daphne out so she could talk to me." A sob caught in her throat. "I'm afraid it might have been the last of her strength. She slumped forward and lost consciousness. Toni is trying to revive her."

"Did she get a chance to talk to you at all?"

"She'd just started when Daphne showed up. Jack, whatever Mom wanted to tell me, Daphne already knows. I'm sure of it. And she doesn't want me to know about it. That's why she's been hovering over me whenever I go in to see Mom." She shook her head. "I can't believe her. She's responsible for what's happened."

"Hopefully your mother will still get a chance to tell you."

"I'm not so sure. It doesn't look good, Jack."

He took a step toward her, and she willingly went into his embrace. He held her, neither of them speaking, until they heard the siren of an approaching rescue truck.

Todd raced down the stairs. "Are they here?"

"They're coming in now," Jack told him.

The technicians came in the house, and Todd directed them to Caroline's room.

"I hope they can revive her," he said as they all looked up at the rapidly moving EMS team. "I've got to say, it didn't look too good. Alicia, you might want to go up."

Jack felt her arms tighten around his waist for a second before she let go and smoothly climbed the stairs.

He turned to Todd. "How's Daphne?"

"Not good," he said grimly. "Apparently, she feels responsible for what happened. She kept saying, 'I didn't mean it. I didn't mean it.' I can't imagine where that came from."

Jack thought of what Alicia told him and thought, *It came from her*, but wisely kept quiet. "You probably should get upstairs to her."

"Yes, I guess so. I finally got her in a chair." He looked into the empty living room. "Any idea where Martha took Fletch?"

"She and Marvin brought him upstairs to bed."

"Good. He doesn't need to see what's going on."

Once more, the family gathered at the hospital for a vigil in the emergency room. This time, though, the outcome was different. The doctor came out and said, "I'm sorry, we weren't able to revive her."

Chapter 25

My Sweet Lord

Several hundred people came to the church in Stamford to pay their respects to Caroline Timberlake. At the funeral service, sitting in the front row with Daphne, Todd, Fletch, and her uncles and their wives; Alicia took the most comfort knowing that Jack sat just two rows behind her, after her cousins and their families.

The flustered feeling she got from being close to him had faded in the past days. Jack was still busy at work completing his project, but he called her often as she worked with Daphne to plan the funeral.

Thank heavens it was nearly over. Her mother was at peace, reunited with the husband she loved so much.

Alicia kept telling herself that was what counted the most. When sadness threatened to overtake her, she pictured her parents dancing together, moving as smoothly as Astaire and Rogers. Still, she was human enough to wonder what her mother planned to tell her in those last moments.

Although everything said that night pointed to Daphne being privy to the contents of the confession, Alicia refused to ask her sister. She simply would not give Daphne the satisfaction of refusing to divulge what she knew. When they gave the history to the doctors at the hospital, Alicia explained that Caroline had become agitated as a result of Daphne's interruption and refusal to leave, an account with which Toni Livingston reluctantly agreed and Daphne vehemently denied. The sisters had barely spoken since. Todd served as a liaison between them during memorial plans.

The service went by in a blur, followed by the drive to the cemetery and the repast at the Mason's lodge, where Fletcher Timberlake had been a member. Only family and close friends returned to the house after the repast.

Alicia sat quietly with Jack in the living room when Sam McDaniel, the family's attorney, approached her. The short, stout dark-skinned man with round cheeks had handled her parents' affairs for as long as she could remember. "I thought this might be a good time to go over the generalities of Caroline's will. We can discuss it in more depth after the New Year. Daphne and Todd are already in the library."

"All right." She turned to Jack. "I'll just be a few minutes."

In the library with its walls of built-in bookcases, Sam sat behind the cherry wood desk as Alicia, Daphne, and Todd faced him in tufted leather chairs.

"I'll be as brief as possible," Sam said. "Caroline's will was relatively uncomplicated. I'm sure you both knew that she retained three life insurance policies. The smallest covered her funeral costs, and she instructed that anything left should be given to the church." At their nods he continued. "The others were both in the same amounts, fifty thousand dollars apiece. One lists Alicia as beneficiary, the other Daphne."

Once again the attorney peered over his bifocals to see if anyone had any questions. "Your mother made a bequest of five thousand dollars to the church, in addition to what will likely be a small amount left from the insurance policy. She left her share of the family business to you girls equally.

"Caroline made very little changes to Fletcher's bequests. Virtually all stocks, mutual funds, and bank accounts have been passed to the two of you equally."

"What about the house?" Daphne asked, sounding anxious enough to make Alicia turn her head to look at her. She noticed her sister's posture had changed so that she leaned forward. She half expected Daphne to hold out her hand so Sam could lay a key in her palm.

"You'll remember that your mother sold the cottage on Martha's Vineyard after your father passed," Sam replied.

Alicia nodded. Caroline explained to her and Daphne

at the time that she couldn't bear to spend the summer there without Fletcher coming out on the weekends to join them. Even Daphne, greedy as she was, couldn't object. Caroline gave both girls part of the proceeds of the sale. "In addition, she gave you each a fifty percent share in the house," Sam continued. "If the house is sold, you each will get fifty percent of the proceeds. As I'm sure you know, the mortgage has been paid off, and the house has appreciated considerably in value over twenty-five years. Any loans taken out will be the sole responsibility of the person doing the borrowing. Defaulting on a second mortgage can lead to losing your interest in the house. Whoever lives in the house is responsible for its upkeep, if both of you live here the maintenance costs and taxes are to be divided.

"Taxes are paid from the rent money received by the Lewis family. Any improvements made must have complete approval of both owners, and they will not be reimbursed unless and until the property is sold. Any disputes are to be handled by myself," Sam concluded, peering at them from over his half-sized bifocals.

Alicia kept waiting to hear more about Martha's family other than that their rent money went toward the property taxes. When nothing else was said she decided to ask. "What about the Lewises?" Did she imagine it, or did Sam suddenly look uncomfortable?

"This is where Caroline made some caveats not in Fletcher's will," he began. "Martha Lewis is to decide whether she wishes to stay on as chief housekeeper and cook."

"What if I decide I don't want her here?" Daphne said.

"And what if *I* decide I want her to stay on?" Alicia countered.

"It is unlikely, after fifteen years of service, that Martha's performance would suddenly become unsatisfactory," Sam noted. "Any disciplinary action must first be brought to my attention. I'll then arrange a teleconference with both of you, possibly with Martha as well, and I will make the final decision. In short, Daphne, you can't take it upon yourself to let her go."

As Alicia expected, Daphne's features contorted into a scowl. "I don't like that at all. You're saying she can tell me to kiss her butt and I can't fire her without discussing it with the two of you?"

"And if I know you, Daphne, you'll goad her into telling you just that so you can insist she be fired," Alicia said.

"I'd do no such thing, Alicia."

"You'd better remember that the rent she pays covers the taxes on this property."

Todd gestured to Daphne to be quiet as Sam spoke.

"There's more involving Martha," he said, speaking slightly louder than before.

"I think you have our attention," Alicia said with a smile.

"Caroline also specified that the Lewises' rent is to be kept up with the rate of inflation and should not increase more than five percent a year without special approval from myself."

"What!"

Alicia gave her sister a triumphant smile. "Planning on hiking up Martha and Marvin's rent, were you?"

"That's ridiculous. For years they paid no rent at all. Even now they're only paying something like seven-fifty. Seven-fifty, for a three-bedroom apartment that's worth three times that much. It's criminal, I tell you!" Daphne said, her voice ringing with righteous indignation.

"Not when you consider that Martha's wages have always been tied in to the rent her family pays," Sam replied calmly. "Fletcher and Caroline consulted me when they made the original arrangements. I know the Lewis family lived in the guest house rent-free for their first two years. At that time Martha was paid two hundred and fifty dollars a month for cleaning the entire house and preparing breakfast, lunch, and dinner."

"Not exactly princely wages," Alicia remarked.

"They still came out ahead," Daphne muttered.

"And that really kills you, doesn't it?" Alicia said in frustration. "Why shouldn't Martha and Marvin get ahead?"

Daphne met her gaze defiantly. "Because they're not the type of people who deserve to live in this area, that's why. They don't fit in. It's not my fault that they lost everything they had in an apartment fire and didn't even have sense enough to buy an insurance policy so they could at least replace their belongings. So they move on up from Bridgeport to Westport and they've lived here fifteen years. That still doesn't mean they belong here."

Alicia stared at her, momentarily speechless. When she found her voice, she said, "You've got an awfully lofty attitude for someone whose father started off as a

stable boy on a Hudson River estate." Caroline may
have been a child of privilege, but Fletcher had told
them of his humble beginnings many times, always
adding where a person came from shouldn't limit what
he or she could accomplish. "Do you feel that Pop didn't
belong in Westport, either?"

"That was different. Besides, I could tell you a thing
or two about—"

"Daphne!" Todd's tone held a stern warning.

Daphne glared at Alicia, who returned an equally
steely and unyielding stare.

"If this afternoon is any indication of what the future
holds, I've got a feeling my services are going to be
needed frequently," Sam remarked. His eyes went from
one sister to the other. "You know, Caroline would be
very sad to see the two of you going at it like you were
raised by wolves."

"I don't care," Alicia said defiantly. "She has no
cause to say that the Lewises don't belong in Westport.
Our parents were both open-minded people who knew
a thing or two about being dismissed on the basis of their
background, specifically race, and in my father's case,
class as well. They believed in helping people. That
was why they took in the Lewis family in the first place.
And they were both proud of what Martha and Marvin
accomplished.

"That guest house is tiny, just over a thousand
square feet, yet it's divided into three bedrooms. No
way is it worth over two thousand dollars as rental
property," she declared.

Sam nodded. "Something else for you to consider,

Daphne. These were your mother's wishes." He paused to let that sink in. "She also willed Martha twenty-five thousand dollars and her jade necklace and bracelet."

At this Daphne opened her mouth, then abruptly closed it.

"There were a few other bequests of jewelry. A pearl ring to the pastor's wife, a few other pieces to her sisters-in-law. That's pretty much it."

Todd got to his feet. "Thank you, Sam." The two men shook hands, and Todd escorted Daphne out of the room.

Alicia remained in her chair. She closed her eyes and sighed. "Sometimes I can't believe my sister and I are related."

"I think Caroline would be tremendously disappointed in Daphne if she witnessed what just happened, and Fletcher, too."

"At least Mom had the foresight to predict that Daphne might try to force Martha out and prevented her from doing it." She yawned. "I'm tired, Sam. I don't think I can take being around any more people. I think I'll excuse myself and let Daphne take over as hostess until everyone leaves."

She returned to the living room to find Jack talking with Pete and Rhonda. Most of her other friends returned to New York immediately after the church service, and Shannon had left shortly after returning to the house. Alicia and Shannon had agreed that it wasn't fair to their administrative assistant, Amy, to have to hold down the fort all alone, and afternoons tended to be busy with requests for court reporters.

Both Jack and the Robinsons looked her way as she

approached them, making her feel a little like a prize hog at a state fair.

"Hi guys," she said pleasantly. "Can I borrow Jack for a minute?"

At the Robinson's urging she took Jack's hand and led him to the kitchen, where she leaned against the counter, pressed her palms against her temples and said, "Ahhhhh!"

"Something must have happened in there to upset you," he guessed.

"I think it's a combination of everything. My sister is behaving like a greedy gut, like no one but her is entitled to any of Mom's things. She truly makes me want to vomit, Jack. I do hope all of my parents' friends leave soon. I can't stand the idea of listening to one more person telling me the same old ridiculous lines, like 'She's in a better place now.' How the hell do they know about what happens after you die? And people saying how nice Mom looked in her casket. Her brothers are morticians, for heaven's sake. Of *course* they'll make her look as good as they can."

"How about a nice walk along the beach before you burst a blood vessel?" he suggested.

She let out her breath and looked up at him with a smile that relaxed her entire face. "You always seem to know the right thing to do. Come on, let's go before anyone comes looking for me."

They slipped out the back door and climbed the low brick wall that separated the back yard from the beach, Jack holding her hand to help her up and then lifting her and allowing her body to slide down. They gazed at each other but did not kiss or even embrace, both of them knowing this wasn't either the appropriate time or place. Instead they began to walk, their arms brushing as they moved.

Jack had never walked along a beach in winter before last week. The sand felt firm under the soles of his shoes, like packed-in dirt.

He listened carefully as Alicia told him about what transpired in the library. That sister of hers was a real piece of work. He wondered if the pair would even see each other after today.

He felt Alicia handled the situation reasonably well. Since Caroline's death he feared Alicia would cope by returning to the excessive drinking he'd noticed when they first met, but he'd had dinner with her twice since that sad episode at the hospital, and she declined his suggestion to order a bottle of wine. Perhaps the source of her stress came from witnessing her mother's decline— which he was sure couldn't have been easy—and now that Caroline's suffering had ended she would revert to the near-teetotaler Pete and Rhonda spoke of.

He felt badly about not being able to spend as much time with her during such a difficult time due to the demands of his position. He'd had the audio/visual guys screen the presentation for him just yesterday, and he spotted some things he wanted changed. His team was working on it now, and he felt a little less guilty about taking the day off to be with Alicia. He only had two days left to give a final green light for the project by the deadline of the first workday of the New Year. Tomorrow was sure to be a marathon day.

He'd been putting in a lot of those lately. The team

members joked that after this was over they all had some Royal Caribbean coming. He liked the idea of taking a cruise with Alicia, relaxing on a sun-brightened deck, enjoying balmy sea breezes and sipping cocktails, and then dancing after dinner. Not the boogie down kind of dancing, but the romantic kind, the kind where you glided across the floor the way his grandparents must have done when they were young.

Between her mother's death and his project, some time to merely enjoy each other was just what they needed. His family, who tried to take a trip together every three years, had a cruise vacation planned for February. Maybe he'd invite her to attend the reunion with him.

The more he thought about it the better it sounded. But he knew this wasn't the right time to mention it to her.

After walking for nearly half an hour they found themselves back where they started, the Timberlake's back yard. Jack checked his watch. Three-forty. His team probably had the video re-done for him by now. He really should check it the first chance he got.

"Alicia, I'm thinking about heading home," he said tentatively. "Will you be all right?"

"Yes, I feel a lot better now. I'll walk out with you and say good-bye to everyone, and then I'm going up to lay down. I feel exhausted, like I just swam the English Channel."

"It's been a big day for you."

She stopped just short of the kitchen door and turned to him. "Jack, I can't thank you enough for being there. You helped a lot more than you think you did. I want to tell you how much I appreciate it."

For one crazy second he considered telling her he loved her. He let the idea go as quickly as it formed. She'd made her feelings about love plain to him the night of the storm. The last thing he wanted to do was give her more emotional issues to deal with. He'd made progress, of that he was certain. Even Pete pulled him aside and told him it looked like he'd been wrong about the low likelihood of him ever getting anywhere with Alicia.

Jack bid the remaining mourners good-bye and walked outside with Alicia along with Pete and Rhonda. A few of Alicia's friends he recognized had attended the funeral, including Jenny Walters and Derek Taylor—the latter keeping a respectable distance—and her business partner, Shannon Anderson, whom he'd met just a few weeks ago when he went to Alicia's office in Lower Manhattan to retrieve his laptop. Shannon introduced him to her parents at the cemetery. She attended the repast, unlike most of Alicia's friends, who returned to Manhattan following the conclusion of the graveside service, but left soon after arriving at the Timberlake home.

Holding Alicia's hand, he walked with her to the Robinsons' SUV and stood while Pete helped Rhonda into the high-sitting vehicle. After the Robinsons drove off with a wave, Alicia walked with Jack to his Aviator, which he'd deliberately parked well down the street out of deference to the many seniors returning to the house.

"If you need me, no matter what time it is, just call," he instructed after using the remote to unlock the door, but before opening it. Impulsively he wrapped his arms around her waist and buried his face in the niche between her neck and shoulder, the warmth of her skin radiating the fragrance he'd gifted her with on Christmas, just a few days before. The corners of his mouth turned up when he felt one of her hands on his shoulder and the other resting on the back of his head, and he allowed himself the luxury of believing it would all work out.

Chapter 26

She's Leaving Home
Westport, Connecticut
Early 2000s

"I can't believe my baby girl is leaving home," Caroline said in a voice that sounded suspiciously like she was about to cry.

Alicia turned from the bag she was packing. "Now, Mom. Aren't you forgetting I didn't live at home when I went to college?"

"But that was different. You needed the experience of being away from home." Caroline sank into a chair as Fletcher's frame filled the doorway. "Besides, you came home every couple of weeks."

Alicia knew what else was different. When she went away to college, Daphne was only twelve years old and still living at home. Now Daphne was married, living in Westchester County with her husband. Alicia's leaving meant there would be no one but her parents in the house. "And I'll keep doing that now. Mom, I'm only going to New York. I stay there a lot now, anyway, with friends." Alicia always told her parents that she stayed with her friends Rhonda, Shannon or Jenny at their apartments in the city when she had dates, when often she stayed overnight at her date's apartment. She doubted they believed she was a virgin at thirty years old, nor did she feel they had to know every detail of her social life. "You'd worry more about me trying to get to Grand Central after dark than you would knowing I don't have to go that far after my classes."

"I don't understand why you have to take up court stenography in the first place," Fletcher grumbled. "If you were interested in the legal profession we would have sent you to law school. You don't have to be a glorified secretary."

"I'm not particularly interested in the legal profession, Pop. All I know is that I don't like crunching numbers. This opportunity with Shannon is going to be good for me."

Fletcher grunted. "I ran into Howard Anderson last week at the golf course. He was never too thrilled about his daughter choosing court stenography for a profession, but at least he's glad to see that she's become a business owner instead of working for somebody else."

"Most court stenographers work as contractors, Pop. They work when they want to."

Caroline took her husband's arm. "Now, Fletcher, I know you would have loved it if both our girls became attorneys like yourself, but what's most important is that they're both doing what they enjoy." She beamed at Alicia.

"Daphne won't be teaching long," he grumbled. "As soon as she and Todd start a family she'll give it up. Although I'm not sure how they'll manage on one salary with Todd still working in the D.A.'s office. I keep telling him he should have gone to work for a private firm. That's where the money is."

Caroline tugged at his arm. "Dear, don't you remember? Florence and Henry own a four-family house in White Plains. The kids are going to move in to one of the two-bedroom apartments as soon as it becomes available. The Scotts won't charge them much rent, so Todd will be able to support them fine on his salary and Daphne won't have to work."

"As long as he's not considering having her go back to work and have my grandchildren raised by day care workers."

"Fletcher, you lived your life the way you wanted to. Let Todd do the same thing," Caroline said patiently.

"I never had anyone give me any breaks," Fletcher declared. "I went straight from law school into a firm, and I was able to support my family comfortably from day one. You never had to go back to work at the funeral home from the time Alicia came on the scene."

"I don't have any plans to get married anytime soon, Pop." She didn't have the heart to tell him that she doubted she'd ever marry.

"Maybe you ought to think about settling down, Precious. You're almost thirty."

"I realize that, Pop."

"Your mother and I are looking forward to having plenty of grandchildren."

Once again Caroline came to the rescue. "It's just that your father and I don't want you and Daphne to wait as long as we did to start families, so you won't have the difficulties we had."

"Women are having babies later nowadays, Mom." Alicia tactfully refrained from pointing out that neither she nor Daphne had the heart ailment that had plagued Caroline for most of her life.

"All I can say is, this house isn't going to be the same without you, Precious." Fletcher sounded a bit sad.

Alicia felt like someone had stuck pins into her flesh. Her parents had suddenly grown old before her eyes. Her tall father, famous for his erect carriage, suddenly seemed slightly stooped over. He was now in his early seventies and fully retired from law after several years of putting in part-time hours. He didn't need the money; he did it because he loved his work. Caroline was sixty-six. Their ages seemed so advanced to be parents of relatively youthful children of thirty and twenty-four.

She found herself wishing that Daphne would hurry and have a child. Her sister believed in doing everything the traditional way, and she'd already been married two years. Wasn't that the norm, to get pregnant two years into marriage? Their parents needed something to look forward to besides regular games of golf. This house would probably seem cavernous to them with no one but themselves living here.

At least they had a good relationship with Martha and Marvin Lewis and their children, who were ten and eleven and attended the local middle school. Sadie had stayed with them from before Daphne's birth until they moved to this house three years later, when she decided to retire. There'd been another housekeeper for ten years who eventually became ill, and then Martha Lewis came to them after that. The Timberlake family watched the Lewis children grow up before their eyes, and the children were frequently in the house helping their mother.

"This whole thing about getting your own apartment in the city," Fletcher continued. "If you ask me, I think it's a little foolish. A woman should go from her parents' roof to the one she will share with her husband."

Alicia could have mouthed his next words, so certain was she of what he would say.

"Like Daphne," he said.

She merely smiled and continued packing, more certain than ever that she'd made the right choice.

Chapter 27

Martha My Dear

Alicia awoke to see darkness outside her window. She reached out and turned on the lamp on the bedside table. Eight-twenty. She'd slept for nearly five hours. She must have been exhausted, both from planning the funeral and from realizing that her mother was really gone. She'd never again lay eyes on that lovely face with the concerned eyes or hear the voice murmur compassionate phrases.

She washed her face in the attached private bathroom, then ventured out into the hall. She saw a light under her mother's room and knocked politely before going in, not waiting for consent. Who was in there?

Daphne and Todd sat on her mother's bed, the doors and drawers of Caroline's walnut jewelry armoire opened and, from what Alicia could see, practically empty.

"What's going on?" It looked like Daphne was helping herself to their mother's jewelry, but Alicia wanted to hear her say the words.

Daphne glanced at Todd before replying. "We're just going through Mom's things."

"It looks more like you're cleaning her out. Where's the pieces Mom promised to our aunts and to Martha?"

"They're there," Todd said quickly.

Alicia's closer inspection found the promised jewelry in one of the drawers, along with loads of costume pieces. Those had been passed over, clearly because they had no value. She faced her sister squarely, hands on hips. "Did it occur to you while you were grabbing everything in sight that *I* might want some of Mom's jewelry?"

Daphne raised her chin. "Let me tell you how things are going to be, Alicia."

"Yes, Daphne. By all means, tell me."

"You can act all cool now. I guarantee you won't be so nonchalant after you hear what I have to tell you." She paused for effect, smiling at Alicia's unchanged expression. "I don't know what I can do about my aunts, but Martha isn't going to get a thing from my mother's estate."

"Since Mom left a will specifying her wishes, I'd like to hear how you plan to prevent that from happening."

Todd spoke up. "We're going to contest Caroline's will. There's no reason for Martha to be awarded all that money. Fletcher and Caroline provided very nicely for Martha's entire family while they were alive."

She looked at her brother-in-law in amazement. "Mom *wanted* to give jewelry and money to Martha, or else she wouldn't have willed it to her. She often said she considered Martha to be like a daughter. And she protected her from what Daph—what you two might do." She'd always thought Daphne behind any attempted shenanigans, but Todd's statement made her think otherwise. She thought of the law degree he possessed, and she began to feel alarmed.

"If you're not well and you've been coerced, what's on paper only *looks* like it's your wishes," Daphne said meaningfully.

"Mom wasn't demented, Daphne. She left Martha that money because Martha took such good care of her. She was hired to keep house, not provide personal care. But in the end she did both."

Daphne's eyes narrowed. "So you're not with me on this?"

"No, I'm not. And personally, I don't think you stand a shot of winning."

"All right, so be that way. Todd is on my side. He'll support me."

"I'll testify on Martha's behalf, Daphne. No one would believe that Mom leaving her a mere twenty-five thousand dollars and a few pieces of jade constitutes coercion."

Daphne smirked in a way Alicia found unnerving. "That and a subway token will get me from the Bronx to South Ferry."

"Don't underestimate my influence. After all, I'm the eldest child."

Her sister grunted. "How appropriate for you to use that term, instead of something like, say, 'first born.'"

"Daphne," Todd said, his voice carrying an admonition.

Alicia looked first at him and then at Daphne. She had a sudden Twilight Zone feeling. Just a few hours ago, when they discussed the terms of their mother's will with Sam McDaniel in the library, Daphne had started to say something and Todd cut her off. "What's going on?" she asked suspiciously.

"I wouldn't be so quick to testify for Martha if I were you," Daphne said.

"I'm not a poker player," Alicia began, "but I can tell when someone feels they're holding a trump card. Go ahead, Daphne. Play it."

"Daphne," Todd warned. "There's no need for any of that to come out."

Her smile was mean-spirited. "If Big Sister feels she can take it, I'll tell her."

Her husband persisted. "Daphne, don't do this!"

"No," Alicia said, holding out a hand to halt Todd. "I want to hear what she knows—what *both* of you know—about me that I don't."

"I don't think that's a good idea," Todd said frantically. "Why don't we just forget it before somebody loses their temper."

"Forget it? No, Todd, it's gone too far for that." Alicia turned expectantly to Daphne. "Go ahead."

She paused dramatically. "You're *not* my sister."

The corners of Alicia's mouth turned upward. "I can't say I find it particularly upsetting not to be related to you."

"You're not even Mom and Pop's daughter."

Alicia stopped smiling. What was this about?

"You're nothing but an orphaned little nobody whose father was killed by your mother's boyfriend. The police found you sitting by your father's dead body. Pop heard about you through his legal connections. You had no family. You came out of the Hartford ghetto. I know I can't get you out of Mom's will, but I don't have to sit back and watch Martha Lewis walk off with one cent of my parents' money."

It took every ounce of restraint Alicia could muster not to crumple at such an astounding announcement, but she knew if she appeared crushed Daphne would never let her forget it. Sheer stubbornness kept her calm. "You can try to contest Mom's will, but I'll see to it that you lose. And since you never bothered to ask me if I wanted any of Mom's jewelry, I'll tell you now that I want Mom's ivory cameo," she said quietly.

"Didn't you hear what I said? Your testimony won't mean a thing. She wasn't your mother. Your real mother got stabbed to death by her boyfriend after he killed your father."

Another blow. Alicia bit her lip and her hands, at her sides, pressed tightly into her thighs to help her stand steady. "I want the cameo, Daphne," she repeated.

Daphne didn't move.

Todd stood up to his full height of six feet, three inches. "Give her the damn cameo, Daphne," he ordered.

She glared at her husband. "Why should I? Do you have any idea what that's worth? She's not a blood relative. It was my mother's jewelry. Why should she get to have it?"

Todd grabbed a large Zip-Loc bag and poured the contents out onto the bed, and began sorting through it. Alicia noticed the multiple other zipped bags lying on the bed. If she hadn't woken up, Daphne would have walked out of their parents' house with every piece of jewelry Caroline had owned.

"Oh, all right," Daphne said, sounded exasperated. "I think it's in this one." She reached for another bag, unzipped it and pulled out the oval-shaped cameo with its black background and gold chain. She handed it to Todd, as if it would be too much to give it to Alicia directly.

"Did you want anything else, Alicia?" Todd asked as he placed the cameo in her palm. At Daphne's audible gasp he snapped, "Be quiet."

She shook her head before accenting it with, "No. That's all I want. If you'll excuse me." She walked out of the room slowly, not wanting to give Daphne the satisfaction of seeing her run to her room to absorb the shocking information just disclosed in private.

Todd turned to Daphne. "That was a truly rotten thing you just did. How could you?"

"I just wanted to see Big Sister lose her cool for once."

"Why have you always been so jealous of Alicia?"

"I'm not jealous of her! Why should I be? She doesn't have a thing I want. Especially now. *I'm* the only offspring of my parents' marriage, Todd. That's why I got all my father's attention. He might have been proud of Alicia, what she'd accomplished and all, considering where she came from, but he *loved* me. Even if I'd dropped out of college and never worked a day in my life, he still would have loved me. He treated me special.

He always did. I just never knew why until Mom told me Alicia was adopted."

"So that's it. You can't stand knowing that you had to share your mother not only with Alicia, but with Martha as well."

She shrugged. "I'm their only *real* child, and that's that. I know I can't get Alicia removed from the will, but I don't think she'll want anything other than the money Mom left her and the share in the funeral homes. She'll probably feel too guilty to want any interest in the house. It'll all be ours, Todd. And one day it'll belong to Fletch and his sibling, when she gets here." She smiled at him mischievously. "That reminds me. Maybe we can start on that project soon. We won't have to worry about money."

He stared at her incredulously. "Daphne, I'm disappointed in you to the point of being outright disgusted. Your mother was just buried a few hours ago, yet you insisted on going through her jewelry box instead of going to bed. Do you really think Alicia is worried about grabbing as much of your mother's things as she can?"

"She can't now, can she?"

He shook his head. "It's bad enough that you told Alicia about her adoption the way you did. You promised me you wouldn't tell her, that you'd speak to Sam McDaniel about it and let him tell her, since he handled all the arrangements. You broke your word without a second thought. But how can you sit here talking about trying to make another baby when your sis—when Alicia is down the hall with her whole world unraveling because of you?"

"I'm sorry I broke my promise. It just burns me up to see her prancing around like she owns the place."

"I've got news for you, Daphne. She *does* own it, as much as you do. And she's as much entitled to live here as you are. There's no reason for her to give it up. In the eyes of the law she is the oldest child of Fletcher and Caroline Timberlake." He turned his back to her as he took a few steps toward the window, then turned back. "You know, this is your father's fault. I can understand how excited he felt to have a child he created after thinking that would never happen, but he went overboard with that whole Princess routine, and it affected you the wrong way. I guess I didn't help. I've always indulged you myself, like the way I agreed with you that Martha shouldn't get that money. *Agreed,*" he clarified at her smile, "as in past tense. I don't feel that way anymore.

"I still don't understand you, Daphne. I couldn't believe the way you acted this afternoon with Sam. You had the worse case of the 'gimme's' I've ever seen in anyone over five years old. You never used to be greedy like this. We're far from rich, but we do all right. I'm six years out of law school, but because we live in an apartment my parents own and our rent is low I can afford to keep you at home with little Fletch. Our situation isn't all that different from that of the Lewis family, when you think about it. We have a good life. But I'll tell you something. Your father and I both did you a disservice by giving you everything you wanted.

"And I'll tell you something else," he added. "This is no idle threat, Daphne, I really mean this. You take one

step to contest your mother's will, and I'll divorce you."
He saw fear in her eyes and knew his words had an impact.

"Now, excuse me," he said. "I have to tell Alicia
something."

Chapter 28

Photograph

Alicia couldn't get to her room fast enough, but once there she didn't fall apart the way she feared she might. Instead she merely felt numb.

Adopted? How could that be? Why hadn't her parents—no, that was no longer the correct phrase—why hadn't Fletcher and Caroline Timberlake told her? She had a right to know. How could they allow Daphne to know and to spring it on her in such a cruel way?

No, that wasn't how it had been. Her mother made at least two attempts to tell her the truth. There was that time back in October when she started to say something but was interrupted by Martha bringing them breakfast.

After that Daphne joined them and stayed with them the rest of the day.

It remained that way almost until Caroline's death.

She frowned as she tried to remember exactly when Daphne started sticking so close to Caroline. The room was still and quiet as she concentrated.

She recoiled when someone knocked on the door. She didn't want to talk to anyone, and she didn't think she could stand to even look at Daphne.

The knock sounded again. "Alicia, can I talk to you for a minute? It's Todd."

She hesitated only a moment. "All right. Come in."

He opened the door and stepped inside. "I won't stay long. Alicia, I'm so sorry for Daphne's behavior. I'm ashamed of her."

"I appreciate that, Todd."

"But I especially wanted you to not worry about her contesting Miss Caroline's will. I'll see to it that she doesn't."

"Thanks, Todd."

He nodded as he stepped backward. "Good night."

After a night of little sleep, Alicia was waiting in the reception area of Sam McDaniel's office in Stamford when he arrived a few minutes after nine the next morning. He took one look at her anguished expression and said, "I think I know why you're here. Come on, let's go to my office." To his secretary he said, "Hold all my calls. I don't want to be disturbed."

He flipped the switch and allowed her to enter, closing the door behind him. Alicia sat facing his desk, and he surprised her by sitting not behind his desk but in another chair just a foot or so away. "You must have found out about the secret your parents kept from you all these years."

"And obviously you knew all about it."

"Of course I knew. I've been your parents' attorney and legal advisor for nearly forty years."

She laughed, a bitter sound. "I guess you got a good chuckle out of my sitting in the library saying I could hardly believe Daphne and I were sisters."

"Alicia, you're not being fair. Caroline told me months ago that she intended to tell you the truth. You weren't old enough to be told at the time of your adoption. Fletcher and Caroline always planned to tell you, but somehow the ideal moment never came up. When I was informed of Caroline's death I kept waiting for you to contact me for more information about your birth parents. When you said nothing I had no recourse but to think that for whatever reason Caroline changed her mind. It wasn't up to me to open a proverbial can of worms she wanted to stay shut. She's my client, and I can't breach confidentiality, even after her death."

"But Mom told Daphne."

"I hadn't counted on that," he admitted. "I got that impression yesterday. It sounded like she was about to say something derogatory about your birth father. Your mother must have told her, unless one of your uncles did."

"I don't think so. My mother's brothers loved her, and they'd never do anything to cause her or anyone in her family grief."

Sam leaned back in his chair. "I know for a fact that

Daphne didn't know about your being adopted at the time of your father's death. I can't understand why she would tell Daphne and not you. But I'm sure Caroline never believed that Daphne would use it against you, even if you girls weren't close. And I'm sure if she told Daphne she intended to tell you." He paused. "Alicia, don't be angry at your parents. They thought they were doing the right thing. They wanted to protect you."

"I understand that," she said quietly. "But it hurts to have it thrown in my face by a vindictive witch."

"I know Daphne wasn't happy with the restrictions Caroline put on her in her will. But it wasn't right for her to tell you like that." Sam leaned forward earnestly. "Alicia," Sam said. "Surely you don't believe Caroline would share your history with Daphne if she didn't fully intend to tell you."

"Sam, I know Mom planned to tell me. She tried to tell me just before she died. Daphne was so desperate to prevent me from knowing—at least being told by Mom—that she started a stink that literally killed Mom." At the quizzical rise of his eyebrows she explained the events of Christmas night. "The blame for Mom's death lies at her feet, Sam. I don't care if Mom only had another fifteen minutes to live. Daphne shortened her life by those fifteen minutes, and she had no right to do that."

"I can't disagree with you on that." Sam pushed his chair back as he eased his bulk out of it. He went behind his desk and retrieved a yellow manila envelope and handed it to her. "I've been saving these for you," he said. "It's all here for you. Newspaper articles, trial transcripts. Go over them, and we'll talk some more."

She took the envelope with a shaking hand but didn't open it. She would do that after she arrived home. This remarkably fresh-looking envelope held the key to her past, and she wanted to inspect it in private. "I understand that she and my father planned to tell me, but I still can't figure why they waited so long. I'm thirty-five years old, Sam, and my…my parents were practically middle-aged when they adopted me. Time was never on their side. Hell, Pop's been dead for two years already." A memory suddenly came flooding to the surface. "When my father had his stroke and was rushed to the hospital, I sat at his bedside just hours before he died. He told me that he loved me and that he was proud of me. Why didn't he tell me then that they adopted me? He was weak and couldn't speak too clearly, but I could still understand him."

"Alicia, you witnessed a brutal, cold-blooded crime, or at least its aftermath. The child psychologist who handled your case insisted that while you showed no signs of having been touched by your father's murder, you would one day suffer from posttraumatic stress disorder. He said you would be a perfectly functioning, happy adult, and then some obscure sighting will trigger the suppressed memories when you were ready to remember. The last time I talked to Caroline about it, she said she knew she didn't have much time left and would tell you at the right moment. When you didn't come to me before or after she passed, I presumed the right moment never came." Sam shrugged. "It wasn't my place to tell you, Alicia. All I could do was hand over the paperwork to my partner when I retire."

She closed her eyes momentarily. "Daphne did everything she could to prevent me from being alone with Mom those last weeks. Mom must have told her during that time."

Sam gestured toward the envelope lying across her lap. "I can leave you alone for a few minutes if you'd like, to let you absorb all of this in private."

"No," she said. "I'll look at it when I get home. What I want from you now is for you to tell me everything you know about my parents."

"I didn't know them, of course, but I read the trial transcripts thoroughly. Your parents were both young. Your mother liked to have fun and felt a little stifled by marriage, motherhood, and housework. She married right out of high school. She began having an affair with a flashy type, a petty criminal in the neighborhood, who'd taken a fancy to her. Your father came home unexpectedly and caught them together. Neighbors heard sounds of a physical disturbance, and the conclusion was that during a fistfight, your mother's boyfriend pulled out a knife and stabbed your father in the abdomen. Neighbors also heard your mother scream. One of them called the police. When they arrived they found your father dead on the floor with you hovering nearby. Your mother and her boyfriend had fled. Three days later your mother's body was found stabbed to death in an alley. She'd been killed somewhere else and her body dumped. Eventually they caught the man who did it. The prosecutor got him to admit on the stand that he killed her when she kept objecting to his killing her husband and making her leave her baby there with his dead body.

"I might as well tell you this now, Alicia. When the killer was asked how he managed to get your mother to leave you with your father's body, he said he told her if she didn't leave with him right away he'd kill you, too."

She bowed her head, stressing her facial muscles to keep her eyes tightly shut to hold in the tears.

Sam covered the back of her hand with his palm. "Alicia, you've been subjected to a tremendous shock. No one could expect you to bounce back into business as usual after learning about your early life. It's as much a trauma to your system as getting hit by a car."

"I'm coping, Sam."

"I don't think you are. You can't do this by yourself, dear. I hope you'll consider counseling."

"Counseling? As in a *psychiatrist?*"

"You don't have to say it like it's a dirty word. It isn't, you know. This is no different than schools bringing in counselors after a school shooting to help students deal with the trauma."

"I'm no student, Sam."

"You've been traumatized nonetheless. Posttraumatic stress disorder is a very real condition, one you can't expect to conquer alone. Because I anticipated your learning about your adoption, I've taken the liberty of contacting the firm your parents consulted shortly after your adoption. You won't remember this, of course, but they brought you in a couple of times to see their child specialist. At the time it was determined that you had no recollection of your father's murder, but they warned that it might be buried somewhere deep within your memory and it might not surface until years later, if ever. They still have your file, and they have practitioners on staff who treat adults as well. Do yourself a favor, Alicia. Go and see them. They're right here in Stamford. I can give you their name and number."

She shook her head. "Maybe. But I'm not ready to call them now. I'll wait and see how I feel."

Alicia got into her Solara and headed for the city, a decision she'd made before leaving Green's Farms. It would be a real pain in the butt to find a parking space and cope with alternate-side-of-the-street parking rules to accommodate the street sweepers, but she'd have to take her chances. Leaving her car at the house she now co-owned meant certain contact with Daphne, the last person she wanted to see. Even if she had to purchase a monthly parking pass in a garage—something that would likely cost nearly as much as the rent on her apartment, it would be worth it.

Taking possession of her car only represented a third of her Connecticut-related concerns. As she drove she made a mental note to make some employment inquiries on Martha's behalf, and to call Martha and ask her to take Lucky out to the guest house before Daphne could get rid of him, at least for the time being.

She knew that in the near future she'd have to make some decisions about her own living arrangements, like considering buying a place large enough where Lucky wouldn't be cramped, but at the moment one issue took priority.

The envelope that lay on the passenger seat.

* * *

Settled on her sofa with the blinds drawn, Alicia carefully undid the metal clasp of the envelope and slid out the contents. She started with the newspaper articles, unfolding them gingerly. Lurid headlines screamed out at her. "Man stabs girlfriend's husband in jealous rage." "Woman found stabbed to death near downtown." Black and white photographs showed Clifton Matthews, the man who'd killed both her parents, being taken into custody, a jacket covering his face. A photo of her parents in happier times, a curly-haired infant in their laps. She looked at the picture more closely. Good Lord, that was *her!*

Her mind, rushing out in a dozen different directions, focused on one thing. Only one baby picture of her existed, a studio portrait with her wearing a pretty flowered dress with a lace trim, sitting up and laughing with her mouth wide open. She was toothless at the time, probably only a few months old. The photo was on display in her parents' bedroom. Her parents, on the other hand, possessed dozens of photos of Daphne to document her babyhood, as well as photos of herself at later stages of her life. Alicia remembered asking them why there were no more baby pictures than the one, and Caroline told her that they didn't have a lot of money in those days to pay photographers. By the time Daphne came along, she said, their fortunes had improved.

Alicia accepted the explanation readily, but now she knew that wasn't the reason at all. This was probably the only photo taken of her alone as an infant. Caroline and Fletcher couldn't very well display photographs of her with her birth parents, unless they were prepared to tell her about her adoption.

She focused on the article. Her mother's name had been Norma Jean Clements. She was surprisingly petite, perhaps five feet two. All her life Alicia believed she resembled Fletcher Timberlake, with her only inheritance from Caroline slightly prominent cheekbones, but now she knew that was mere coincidence. Alicia's real mother, Norma Jean, had been blessed with high cheekbones, and that was the source of her own bone structure. She looked sweet and fun-loving. What had induced her to seek fulfillment in the arms of another man, a man so cruel he could make her choose to leave her toddler alone with the body of the man he'd just killed or he'd kill the child as well? Had her father been some kind of brute?

Benjamin Clements had been a tall man, well over six feet. In the photo his large hand covered her shoulder and upper arm to keep her from falling over. She smiled at the protective gesture. Her father loved her; that much was clear. Then her eyes moved to his face, and she gasped in shock.

Her father looked just like Jack Devlin.

Chapter 29

Whatever Gets You through The Night

She stared open-mouthed at the reproduction. Benjamin Clements had a close-cropped haircut in an era where many men wore three-inch or longer Afros. Like Jack, he wore no moustache, no beard. He was tall, perhaps even taller than Jack, with broad shoulders. But what struck her immediately was his piercing dark brown eyes. No wonder she felt from the beginning that she had seen Jack before, that they had a prior history together. Jack's appearance stirred up memories of her birth father.

A memory came to the forefront of her mind, so strongly that her shoulders jerked. She remembered

being carried about on broad shoulders in the years
before Daphne's birth, remembered feeling like she was
high enough to touch the sky. All this time she believed
those shoulders belonged to Fletcher Timberlake, but in
that one instant she saw it clearly.

Her birth father, Benjamin Clements, had been the
one to carry her that way.

She closed her eyes tightly. Surely there had to be more
memories that she'd buried in her subconscious.

Alicia sat quietly for a full five minutes, but nothing
came to her. She realized that memories worked like in-
spiration…they couldn't be forced.

She leaned forward and cradled her forehead in her
hands. Not only was she *not* the daughter of the only
parents she clearly remembered, but her birth father bore
a remarkable resemblance to the man she was dating.
Either one of those by itself would be difficult to cope
with. This reminded her of what political pundits coined,
"an October surprise," revelations about candidates that
came to light in the weeks just prior to the November
election that contained enough substance to affect the
outcome. It might be December, but these were her
October surprises. Her whole life had been changed
because of the new information she now possessed.

What a way to wind up the year, especially when
considering the event that triggered it all. The death of
her mother—no, she couldn't even accurately refer to
Caroline Timberlake that way anymore—had come as
a blow, but it hadn't been unexpected.

Alicia recalled that day in October, right after she met
Jack and waited impatiently for him to call. She'd gone

to her mother's room Sunday morning—doggone it, she couldn't just up and stop thinking of her that way, not after nearly thirty-five years—and Caroline had started to tell her something, but stopped when Martha came in with a breakfast tray. At the time Alicia thought her mother intended to say nothing more than continued concerns about possible effects on her because of her father's preference for Daphne. But what was that she'd prefaced with? Something about how lost she felt before Alicia "came along," and how much she meant to her? No, she planned then to tell her about the adoption. Martha came in with breakfast, the three of them talked a bit while they ate, and then Martha took the tray down to the kitchen, promising to return to help Caroline dress, and Alicia went to get ready herself. There hadn't been another chance for them to talk privately the rest of the day.

Of all times for Martha to join them. If only she'd taken a few more minutes to prepare that food….

Alicia knew she couldn't fault Martha for her timing. She had no way of knowing.

But she couldn't help wondering how different things might have turned out for her if Caroline told *her* the truth about her past, rather than Daphne.

Jack frowned. Alicia's greeting sounded barely intelligible, completely unlike her usual crisp diction. "Alicia, it's Jack. Are you okay? You sound funny."

"No, Jack, ahm not okay. In fact, I'm not even sure ahm even A-*lee*-see-a." She mimicked his pronunciation of her name.

He took a moment to absorb what he heard. He immediately recognized the signs of excessive drinking in her slurred words, but he struggled to come up with a reason why she would express uncertainty about her identity. He could think of nothing except something must be terribly wrong. That, of course, meant she shouldn't be alone.

He didn't hesitate to make the suggestion. "I'd like to come over, if that's all right with you."

"Sure. Just as' fo' the li'l nobody when you ring the bell."

His forehead wrinkled in confusion. What the heck was she talking about?

He packed a suit, shirt, socks, and underwear for work tomorrow and some toiletries and threw everything in a black nylon garment bag. At the last minute he tossed in an extra shirt. He didn't stop to dial Rhonda until he'd gotten on a train headed for the city.

"Rhonda, have you spoken with Alicia today?" he inquired without preamble as soon as she answered the phone.

"No, Jack, why?"

"I called her a little while ago. She sounded awful, like she's been hitting the bottle again."

"I don't understand what's gotten into her lately. She barely used to touch a drop. And here I was thinking that since her mother passed she'd probably cut it out."

"People who only drink when they're stressed over something often become alcoholics," he remarked. "But there's more to it than that. She said some things to me on the phone that just plain don't make sense. I think something happened to her today, or maybe last night."

"I can get Pete, and we can go down there to check on her."

"No, you stay put. I'm already on a train. I'll go to work straight from her apartment."

"Will you call us, let us know what's going on?"

He recognized the concern in her voice. "I promise. Try not to worry."

In a hurry to reach Alicia, Jack took a cab to her apartment from Grand Central. He rang her bell, then rang it again when she hadn't answered after a minute. He had his cell out to call her when her voice came through the speaker. "Who'zit?"

He started to call out her name, then rephrased. "It's Jack. Let me in."

When the buzzer sounded he pulled the door open and proceeded to take the stairs two at a time until he reached the fourth floor landing.

When she opened the door, after what seemed like an eternity, he immediately forgot his promise not to use her first name. Her hair was loose and uncombed, her eyes puffy and bloodshot, her face showing intense strain. His beautiful Alicia looked almost seedy. "Alicia! What happened?"

She fell into his arms, her hands clutching his back like he alone could save her from her demons. Jack quickly glanced in the hall to see if anyone witnessed what should be a private moment. He gently eased her backward and closed the door behind him, then let the garment bag slip from his hand and fall to the floor in a heap. He used both hands to hold her to him and whispered in her ear. "It's all right. I'm here. I'll stay as long as you want me to." He paused. "Do you want to talk about it?"

"No, not now," she whispered back. "It hurts too much."

"You don't have to," he said quickly. He felt her hold on him lessen.

"I look a mess," she said dully.

Jack wasn't sure that agreeing with her would be such a good idea. Instead he said, "Did you want to clean up?"

She reverted back to her whisper. "Yeah."

"Go ahead. I'll just make myself comfortable."

He hung up his garment bag in the coat closet, then removed the throw that lay across the chaise in the corner and sat down, kicking off his shoes to rest his feet on the matching ottoman. He noticed an empty bottle of Australian wine on the coffee table, as well as the martini pitcher partially filled with an unknown beverage. It broke his heart to think of her in this apartment alone, drinking to drown her pain. Thank God he'd called.

He glimpsed her leaning over an open drawer of the Bombay chest, her upper body bent but moving up and down a few inches in an inadvertent rocking motion. When she straightened up, fresh clothes in hand, and disappeared into the bathroom, he got up and discarded the empty bottle, washed out her glass, and returned the martini pitcher to the refrigerator.

Other than the ingredients of binge drinking, the

apartment looked fine. Her bed at the front of the apartment remained neatly covered with pillows, as usual. She had apparently sat in the chaise and drank until she fell asleep.

Fifteen minutes passed before Alicia emerged from the bath, wearing a blue cotton blend knee-length bathrobe that completely concealed whatever she wore beneath it. He looked up expectantly. She looked a thousand percent better. Her hair had been brushed and caught with a coated rubber band at the nape of her neck. He still saw stress in her face, but not as much. "Feeling better?"

"Yes, much."

She didn't seem to want to talk, so he didn't press the issue. She'd tell him what had her unglued when she was ready. "I thought I'd order in," he said instead. "What do you feel like eating?"

"That's a great idea. I don't really want anything exotic, like Chinese or even pizza." She took a moment to think. "You know what I could really go for? A big, juicy hamburger. But the people who make the best burgers don't deliver."

"That's not a problem. I'll pick them up." He had no idea how far he had to go, but if that's what she wanted, he'd find the place, wherever it was.

"No. I don't want you to leave. We'll send them by cab."

He looked at her incredulously. "Hamburgers delivered by cab?"

"Sure! From Luger's in Brooklyn. I've done it before."

An hour later Jack completed eating the best hamburger he'd ever eaten. "This is delicious," he said.

"There's nothing like a burger from Luger's. In my opinion they're the best in New York." She yawned. "Excuse me. I know it's bad to eat and lie down, but I'm still tired."

"Go ahead. I'll be right here."

He watched a documentary on the Civil War for the next two hours. Frequently he walked over to look in on her. She appeared to be sleeping, but at one point she rolled over on her stomach and whimpered into her pillow like a hurt animal.

Jack felt utterly helpless watching her. Never before had he witnessed such deep pain. He wished he had a way to get in touch with Martha. She might know what happened.

No, he thought. Martha wouldn't know, unless she'd witnessed it herself. Alicia didn't confide in people, not even someone as close to her as Martha. The only person she might talk to had just been buried.

Could Alicia's torment stem from grief? She'd cried a little at the cemetery, not wracking sobs like Daphne, but dignified tears, like those of her uncles.

No, that wasn't it. She grieved for her mother, no doubt about that, but this was something deeper. Something unimaginable.

He sat on the edge of the bed and rested his palm lightly on her back, remaining there for nearly ten minutes, until her breathing returned to normal. She didn't wake up at all during the episode.

Jack wondered how long it would be until she felt she could share the source of her pain with him, put it into words. A day? A week? Longer? Even as he mused, he knew that however long it took, he would be by her side while she dealt with her anguish.

When Alicia's cell phone, laying on top of the coffee table, began its distinctive ring he looked at it uncertainly, then made a split second decision. "Hello."

The hesitation on the other end of the line told him the caller was a male. Jack expected as much; it was after ten.

"May I speak to Alicia?" the caller finally asked in a confident voice.

"I'm sorry, she's not feeling well at the moment."

Another pause. "Who's this, anyway?"

"This is a friend of hers."

"So am I."

"Good. I'll tell her you called." Jack's finger poised to hit the End button when the man on the other end spoke.

"Wait a minute. You don't even know my name. How can you tell her I called?"

"I'll just tell her a friend of hers called."

"My name's Derek, man. Is there anything I can do to help out?"

"That's nice of you, Derek, but I'm taking care of her." He decided that Derek was entitled to know his identity. "This is Jack Devlin. I think I met you here, and I saw you at the funeral."

"Yeah, I think so. Well, let me know if I can be of any help. Alicia's my girl. I gotta make sure she's okay."

He said it in a casual rather than possessive manner, with the emphasis on "girl," not "my." Still, that was the last thing Jack wanted to hear Derek say. "No, Derek, she's *my* girl." He hung up, smiling. He'd shifted the emphasis a word ahead to leave no doubt about his intentions. He knew Derek understood exactly what he meant.

He went to use the restroom, pausing by where Alicia lay on the way back. She'd climbed between the sheets of the medieval-looking sofa that served as her bed, hiding in plain sight. In sleep she looked completely peaceful, stress-free. She slept on her side, one arm partially obscured by her pillow, the other outside the blanket. A spaghetti strap of a tan nightgown peeked out from under the covers.

He gazed down at her for a few moments, then reached out to lightly caress her bare shoulder. Her skin felt soft to his fingertips. In spite of himself he ran his hand down the length of her arm.

In an instant she opened her eyes and reached out with her other hand, clamping it around his arm. Their eyes met and held. "Lay down with me, Jack," she said softly.

He couldn't refuse her. He nodded, and she let go of his arm. He slipped the covers back and slid between the sheets, on his side, facing her. The double bed seemed very small. He moved as close to her as he dared. Feeling an overwhelming need to touch her, he reached out, aiming for a part of her that would be covered. He didn't know if he could handle touching bare skin.

He settled for her lower back, just above the curve of her hips. A satisfied sigh escaped from Alicia's lips as she stretched her body lengthwise against his. Her head fit nicely in the niche between his chin and his chest. Her left arm reached out and settled near his arm, her hand resting on his shoulder.

Lying and holding each other this way gave him the wonderful sense of intimacy, and he knew he wanted to take care of Alicia forever. He still didn't know what had caused her to go on this bender, but he felt confident that she would tell him soon.

Jack opened his eyes. He realized immediately that he'd dozed off. Alicia's soft breathing next to him told him she, too, was sleeping. The bed's high head and foot boards blocked out much of the light, but he could hear the TV playing softly behind them. He hadn't bothered to turn it off.

He slipped out of bed and turned off the set with the remote. It only took a few seconds, but when he returned Alicia startled him by saying, "Weren't you going to say good-bye?"

"No, because I'm not leaving. I just got up to turn off the TV." He lifted the covers to get between them.

"Do you always sleep in your jeans?"

He hesitated. They were getting into territory that he wasn't sure she was ready for, at least not emotionally. "No."

"Then take them off."

The room was completely dark, but his eyes had focused enough to see that she propped her upper body on one elbow. The spaghetti strap of the elevated shoulder had fallen down. He could create a sticky mess in his shorts just thinking about the curves and warm skin beneath that nightgown.

Quickly he stripped to his shorts and got back into bed, laying on his back so she wouldn't feel his arousal. This wasn't the right time to make love.

Alicia snuggled against his side, and his arm went around her.

"I'm glad you came to me tonight, Jack," she said softly. "I wanted to call you. I guess I was too proud. But I'm glad you called me."

"I was worried about you." His arm inadvertently tightened around her shoulder.

"Sometimes pride can be a terrible thing," she said, so faintly he could hardly hear.

"Don't worry about it," he mumbled, already falling asleep.

The feel of something wet on his shoulder woke him. He glimpsed at the large red digits of the alarm clock on the Bombay chest. Two-forty-five. Alicia's face still nuzzled against his shoulder. He quickly realized the source of the wetness.

It was tears.

He shifted position, facing her. "Alicia, what's wrong? Why are you crying?"

"I'm all right."

"The hell you are. People don't cry for no reason."

"I'm not crying. I just got a little emotional, and one tear slipped out of me."

"You know you can talk to me about it any time you want," he said gently.

"I know. I'm not ready yet. I'm all right, Jack. Go back to sleep."

"All right." But Jack had no intention of going to sleep. Instead he lay awake and listened carefully for any sounds of crying. When her even breathing took over, he impulsively pressed his lips to her now-dried cheek. Alicia stirred, moving her head so that her lips replaced where her cheek had been moments before. Her arms went around his neck as they kissed deeply.

His reservations about making love to her quickly melted away. She clearly wanted and needed him as much as he did her. In a blur of movements they shed their clothes. "I've got protection in my wallet," he said breathlessly between kisses.

"For God's sake, hurry up."

Afterward they snuggled together on their sides, facing each other. He dozed off and on, not wanting to fall asleep until Alicia appeared to be resting comfortably. The sound of her even breathing made him relax. Obviously something happened in the elapsed time between leaving her mother's home yesterday afternoon and this evening when he called her, something that disturbed her even more than the death of her mother.

He just couldn't imagine what it could be.

Chapter 30

All Things Must Pass

He found himself glad he'd thought to pack that extra shirt. Just before leaving for work he sat beside her on the edge of the bed. "Alicia, I'm about to leave. You'll have to come and lock the door behind me." When she didn't respond he shook her shoulder gently.

She slowly opened her eyes. "My head hurts," she announced.

"I suppose it does. I saw that pitcher of liquor." The mixture had the same coloring as the Kamikazes she'd mixed the first night they met, back in the fall. "It was nearly empty. Alicia, you can't continue drinking like that."

He expected her to argue, but she merely said in a meek voice, "I know."

"I've got to go, but can we talk later?"

"Yes, definitely."

"We'll go get some dinner when I get in. Can I call anyone for you?" As he promised to do, he called Rhonda last night while Alicia showered, just to let her know that no harm had befallen her.

"No, thanks. I'll call Shannon and let her know I won't be in again today."

When he returned after work she looked much more like herself. Her face looked back to normal, and she wore jeans and a striped sweater.

"You look great," he said, smiling.

"I don't feel too bad, either. I took a nice long shower. And I haven't had anything to drink. You can check the pitcher."

"I don't have to check, Alicia. I believe you." He patted the pockets of his overcoat. "I guess there's not much point in my taking off my coat. You look ready to go."

She glanced at the sports coat and tie he wore under his unbuttoned coat. "Maybe I should change. I'm a little underdressed—"

"Don't worry about it. You'll still be the best-looking woman at the restaurant." He loosened, then removed his tie. "Is there anyplace in particular you'd like to go?"

"There's a Mediterranean place down on Seventy-Seventh that I like. It's quiet, so we can talk."

As they walked Alicia relayed what happened the day before, her shouting match with Daphne, and her visit with Sam McDaniel. She left out the circumstances of her parents' deaths, only saying that they died, leaving her an orphan, or as Daphne had put it, "an orphaned little nobody." It was all too raw, too new. Eventually she'd tell him about it, but right now she couldn't handle it. It wasn't a lie, not really…just not the whole truth.

"Alicia, I'm…speechless," Jack said honestly when she was through. "I understand why you went on a bender. I'd probably do the same thing if I suddenly found out I wasn't who I'd always thought I was. And what a terrible way to find out." It would have been so much better if Alicia heard the truth from Caroline, a loving mother figure, than a spiteful creature like Daphne.

"I woke up yesterday thinking I was Alicia Timberlake," she concluded. "I went to bed as Alicia Clements."

"You're still Alicia Timberlake," Jack pointed out. "Your name doesn't mean anything. And it's just your last name at that."

Their conversation temporarily stopped as they arrived at the restaurant, were seated and looked over the menu.

After they placed their orders—neither of which included alcohol—Jack smiled at her across the table. "So what happens now?"

"I'm going to see if I can track down anyone in Hartford who knew my parents."

He hesitated, not wanting to offend her on what obviously was a sensitive topic. "Alicia, I can readily understand your wanting to talk to people who knew your parents, but do you think that's wise? A lot of neighborhoods that were merely poor forty years ago have become unsafe now."

"You're absolutely right. But when I said 'I,' I didn't mean it literally. I intend to hire a PI."

"Won't that be expensive?"

"I'm sure it won't be cheap," she admitted. "But it's not like I can't afford it, Jack. My father left me money when he died, and I just inherited more from my mother." Her attempt at a chuckle sounded like she was choking. "My mother, my father. I don't know how to differentiate my two sets of parents."

"Isn't it safe to say that when you make that reference you mean the Timberlakes? They're the ones who raised you, Alicia, the ones who gave you a good life. You have no reason to feel guilty. If anything, your birth parents would be happy that you were so well taken care of." Personally, he felt that the Timberlakes deserved to be identified as parents. It wasn't the fault of Alicia's birth parents that they both died young, but the fact remained that Mr. and Mrs. Timberlake provided the parenting.

He wondered what happened to the Clementses, how they died.

"Yes, I suppose so."

He shifted in his seat, another question on his mind. "Alicia, what about you and Daphne?"

"Who?"

The I-don't-know-who-you're-talking-about attitude told him Alicia had no intentions of having any further contact with her sister. "I guess that answers that."

"It's easy for me to not see her, but I feel for Martha. Daphne will make her life miserable. If I know her she'll have poor Martha peeling grapes for her...at three in the morning."

"So Martha's going to stay on?"

"For the time being. I haven't had an opportunity for a real heart-to-heart with her, but we've spoken about what would happen after Mom passed. She said that she and Marvin want Tyrone and Melody—their kids—to graduate from Staples High School in Westport. For one thing, it looks nice on a college application. For another, both Tyrone and Melody have friends there, and they're active in several sports. Transferring to a high school in Bridgeport will not only compromise their education, but disrupt their athletic programs and social lives as well.

"That's something else on my to-do list," she said. "Put in some inquiries about anyone who's looking to hire a live-in housekeeper. I'm not sure how many estates have housing for a family of four, unless their caretakers live in. That's what makes the Lewises' situation different. In many cases the caretaker and the maid are married and they have a one-bedroom cottage on the property, but Marvin never took care of the grounds at my…at my parents' house, we always used a service for that. And they have a son and a daughter, so they would have to have three bedrooms."

"That'll be nice if you can find something for her."

"At least Mom left instructions that give Daphne no power to let her go without an investigation by the attorney and myself. Mom didn't try to force Daphne to be close to Martha, but deep down, I think she knew what Daphne would try to do, or else she wouldn't have left instructions limiting her power."

"Why does Daphne dislike Martha?"

"Because she knew how fond Mom was of her, and she hated that. Daphne wanted Mom all to herself. She already knew she had Pop twisted around her little finger, but that wasn't enough for her. She felt Martha wasn't worthy of Mom's affections because she didn't have a privileged background and she worked as a housekeeper. So of course Daphne had a field day when Mom told her about me."

He reached across the table, where her hand rested, and covered it with his. "Alicia," he said gently after taking a moment to think, "this is a lot for any one person to absorb. A shock like that after thirty-five years. It's something that can be hard to recover from, maybe impossible." About to suggest that she consider counseling, he stopped when he felt her hand, so relaxed just a moment before, suddenly stiffen under his. "Something wrong?"

"It sounds suspiciously like you're about to make the same suggestion that my parents' attorney made."

"What did he suggest?"

"That I get psychiatric counseling."

"I get the impression you don't think much of that idea."

"No, Jack, I don't."

Her words came out flatter than the Midwest prairie, he noted. He gave her hand a reassuring squeeze before pulling his arm back. "I'm not going to preach on the subject, but I will say this. There's nothing shameful about seeking out professional counseling. It can be an important factor in both acceptance and healing." When she opened her mouth to object he pressed his index

finger vertically against his lips. "Why don't we just let
it drop? Besides, our dinner's here." He pointed with his
chin toward the server, who rapidly approached their
table with two plates balanced on a tray held on her
shoulder.

After dinner he paid the check and they set out to
return to her apartment. "Are you up to walking back,
or should we get a cab?" he asked.

"Oh, let's walk. I like walking after eating, especially in the winter."

The late December air felt crisp and clean to Jack's
nostrils in a city not known for good air quality. Holiday
decorations brightened the restaurant and shop
windows. He captured her gloved hand in his. "Alicia,
my family is taking a reunion cruise in February. We try
to do something together every couple of years where
everyone participates. The ship leaves from Fort Lau-
derdale. We'll be out for five days and four nights. I'd
like you to come with me."

"Oh, I don't know, Jack. I'm not much for family
gatherings."

He'd expected her to hedge. "I think it'll be good for
you." He wanted to tell her his family would love her,
but instinct told him not to press the issue.

Now that he knew of Alicia's adoption, her negative
views on love had started to make more sense to him
now. Surely nothing in her life with the Timberlakes had
given her cause to feel that love equated weakness. He
wondered if she'd unknowingly harbored in her uncon-
scious her time as an orphan, her parents suddenly gone

from her as a child too young to understand their disappearance. The confusion she undoubtedly felt paired with other experiences in those early days might have affected her way of thinking to this day.

Not that he had the qualifications to make any diagnoses. It would take a skilled psychoanalyst to figure that one out.

"All right, I'll ask you something more immediate," he said lightly. "What are you doing New Year's Eve?"

Chapter 31

I'm Happy Just To Dance with You

Jack watched in amusement as his siblings, sitting out on deck having a late breakfast, filled Alicia in on every embarrassing detail of his childhood. They told her about the time he lied to his parents about losing the third house key they'd had made for him in as many months, saying he accidentally threw it in the garbage. His father brought him to the trash pile and was about to make him go through it with his bare hands until he found the key when a fearful Jack confessed he'd lost it, earning a spanking. They also told her about the time he locked his sister Felice in a closet for a full half hour because she'd tattled on him. He'd gotten his butt whipped for that one, too.

He didn't mind Alicia knowing about the trouble he got in as a boy. He liked the way she fit in with his family members, never forgetting a name, or who was married to whom. They all liked her immediately, and he'd been asked more than once if he had any plans to settle down. He always made the same response: "By the time your youngest child graduates college, I *promise* I'll be married." It would be several years before any of his nieces and nephews even graduated high school, much less college, so the response hardly revealed anything imminent.

His parents made no secret of the fact that they thought Alicia a wonderful girl, but he kept equally mum with them, evading their questions about his intentions to stress that they hadn't known each other very long. His mother smiled, stating that was often plenty of time to recognize Ms. Right. Funny how people tended to think that all a man had to do was tell a woman he wanted her always and she would be his. The way he saw it the man didn't do the choosing; the woman did. If there was one thing he knew about Alicia, it was that she wasn't to be taken for granted. They were together right now and having a wonderful time, but he had no assurances she would be around in another month. He only knew that he intended to do whatever he could to keep her in his life.

A cruise, in Jack's opinion, presented the perfect opportunity to get together with family without constantly being in each other's way. He and Alicia had plenty of time to themselves. They usually spent a part of each day in the lounge listening to a singer accompany himself on the guitar, while most of the others preferred to listen to the jazz pianist who played near the dining room. They frequently went dancing after dinner, and they saw all the shows the shipboard entertainers put on. They spent perhaps a half hour in the ship's casino daily. Like him, she disliked slot machines. He'd been surprised at her skill at blackjack; she'd actually come out ahead of him.

But he and Alicia sometimes went their separate ways as well. She enjoyed morning stretch classes on deck and shopping in the ship's boutiques with his sisters and sisters-in-law. He'd even found her once in the café, having pastries and coffee with his parents. She was so personable. No wonder everyone wanted her to remain in his life.

Jack's favorite public activity by far was dancing with her. He enjoyed holding her, nuzzling her neck and swaying with her, either on a hardwood floor inside or out on deck under the stars, surrounded by other couples. At last he'd found the woman for him.

Just like his mother said he would.

Alicia closed her eyes, loving the feel of Jack's hand pressed against the small of her back. She'd had such a wonderful time on this trip. The Devlin family treated her with genuine affection. Jack's sister Felice confided that he hadn't brought a companion to a family function in years, adding, "You must be quite special to him."

She'd merely given a noncommittal Mona Lisa smile in response to Felice's comment, but secretly she wondered if she and Jack had indeed embarked on what could possibly become a permanent bond. That in itself represented an epiphany. It amazed her that she could even consider settling down with one person, but her daydreams certainly had merit. She and Jack got along so well, sex was dynamite, and, perhaps most important of all, he'd been right at her side through the ordeal of losing her mother and the shock of learning of her adoption.

Derek Taylor told her that Jack literally told him to get lost when he called to check on her the night after the funeral, that awful night when she gave into despair after Daphne's cruel announcement.

Normally, learning of such a possessive action would have her grinding her teeth in anger, but this time she merely laughed it off. Maybe she was softening…or maybe—and she tried not to consider this, preferring to tell herself she didn't care—deep down she felt relief that her less-than-stellar family background hadn't affected Jack's opinion of her.

She knew that one day she'd have to tell him the whole story about the death of her parents, that there was much more to her background than just being the daughter of a poor young couple from Hartford. And one day she would show him how much he looked like her father, once she had more time to get accustomed to the idea. She chuckled. That obscure sighting Sam referred to that would trigger long-dormant memories had come, all right, in the form of Jack Devlin. She just didn't understand why until she saw her father's photograph.

Part of her envied Jack for his secure position as part of a large, loving family. Alicia's brother-in-law, Todd, had called her a few times to see how she was doing, even spoke about bringing little Fletch down to see her, but she never expected to see Daphne again.

Alicia felt she had done a fine job of accepting her past, and all by herself. Contrary to what both Sam and Jack said—Jack without benefit of knowing the full story behind her adoption—she needed no professional sessions lying on a couch pouring her heart out to a stranger to help her cope. She'd just hired a P.I. to do a search for neighbors of her birth parents to help her learn about them, just so she could have a clearer picture of their personalities.

She couldn't deny a healthy curiosity about certain aspects of her psyche, like why she had retained vague memories of her birth father but virtually none of her birth mother. Caroline Timberlake was the only mother she remembered. Was that why she formed such an attachment to Caroline but not to Fletcher?

Then and now, Alicia shrugged off her interest as being natural. It certainly didn't keep her up nights.

Suddenly aware that Jack no longer guided her and they'd stopped moving, Alicia opened her eyes. The musicians had stopped playing. She'd been so lost in her thoughts she hadn't realized it.

Tomorrow they would leave all this behind and fly back to New York. Still, she had high hopes for a continuing relationship with Jack after a sharp change of environment, from balmy breezes and temperatures in the eighties to the harshness of February in the Northeast.

In the meantime, there was always tonight, the two of them together in their cabin's queen-sized bed.

Chapter 32

All You Need Is Love

Alicia rolled on her back to shut off the CD that began playing promptly at six-thirty, signaling it was time to get up. Then she returned to her side and snuggled up to Jack like she'd been doing before the alarm. "I *knew* I should have told Shannon I'd take today off," she said.

"I thought you were nuts, going in the day after we got back," Jack said sleepily.

"I know. I just felt a little guilty because of all the time I took off last month."

"I'm sure she didn't expect you to go right back to work the day after your mother's funeral. Besides, you're an owner, not just an employee."

"Yes, but I'm not a fifty/fifty owner. I only own thirty-five percent of the business. Shannon has the rest."

His muscular brown arm tightened around her waist. "Don't go yet," he mumbled. "Stay here with me a little longer. You might not be a fifty/fifty partner, but you're a salaried employee. It's not like you have to worry about having your pay docked if you don't get in until ten."

Alicia made no attempt to move. She felt as content as Jack to simply lie here, listening to the sounds of the city traffic four flights down. He'd spent a lot of time here with her so far this year. On New Year's Eve they ventured down to Times Square in the cold to watch the apple drop, along with thousands of other New Yorkers. She found that she liked his being here, and she'd never invited any other man to spend as much time with her at home as she had Jack.

The old unstrung feelings had dissipated once she understood what caused them. Funny how the human mind worked. Jack's showing up at her doorstep that night last October brought back memories of the features of a father she barely remembered.

She hadn't told him yet of his resemblance to Benjamin Clements. He'd probably find it amusing, but she still wasn't ready to discuss the details. Maybe after the detective she hired to track down former neighbors of her birth parents came up with some names and addresses for her.

She hadn't discussed Benjamin Clements' resemblance to Jack with anyone. The only other person she'd discussed her adoption with besides Jack and Sam McDaniel was Martha. She'd taken a day off to drive up to Green's Farms and check in with Martha, and with Lucky as well. Martha told her that the setter had been whimpering daily, not understanding what happened to his mistress, or why he'd been banished to the guest house.

From Martha, Alicia learned that Daphne and Todd planned to move in to the house on February first. Daphne, who stopped working as a second-grade teacher when she became pregnant with little Fletch, came by the house regularly to clean out Caroline's things. "She always leaves a mess for me to clean up," Martha said with a chuckle. "I think she wants to make sure I have plenty to do."

Alicia found herself smiling at Martha's good-natured reaction to Daphne's antics, but then pushed the thoughts of Daphne and even Martha out of her mind and concentrated solely on Jack. She'd never experienced such easy camaraderie with a man before, and she enjoyed it thoroughly. Again she wondered if this was the type of relationship Rhonda and Pete had. Maybe it wasn't so bad, if you took away the part about having your life turned upside down in order to accommodate someone who should be able to take care of their own basic needs, like feeding themselves or pressing a clean shirt or pushing a vacuum cleaner. Marriage shouldn't reduce an independent person to a pathetic shell of their former, single self. Yet, strangely enough, she didn't feel hemmed in, even with her being against the wall and Jack's solid frame lying between her and the edge of the bed.

With her index finger she began tracing a straight line

down from his throat to his chest, down to his belly button and beyond, clamping on his morning erection with a delighted gasp.

His words came out as a growl. "Don't start anything you can't finish."

"I guess I'll have to be more than a little late for work," she said matter-of-factly.

Jack instantly came to life. "In that case I'm all yours. Have your way with me, pretty lady."

Climbing atop him, she proceeded to do just that, pausing only to pull a condom packet from a small crocheted bag under her pillow.

Jack watched, incredulous, as she proceeded to apply the prophylactic. He'd dated women who kept a supply of protection, but he'd never have one put it on him before.

He moaned in pleasure as their bodies connected. He gripped her firm thighs as she raised and lowered her hips in fluid movements, looking at her through heavy-lidded eyes. *What a way to wake up in the morning.* He would walk on hot coals for the love of Alicia.

He felt her body quake on top of him, and she collapsed forward into his arms. "Oh, Jack," she said breathlessly.

He wrapped one arm around her back and stroked her hair with his free hand. "I know, sweetheart."

"We work pretty well together, don't we?"

"Yes, we do." He paused. "Alicia, you do realize I love you, don't you?" He wished he could see her face, but it was turned away from him. At least she didn't go rigid in his arms.

"It's occurred to me, yes," she said softly.

"It doesn't frighten you?"

She shook her head. "Not like I thought it would."

"Look at me, Alicia."

She turned her face to him.

"Let me tell you something. Loving someone, and being loved, is the greatest thing that can happen to anyone. It doesn't mean you're weak. You don't know how it pleases me to know that you've needed me these last few weeks."

She abruptly jumped out of his embrace and sat up, pulling the sheet up against her. *"Need?"* she repeated in obvious distaste. "We were talking about love, Jack. Now all of a sudden you say I *need* you."

He stared at her incredulously. "You say it like it's a dirty word."

"It *is* a dirty word," she shot back. "And it doesn't apply to me. I've spent time with you because I've wanted to, Jack, because you were the only one I wanted to share my pain with. Get it? I *wanted* to. *Not* because I needed to be with you. I don't need you, Jack. I don't need anyone."

Caught off guard by her outburst, he now sat up in bed. "Alicia, that's the most childish thing I've ever heard. You've got to grow up and climb out of this vacuum you've created for yourself and allow yourself to feel normal emotions. You might want to try imagining where you'll be in twenty years. In your mid-fifties, still falling into bed with old boyfriends for old time's sake? It's—" he groped for a word that fit "—Freudian, for heaven's sake."

"Freudian? *Freudian?*" She practically screamed

the word. "I'll show you Freudian." She yanked the bathrobe that hung over the headboard and slid her arms through it, knotting the sash furiously around her waist. With agile ease, she climbed over him and out of bed, crossing to the Bombay chest on the opposite wall, where she kept the envelope Sam McDaniel had given her.

"Here," she said, thrusting the newspaper article in his face. "Take a look at my birth father if you want to see Freudian. Does he remind you of anyone?"

Jack's eyes grew wide as he stared at the photograph, then skimmed the accompanying article. "My God," he whispered. Then he looked at her accusingly. "Why didn't you tell me?"

"I was about to, before you made that crack about my behavior being straight out of Freud."

His shoulders slumped as he skimmed the article. The contents stunned him. Not only did Alicia's late father bear a striking resemblance to him, but her parents had been murdered, with three-year-old Alicia found at home with her father's body. All she told him was that her parents died at young ages. She said nothing about them having been killed. He'd thought he'd gotten through to her at last, that she felt she could trust him, but that invisible wall had come between them once again, keeping him shut out and in the dark.

Jack stared at the picture again. If he hadn't known from his family history that no one on either side of his family had made their way from Alabama to Connecticut, he would have sworn Alicia's father was a relative of his. He knew that was impossible, that often complete strangers looked alike. Still, this photo, and the story, made several things clear to him.

Like the way she sometimes seemed so nervous around him, the way he could feel her trembling in his arms when he went to kiss her, and how she tried to cover it up by drinking more than she could hold. And during their first conversation she asked if they'd met before. It all came together for him now.

His heart wrenched at the confusion she must have felt. Subconsciously he reminded her of her father, not Fletcher Timberlake, but Benjamin Clements.

He also understood why Caroline Timberlake looked at him the way she had. Surely she had seen this photo in the newspaper. He considered it a stroke of good fortune that she didn't slump to the floor at the sight of him.

"Alicia," he began. "I'm sorry. I didn't know about the details of your parents' deaths. I wish you'd shared it with me."

"I wasn't ready to," she said defiantly. How could she, when she had just begun to understand the significance of the resemblance between two men with very different roles in her life herself?

"I can understand that. But now that I do know, let me help you through this, help you work it out."

"Why?" she countered. "So you can pat yourself on the back and be a big man because you feel I *need* you? I'd rather do it myself."

"With what, a bottle?"

"Why not?" Barefoot, she plodded toward the other end of the apartment, where the kitchen was located. Moments later he heard the sound of a cork being popped and liquid being poured. So she preferred a cold, impersonal bottle of wine to the encouragement, understanding, and love he could offer her, did she? Maybe he'd made a terrible mistake. Pete might have been right about Alicia all along. The wall she built around herself really *was* impenetrable.

He climbed out of bed and threw on his clothes. His bags were still in his truck parked several blocks away after he retrieved it from a lot near the pier. He splashed some warm water on his face and had his coat on by the time he ventured around the corner of the *L* of the apartment layout.

Alicia stood in the corner, her back to him, wine glass in hand. It was already three-quarters empty.

He shook his head. "You know, I really thought I'd gotten through that wall you keep around yourself. I thought you had softened toward the idea of a love that lasts, not meaningless affairs that start in the fall and are over by the time winter ends, or run from spring to summer." He wanted a love for *all* seasons, not a series of short-term relationships that petered out after a few sweet months together. "You're thirty-five years old, Alicia. You're a mature woman in every way but one, and I think it's high time your feelings regarding love caught up with the rest of you. I'm not ashamed to say that I need you in my life. But not like this. Not with you equating what I feel for you with weakness or spinelessness."

She didn't turn around to face him, nor did she take any sips from her glass. But she didn't say anything in response, either. Suddenly he knew that continuing to pursue her would only break his heart. *I'm through.*

Wordlessly he took his coat from the closet and left. She would know to lock the door behind him.

He walked four blocks to where he parked his car and got in, driving off to a future without the woman he would somehow have to stop loving.

Chapter 33

She opened her eyes at the sound of the raised voices, rubbing her eyes as she clumsily sat up. Mommy and Daddy were yelling at each other again. They woke her up.

No, that wasn't Mommy and Daddy, she realized; it was Daddy and somebody else, somebody she didn't know.

She sat up, rubbed her eyes some more and climbed down from the bed. She wanted to let them know they'd woken her up. Maybe then they'd stop. She hated all that yelling.

Before she got to the doorway she heard the rumbling sound. Her mommy screamed, "Stop it!" over and over.

Her breath caught in her throat. Daddy and another man, the man she knew as her mommy's friend, rolled on the floor hitting each other. They both looked real mad. Maybe she should just go back to bed, or Daddy would really be mad. He never yelled at her, only Mommy.

But she couldn't move, and nobody saw her standing there, anyway. She wished Mommy's friend would go away. She didn't think he'd ever been here when Daddy was home. And she'd never seen Daddy so mad before. It looked like he was really hurting Mommy's friend. He held him down, and his hands were around his neck. Daddy was yelling at him, but Mommy's friend just made funny noises. Now Mommy was yelling at Daddy—only she never called him "Daddy," but "Ben"—to stop it, but he didn't even look at her.

Mommy's friend—that was what she always called him, her friend—had one hand on top of Daddy's hands and the other in his pocket. She saw something shiny, and then all of a sudden Daddy made a funny noise and fell forward onto Mommy's friend.

Mommy ran to him, but instead of sounding mad she sounded like she was crying. "Cliff, what have you done?"

She decided that Mommy's friend's name must be Cliff, just like her name was 'Licia.

She watched as Mommy held Daddy, but Daddy didn't say anything. It was like he'd gone to sleep, and Mommy couldn't wake him up.

"Daddy!" she cried out.

Alicia's eyes flew open, and she sat up with a start.

When she realized she was shivering laid back down and pulled the covers over her head, leaving only her face exposed. She'd just seen it, the tiny apartment with its beat-up furniture, the fight her father had with Clifton Matthews before Clifton stabbed him to death. She could actually hear the rumbling noise as they rolled on the floor. While being choked, Clifton managed to pull a knife out of his pocket and stab her father in the abdomen. She'd read somewhere— probably while doing her scoping, or fine tuning, of one of the court stenographers' transcripts during a murder trial—that those types of wounds bled very little, although they were deadly. But that was cold comfort to her now.

Even with all the covers, she still shivered. Why couldn't she get warm? And would she ever be able to get back to sleep, or would fear of what she might see in her dreams keep her awake until dawn?

"There you are," Shannon said brightly as she stood in the doorway to Alicia's office. "I'm glad you're here. I've got a nine o'clock with Doretha McCann. I had a call from the secretary of a judge. Doretha transcribed a deposition in his office the other day, and he didn't like the way she was dressed. I think the girl's been watching too many TV dramas, wearing all those low-cut blouses to work. I'm going to tell her she dresses inappropriately for court, and if she doesn't comply we won't use her services anymore. Did you want to sit in?"

"No, not this morning. I've got a headache. Didn't sleep too well last night."

Alicia felt Shannon's eyes studying her. "Are you all right? You had a headache when you came in yesterday."

From the wine, Alicia knew. Yesterday she'd come in late and left early. "It went away, but now it's back."

"I've got to tell you, Alicia, you don't exactly look like you just spent five days on a Caribbean cruise. Truth be told, you look like hell. What's wrong? I'm really starting to worry about you."

"There's a lot going on in my life right now, Shannon. I don't mean to be evasive, but I don't want to say any more than that."

"Why don't you go home and try to sleep?"

"No. I've been out of the office way too much. I'll work through it."

But even as Alicia said the words, she acknowledged that after last night's flashback dream it had just become a heck of a lot more difficult.

Alicia fell asleep as soon as she got home. Her slumber was deep and dreamless. When she awoke before dawn the next morning she felt grateful, seeing it as a sign that the disturbing dream of the previous night had been no more than a reaction to the breakup with Jack.

She would make it after all.

Three days later she had another dream, this time seeing images of herself as a toddler being carried way up high on her father's shoulders. It was springtime, and she wore a pink windbreaker and white socks under brown sandals. They took a walk in the park, and he bought her a vanilla cone of soft serve custard.

The scene faded, soon replaced by another. This time

he was taking her out of the tub and drying her off, making a game out of it. As he helped her dress he told her, "You're Daddy's girl, Alicia, and Daddy loves you very much."

Once again she woke up shaken and shivering in the middle of the night, and she knew she had to get help.

Chapter 34

Help!

Dr. Allison Tucker took a few moments to go over the paperwork Alicia filled out. "No history of depression, no history of mental disorders. Tell me why you're here, Ms. Timberlake."

The question irked Alicia. "Didn't they tell you that I was seen here over thirty years ago, as a child? My attorney suggested I come here because my old records are here."

"Yes, and I've studied the records." Dr. Tucker, an attractive if too thin woman with ash blond hair in her fifties, appeared unruffled by Alicia's agitation. "But I'd like to hear it directly from you. What motivated you to pick up the phone and make this appointment?"

"I didn't want to," she admitted. "But my mother passed away Christmas night, and shortly afterward I found out I was adopted, and that my birth parents were both murdered. The last week-and-a-half I've been having these dreams every couple of nights, bits and pieces mostly, from when I was little and living with my birth parents. I even dreamed about the night my father was killed." She explained the circumstances under which her parents died. "I haven't been able to sleep on the nights it happens, and I don't know how to stop them."

Over the next hour she told Dr. Tucker more about herself than she'd ever shared with anyone; her loving relationship with Caroline Timberlake, her lifelong bickering with Daphne, and the partiality Fletcher Timberlake demonstrated for Daphne. "My mother told me they were on the verge of despair when I came along, fearing they would never have children," she recalled. "Obviously my father forgot all about that when my sister was born." She gasped when she recognized the anger Caroline always said she should have. At last it had flared up. Her mother had been right to say it wasn't normal to have no feelings at all about her father's treatment of her. He'd been good to her, of course, left her an equal share of his estate with Daphne, but he'd clearly loved Daphne more.

She concluded with Daphne's efforts to prevent her from spending any time alone with Caroline in the last weeks of her life, and Daphne's revelation to her that she'd been adopted.

Dr. Tucker studied her carefully, typing notes into a laptop computer. She looked at Alicia expectantly, as if she waited for her to say more.

When Alicia shrugged the doctor said, "Alicia…may I call you that?" At her nod she continued. "I get the feeling there's something else you're not telling me. I can't help you unless you're completely honest with me."

"Wow, you're good," she said with a laugh. "All right. I did leave something out. There's this man—" She told the doctor all about Jack Devlin, how she'd gotten a sense of déjà vu the first time she laid eyes on him that lasted for months, especially when she was close to him, and how she discovered his resemblance to her birth father. Feeling more comfortable in Dr. Tucker's almost homey office, in which she sat upright on a loveseat rather than stretched out on a couch, she left out nothing. She included her out-of-character drinking to help quell her uneasiness at being around him…and most recently, to try to chase away her haunting dreams in which bits and pieces of her past came to life; and she provided the doctor with an accurate account of their breakup. Before she knew it she had spoken for nearly an hour.

"Alicia, do you have any idea why your adoptive parents didn't tell you the truth about your background? It's rather unusual for adoptees in the last sixty years or so to not be told they were chosen by rather than born to their parents."

"I always thought it was because they didn't want to have to tell me about what happened to my real parents. It wasn't really a big news story, but it did receive media attention locally. But I'm sure you already knew that."

"Yes, I've read the newspaper articles. You're very perceptive, Alicia. Of course, I wasn't on the staff when your parents brought you here thirty-two years ago, and after a thorough series of interviews, it was determined that you had no recollection of your father's murder, and that you seemed well adjusted in your new life. According to the chart notes, they were advised to tell you that you'd been adopted around the time you entered kindergarten, with a gradual revealing of the details much later, when you were old enough to understand. Obviously, they never did."

"I wish I knew why."

"I'm afraid we'll never know the reason. But I know it was difficult for you to come here today. I'm going to advise a return visit, but since I'm not sure you'll comply, I'm going to give you my impressions and recommendations now."

Alicia leaned forward. "And what are they?"

"I think you're suffering from a posttraumatic stress disorder, or PTSD. In my opinion you should stop running away from your past. You've repressed your earliest memories since the night your father was killed, and now they're fighting to come to the surface. There's no way for me to know how much of that night you really remember and how much might have been your imagination at work. We've had some success with hypnosis—"

"Forget it," she said flatly. "I refuse to give anyone that much control over me. I'm sure your ethics are in the right place, Dr. Tucker, but I still won't consider it."

The doctor smiled. "Many people feel that way. I'll just tell you this, then. Don't fight your memories, Alicia. Stop trying to drown your pain in alcohol. Nothing good can ever come out of that. Embrace them. By all means pursue people who knew your parents. It sounds like you were quite happy with your father and perhaps resented your mother for bringing her boyfriend into your lives, an action that in the end destroyed your family.

"My feeling is that after your father's death you felt lost and alone. All the love you reserved for him you transferred to Caroline Timberlake, the new mother figure in your life. From virtually everyone else in your life you remained detached, even from your closest friends. You're a caring person, Alicia, always thoughtful and considerate of others, but there's no real bond with anyone other than your mother.

"You might have sailed through your entire life with no emotional attachments, but then Jack Devlin showed up on your doorstep and began to stir memories that had been dormant for years, because he reminded you of your birth father. You felt flustered just being around him, and you had conflicting emotions about physical intimacy with him because subconsciously he reminded you of your father. But you weren't ready to accept his love. You rebelled when he spoke of loving you and needing you, and of your needing him.

"My advice to you on that front is not to let him go. From what you've told me he cares for you deeply. It would be a terrible mistake to end such a promising relationship just because you want to be stubborn." Dr. Tucker paused. "Let Jack Devlin into your heart, Alicia."

Chapter 35

Alicia rubbed the top of Lucky's head. The dog had climbed onto the center console and whimpered. "We're almost there," she said affectionately.

Alicia drove down the street at a speed of about fifteen miles an hour, which allowed her to take in every detail. The block on the outskirts of downtown Hartford looked much like any other urban neighborhood. The streets were quiet at the noon hour, with a few elderly pedestrians carrying grocery bags, young mothers pushing baby strollers, and a few young people, probably unemployed, entering the pizzeria around the corner. A few hours from now the block would probably come alive as children arrived home from school. She could picture them stopping in at the corner store for potato chips and soda, or at the pizzeria for a slice. She'd driven past a liquor store with a walk-up window, and there was a bus stop at the corner. A few older model vehicles were parked on either side of the street, with plenty of spaces still available while most people were still at work.

Alicia pulled into a vacant space across the street from the four-story walk-up apartment house, its dark brick in need of a good steam cleaning. No doubt about it, she was looking at a poor neighborhood. She doubted the block looked any more prosperous even thirty-five years ago. The people who lived here kept a roof over their heads and kept their children fed and well-dressed, but probably could afford few extras. Instead of flying down to Disney World in Florida, children here probably got treated to the Six Flags Amusement Park in nearby Agawam, Massachusetts.

She leaned on the steering wheel and gazed at the structure, waiting for memories to stir, but none did. She might as well be looking at her own apartment house on West Eighty-Fifth Street. The best she could do was wonder if any of these front windows belonged to her birth parents' former apartment.

The apartment building stirred no memories, but the park down the street did. Alicia kept staring at it from her seat behind the steering wheel. Finally she got out of the car and walked half a block down the street for a better look, holding on to Lucky's leash and keeping him close so he wouldn't step on any of the broken glass that littered the sidewalk.

She stood on the sidewalk looking in at a sadly neglected play area. The fence separating it from the sidewalk had been bent in spots. The swings looked rusted and decrepit, and neither of the two basketball hoops had nets. An unknown whitish substance streaked the slide, and it looked like the monkey bars had been removed entirely. A wire trash bin was only half full, but the ground around it was littered with crushed plastic pop bottles, empty potato chip bags, and candy and gum wrappers. Surely no one played in such a dismal park anymore; it was probably used for drug transactions.

The detective she hired managed to track down a woman who lived downstairs from her parents nearly forty years before, a Mrs. Geneva Kelly. He contacted her on Alicia's behalf, and Mrs. Kelly agreed to speak with her. She now made her home with her married daughter and was in failing health. Alicia hoped her memory proved to be as sharp as she told the detective it was.

Alicia consulted the directions when she exited the highway. Her detective provided her with excellent directions, and she soon drove up to the blue shingled Cape Cod house on a quiet street. Carefully tended shrubs lined the front of the house, and black shutters and dormer windows on the upper level gave it a homey look. She felt grateful that Mrs. Kelly agreed to talk to her.

"Lucky, I'll have to leave you here," she said. She'd stopped at Martha's and picked up the dog, a wise move on her part. She felt much more at ease with Lucky in the car with her. "I'll be back in a little while. Wish me luck."

She rang the doorbell, which was promptly answered by a woman in her late forties, a man about the same age hovering behind her. "Miss Timberlake?" the woman said.

"Yes. You must be Mrs. Clark."

"This is my husband, Larry."

Alicia nodded. "Mr. Clark. Thank you so much for allowing me to come to your home. Mrs. Kelly was the only neighbor my detective was able to track down after all this time, and it's very important to me that I get to talk with her." She doubted that a typical Thursday afternoon would find a couple in their forties around the house, but she understood their concern about a stranger coming to question Mrs. Kelly.

"I understand completely," Mrs. Clark said. "Please come in."

Alicia wiped her feet and entered the house. An elderly woman of seventy-odd sat in the living room, her Reddi-Whip white hair, styled in a bun at the top of her head, a striking contrast to her brown face. Fingers slightly bent from mild arthritis worked a crochet needle, expanding a blue-and-white square.

"I'd know you anywhere," she said in a deep, rich voice that reflected her many years of living. "You look just like Norma Jean."

Alicia smiled. "I do?"

"Absolutely. Come right here and sit down." Mrs. Kelly patted the empty space on the sofa.

"Thank you." She did as she was told. "Mrs. Kelly, I wanted to thank you for agreeing to see me today."

"No need for that." She removed her glasses and beamed at Alicia. "I've often wondered what became of you. My husband and I offered to take you in ourselves, but the police were worried that we might be putting ourselves in danger if Norma Jean and Cliff came back for you, so they put you in a foster home."

"I appreciate that, Mrs. Kelly."

"After…after everything was over we did speak to Social Services about raising you as one of our own. I used to take care of you a lot while your mother slipped out for a few minutes."

"To be with Cliff?"

The old woman nodded. "My husband, Joe, told me to stop. He'd already heard rumors about Norma Jean being seen with Cliff, and he said it would only be a matter of time before Ben found out. He worked hard, your father."

"At the dairy plant?"

"Yes, but he also had a second job, as a short-order cook at a bowling alley. He wanted to provide well for you and your mother, but he was out working so much of the time, and Norma Jean felt neglected." Mrs. Kelly sighed. "Your mother was really a sweet girl, but she'd taken on marriage and motherhood too young. She was just twenty-two years old, and your father two years older."

Alicia nodded. She'd read all about it in the newspaper. "I know."

"Norma Jean married Ben right out of high school. She grew up in the foster care system and was probably anxious to have a family of her own, even though it turned out not to be nearly as exciting as she thought it would be. As for Ben, he practically raised himself. His mother died when he was about eight, and his father barely kept a roof over their heads." She shook her head. "That boy had it tough. And because of that he wanted all the best for you, Alicia."

"You knew my grandparents?" she asked, surprised.

"I knew Ben's father. I don't think I ever saw his mother around much, probably because she was ill a lot of the time and stayed inside. We all lived in the same neighborhood, and everybody knew at least a little bit about everybody else. I didn't know Ben other than by sight until he and Norma Jean moved in upstairs from us. But everybody knew old Mr. Clements. We'd see him Sunday mornings, coming in from his latest drunk. He'd been a heavy drinker even before his wife died. After she passed he just lost it. They only kept him on in the shipping department of that manufacturing plant because he'd been there for years, and because he had a son to support. Poor Ben did what he could to take care of his father." Mrs. Kelly's eyes took on a faraway look. "A fine young man, he was. If things had worked out…if Norma Jean had never taken up with that no-good Clifton Matthews…."

"What kind of relationship did I have with my parents, Mrs. Kelly?"

"You were a daddy's girl. No doubt about it. He used to take you out in the neighborhood all the time, bring you to the store for little treats, or to the playground. He just adored you.

"You loved your mother, of course," she added hastily. "But she could be impatient with you, a little sharp. I witnessed it many times. She didn't mean it, Alicia. She just felt frustrated with the repetitiveness of her life. She wanted more. Clifton Matthews represented excitement. He was a minor drug dealer and had been to jail numerous times. It was rumored he had a cut in a huge supermarket robbery. He was a flashy dresser, drove a nice car and always had money in his pockets. Norma Jean was a pretty girl, and still young.

"Like I said, I used to keep you when she went out to meet him until my Joe told me to stay out of it, that Ben would be angry at us for accommodating Norma Jean when he found out. Norma Jean didn't like it much when I told her. She got real bold then, inviting Cliff to the apartment when Ben was at work.

"Were you the one who called the police that night?" Alicia knew Mrs. Kelly would know what night she referred to.

"Yes. Joe and I were watching *McMillan and Wife* on TV, so it must have been a Sunday night. Our daughters were getting ready for school the next day. We heard shouting coming from your apartment. That in itself wasn't unusual. Ben and Norma Jean were always arguing about this or that. But it wasn't Ben and Norma Jean. Ben was arguing with another man. I remember Joe saying to me, 'That must be Cliff.' I knew then there would be trouble.

"Ben screamed at him to stay away from his wife. I hoped Cliff would just leave, but in hindsight I know he went over there looking for trouble. When we heard the two of them rolling around on the floor I told Joe to call the police. We went upstairs behind them." Mrs. Kelly's eyes filled with tears. "Your father lay face up on the floor, and you were sitting beside him, trying to wake him up. You thought he was sleeping." Mrs. Kelly bent her head to wipe her eyes.

"Your parents were nice people, Alicia. They made a good-looking couple, your mother so short and your father easily a foot taller. A lot of neighbors painted her as the bad girl in what happened and your father as an innocent victim. I don't agree. It's true that Ben only wanted the best for his family, but Norma Jean wasn't a bad girl. She just made a bad decision, one that eventually had a high price." Mrs. Kelly looked up as her daughter entered the room. "What's this, Jackie?"

"I thought you two might like a little snack." Jackie Clark set a tray down on the coffee table, within easy reach for the women. It contained two glasses, a small pitcher and two small plates, one holding a cheese ball and crackers and the other assorted cookies. "Enjoy."

"Thank you, Mrs. Clark," Alicia said, reaching for a glass. She'd been so mesmerized by what she'd learned from Geneva Kelly that she hadn't realized she was thirsty.

"You're welcome. And call me Jackie." She disappeared into another room.

"You'd better get some sleep," Mrs. Kelly called after her. To Alicia she said, "Jackie is a nurse on the night shift. She works ten-hour shifts three nights a week, thirty hours total. They consider that to be full time, so she gets all the benefits. Plus she gives me my dialysis treatments here at home."

"It's convenient to have a nurse in the family, isn't it?" she said politely.

"I'll say. The best I could do was working in the hospital laundry. But Joe and I saw to it that both our girls got good educations. My other daughter lives in Springfield. She's got a good job at an insurance company." The pride in Mrs. Kelly's voice was undeniable.

During the rest of their time together, Mrs. Kelly provided Alicia with anecdotes about her and her parents. In turn, Alicia brought Mrs. Kelly up to date about her life, covering her adoption by the Timberlakes, her privileged upbringing, first in Stamford and later in Green's Farms, the death of her adoptive parents, even about the court stenography business she owned a piece of.

"What about your personal life, dear?" Mrs. Kelly asked. "You're such a pretty girl. Do you have a fella? Or maybe you're already married with children of your own."

Alicia shook her head. "I broke up with someone a couple of weeks ago, so I'm back on the market."

"I hope you find someone, dear. My girls have both been fortunate in that respect. They got good husbands. My son-in-law is an angel. He takes as good care of me as Jackie." She patted Alicia's hand. "But you'll find someone."

Alicia merely smiled, but inside she thought of Jack and suddenly felt like crying.

When she bid Mrs. Kelly and her daughter and son-in-law goodbye nearly two hours later, Alicia felt cleansed and comforted. Mrs. Kelly had done something all the newspaper articles and court transcripts couldn't do—she brought her parents to life. Alicia could sense her young mother's boredom, her despair that life was passing her by, her viewing the man who would eventually end her life as exciting rather than a no-good small time criminal. Her memories of her father were clearer, but thanks to Mrs. Kelly she understood him better as well. She could feel how much he loved her just like she could feel her shoulder bag bouncing off her hip.

She waved to Mrs. Kelly as she drove away, then patted Lucky's head. "Well, chum, I'm having no more of that orphaned little nobody stuff," she said to the dog. "I'm one lucky girl."

She didn't plan to go back to Dr. Tucker, but she did hold on to her telephone number just in case. The most pressing issue was behind her now. She knew where she came from. All that remained was to try to forget about Jack Devlin. She simply wasn't ready to be taken over lock, stock, and barrel, like a brand-new Chevy, and that was what he wanted.

Something told her this would be the hardest chore of all.

Chapter 36

I Forgot To Remember To Forget

Jack raised his racquet to return his opponent's serve. He enjoyed playing racquetball. He found it an excellent way to burn off stress...an emotion in no short supply these days.

He'd earned accolades at work for the project he'd overseen that was unveiled back in January. The country boy from Alabama had impressed the big boys, even the small boys who didn't think him sophisticated enough to be a major player. The campaign he designed to help combat the negative press after a highly touted new drug performed poorly in tests resulted in an impressive holiday bonus for him. He'd promptly been handed another major assignment.

He didn't complain; it kept him busy, which meant he had less time to spend thinking about Alicia.

He hadn't seen or heard from her since the day he left her apartment the morning after their huge blowup, and he missed her terribly. In spite of the emotional turmoil he felt, he knew that unless she changed her views on love that they would never be happy. Breaking it off now would possibly save him years of frustration.

His social life had been reduced to impersonal games of racquetball with whoever was around, once weekly drinks with members of his staff at a bar near the office, and an occasional dinner with Pete and Rhonda. At the last one a week ago, Rhonda, now visibly pregnant, announced happily that they had a plan to accelerate their savings and help them get into a home of their own within eighteen months.

"Rhonda," Pete said in a warning tone.

"Why shouldn't he know?"

Jack hated it when people talked about him like he wasn't there. "What shouldn't he know?" he said dryly. "You're moving in with Rhonda's parents or something? What's so secret about that?"

"Sorry, Jack," Pete said sheepishly. "I didn't know if it would be a topic you'd want to hear about. It involves Alicia."

The Robinsons knew about the breakup, but tactfully refrained from asking questions…or from saying the dreaded, "I told you so." Jack tried without success to keep the anxiousness out of his voice. "Alicia? What about her?"

"Rhonda and I are going to sublet her apartment. It's

small, but she'll rent it to us for half of what we're paying now."

"That's why we figured we'd only stay for a year, a year-and-a-half tops," Rhonda added. "By then we'll have plenty added to our house fund, and the baby will just be starting to walk."

"It was either that or move in with my in-laws," Pete said. "I'd rather live in one large room than have my mother-in-law around every day."

"Watch it, Pete," Rhonda said, her grin proving that her threatening tone wasn't meant to be taken seriously. "That happens to be my mother you're talking about."

"I love your mother, baby. I just don't want to live with her, that's all."

The exchange hardly registered with Jack. "That's awfully generous of Alicia," he remarked, thinking of what she said about inheriting additional money from her mother. "I guess she's picking up the difference?"

"No, actually she's making a few dollars on the deal. Her rent is only six hundred and something. We'll pay her seven hundred."

Jack found that incredible. "I know it's only a studio, but I thought that in New York even one-room apartments rented for over a thousand dollars. How can a place as nice as hers rent for only six hundred a month?"

"Six hundred thirty-seven dollars and eighty-three cents," Rhonda said. "But it wasn't so nice when she first rented it, oh, I don't know, six or seven years ago. Remember, Pete?"

"I'll never forget it." Pete wrinkled his nose. "Picture

it, Jack. Layers of filthy linoleum filled with cigarette burns, the floors sinking in some areas, yellow-stained walls, and holes everywhere. It took a heck of a lot of tubs of compound to fill in all those holes. And the bathtub was so badly stained with rust that Alicia had to get a professional to re-glaze it."

"It sounds like it should have been condemned."

"The landlord hadn't done any maintenance on it in years," Rhonda said. "The former tenant was an elderly gentleman who suffered from dementia and wasn't too keen on housekeeping. Alicia made an agreement with the landlord to rent it for the current rent-controlled rate if she cleaned it up herself."

"If he'd done it he's allowed by law to raise the rent significantly, but he just didn't feel like being bothered," Pete explained. "Rhonda and I, plus some other friends, helped her make it livable. It took us over a month. I can still remember how my arms ached from all that painting. The walls required three coats."

"What about Alicia? If she's renting you two her apartment, where will she live?" The way Pete and Rhonda looked at each other told him that he wore his heart on his sleeve, but he'd never said he no longer cared about her. He just couldn't invest any more effort into a relationship that was doomed to fail.

He held his breath as he waited for someone to tell him, knowing it would hurt as bad as surgery without anesthesia if she'd decided to move in with one of her male friends.

"She's still not sure," Rhonda answered, easing his fears. "She's looking all over the place, Brooklyn, the island, Jersey, even Connecticut. She wants to buy a house, someplace where her dog Lucky can have some space. Right now he's staying with Martha and her family, but Alicia wants him with her. She's already said that she plans to hang on to her apartment even after we move out. Maybe rent it out to people visiting New York. Lots of folks do that, you know."

"She'd better hope the landlord doesn't find out," Pete pointed out. "As it is, you and I will have to keep a low profile and get Alicia to visit often so it looks like she's still living there."

Hearing about Alicia made Jack long to hear her voice again, to try one more time to convince her to give love a try. He kept telling himself to leave it alone, that he'd done the right thing.

And he wondered how long it would take to get over her.

Alicia could hear the surprise in Derek's voice. "Hey!" he exclaimed, clearly glad to hear from her. "I didn't think I'd be hearing from you anytime soon. I thought your man cut me out of the picture."

His phrasing riled her, serving as a reminder that Jack wanted to put her in a cage like a pet parakeet. "No one has the right to cut anyone out of my life but me," she declared, thinking of how she'd severed ties to Daphne.

"There you go. When I told you about it, I thought you'd lost your, what my grandfather used to call 'gumption.'"

"I guess I did, but it was only temporary," she said bitterly. "I've reclaimed it."

"That's my girl. How about having dinner Friday night?"

She didn't hesitate. "I'd love to."

The cold March air held no hint of the spring that was just around the corner. Alicia and Derek had dinner at a Thai restaurant on Columbus Avenue and set off for her apartment. They'd lingered for nearly two hours, catching up, but Alicia mentioned nothing about the adoption. She'd already decided that no one need know about the emotional trauma she'd been subjected to. She hadn't even filled Martha in, although she felt that one day she would. Right now it still hurt too much. She'd already decided not to tell anyone else; she saw no need. She knew that Jack had seen Pete and Rhonda Robinson, but she also knew he would not betray her confidence.

She absently wondered if Jack was seeing anyone, so much so that she barely noticed Derek reach for her hand as he pushed the door to her building open and handed the key back to her. She knew what he expected, and up until now she expected it, too. It was the one step she could take to prove to herself that she was over Jack.

Now, her mind filled with thoughts of him, she knew otherwise.

They climbed the stairs, and she unlocked the door to her apartment. Instead of going in with Derek following, she crossed the threshold and turned to him. "Derek...I'm sorry. I'm going to say good night."

His surprise showed on his face. "Good night? Come on, Alicia. What is this, a joke? You're actually saying I can't come in?"

"If you come in you won't leave until the morning."

He leered at her, and she found it repulsive. "Yeah, and what's wrong with that? That's the usual routine, isn't it? I know you're packing up your stuff, but isn't it just clothes and electronics? You said Pete and Rhonda are taking over your apartment furnished and are putting their things in her parents' basement."

"It isn't just that I've got some boxes scattered all over the place. It's much more than that. I can't explain it. I'm sorry, Derek. I can't do this, not tonight. Maybe not ever again."

He opened his mouth to object, then shut it and shrugged. "If you say so. I don't want you to do anything you don't want to. It's always been something we both wanted."

"Yes, it was."

"I think I know the problem. There's only one reason why you don't want to be with me. It's because you want to be with someone else. I'll bet I know who he is, too." Derek winked at her. "Go to him, Alicia." He bent and kissed her cheek. "Good night…and good luck."

She closed the door behind him and leaned against it, her eyes shut tightly. She didn't understand what was happening to her.

She only knew that Derek was right; it had everything to do with Jack.

Chapter 37

The Long and Winding Road

Saturday morning Alicia woke up and knew what she had to do. She walked over to Eighty-Seventh and Ninth Avenue, where she'd parked her car, and got in, heading north on the West Side Highway. She crossed into Connecticut on the Hutchinson River Parkway.

As she approached Stamford she began to experience misgivings. What if Jack wasn't home? Worse, what if he was entertaining female company overnight? It had been weeks since they broke up. She couldn't just show up on his doorstep and say, "I'm here!" Besides, in spite of the directions she'd printed out on the Internet she wasn't sure she could find his condo. Best to call ahead.

If he didn't want to see her she could simply turn around and drive back to the city, or keep going until she reached Green's Farms.

Her house hunting hadn't been successful; everything she saw that she liked she couldn't afford. She decided to move into her parents' home until she knew for sure where she would settle. Daphne, Todd and little Fletch lived there now as well, and she knew Daphne wasn't happy about her decision, but Alicia knew she had a right to stay in the house she owned fifty percent of. Besides, she didn't want to hold up Pete and Rhonda, who were anxious to take over her apartment and the low rent that came with it. If Jack didn't want to see her she would leave New York and make a new start somewhere new. She would still retain ownership of the court stenography business, and Shannon could always hire someone to take her workload. Maybe she'd start a new one someplace.

She pulled over in a strip mall and haltingly dialed his number. The time had come to find out her destiny.

Jack planned to get in a few games of racquetball this morning, before the rain that had been predicted began to fall. The racquetball court was indoors, but he didn't feel like going outside in a cold March rain. Days like this were meant for lounging, or in his case, work. His creative side always thrived in inclement weather.

He had just grabbed his car keys when his phone began to ring. He hesitated for a moment, then realized it might be his parents or siblings calling with something important. He went to the phone. "Hello."

"Hello, Dev."

His jaw went slack. Only one person called him that. "Alicia." He closed his eyes, savoring her name on his tongue. "Where are you?"

"I'm here, in Stamford. I had this overpowering urge to see you, Jack."

"Tell me where you are. I'll be right there."

He drove like a madman to the strip mall she named. He didn't know what had brought her here, but it could only be a good sign. He knew her well enough to know how difficult it was for her to reach out.

He spotted her car from the corner, but a traffic light prevented him from proceeding right away. He impatiently tapped on the steering wheel of his Aviator as he waited for the light to change.

Alicia saw him approach and got out of her car. Jack careened into the parking lot like a man driving under the influence, braking the Aviator to a jerky stop just a few feet away from her Solara. She simply stood looking at him for several seconds, then ran to him.

Jack held her to him, pressing his cheek to hers. He didn't care if anyone watched them embrace. He knew from the way she ran into his arms that she was there to stay.

She pulled back a little so she could see his face. "You were right, Jack," she said. "I was being childish. I haven't been right since you left. I keep feeling like something was missing, and it was. You."

Suddenly he could stand it no longer. He kissed her, hungrily, right there in broad daylight on one of Stamford's busiest avenues.

"I went to therapy," she managed to say when he tore his lips away from hers. "I talked to someone who knew my parents and knew what happened that night. And I'm moving into my parents' house. Daphne might live there, but I have a right to live there, too."

"It sounds like you've accepted your past without giving up on who you are."

"Oh, I am." Then she cupped his cheeks with her palms and said the words he thought he'd never hear.

"Jack…I need you."

Chapter 38

When I'm Sixty-Four
Docena, Alabama
One year later

" 'Til *death* do us part," Alicia repeated. Her emphasis on the word "death" made their guests chuckle. She wanted to remind Jack that they would be together the rest of their lives, grow old together…and that he'd better not even think about leaving her. He'd walked out on her once. She'd see to it that he'd never do it again.

A few minutes later they sealed their vows with a kiss to raucous applause. All of Jack's nieces and nephews were present, with the youngest two serving as flower girl and ring bearer. Jack suggested that little Fletch fill the latter role, but Alicia pointed out that at not yet four he was still a little young to handle the spotlight. Besides, she said, the logistics wouldn't work. She and Jack decided to be married in the small church in Jack's hometown, where his family had worshipped for generations. Alicia attended services there on her first trip to Docena with Jack and immediately fell in love with the well-tended country church with huge oak trees on both sides and a cemetery containing the graves of former parishioners about twenty yards away. She knew that Daphne would never consent to traveling to Alabama, which she regarded as a totally unsophisticated place. Besides, Daphne was now five months pregnant with her second child, which gave her an ideal excuse for skipping the festivities.

Alicia hadn't even been upset when Martha confided that Daphne commented, "Who the hell takes a dog on a honeymoon?" It sounded like such a typical Daphne observation.

It delighted Alicia to be part of a family again. Because she had moved back to the family home she and Daphne did see each other, but they had little to say, behaving mostly like polite neighbors. Alicia spent most of her time with Jack in his condo in Stamford, and when they returned from their leisurely cross-country drive that would be their honeymoon she would officially move in.

They wouldn't leave on their trip until Monday morning, after rush hour ended. They wanted to spend the next day enjoying their guests. Her new sisters-in-law, Felice and Donna, were holding a brunch tomorrow for the family and close friends that would probably last into the afternoon. Monday they would say goodbye to Jack's parents, pick up Lucky, who stayed with them and had made friends with their pet Dachshund, and hit the road from there.

The ceremony over, the newly married couple stood in the back of the church to receive their guests. They had done away with the customary bride's guests on the left and groom's guests on the right because the majority of the guests had been invited by the Devlin family.

Alicia did feel fairly well represented. Most of the people who counted the most in her life had booked travel to Birmingham, staying at the Wyndham Tutweiler Hotel, where the reception would be held. One by one she greeted the guests, many of whom she met for the first time. She graciously accepted their good wishes and thanked those who told her she made a beautiful bride. She wore a simple sleeveless white chiffon dress and white sandals, with a short veil, in line with her nature of not liking anything fussy. But she was happiest when she saw familiar faces: Her good friend Jenny Walters, Shannon and her new lawyer boyfriend, Pete and Rhonda, who'd left their nearly year-old son in the care of his grandparents, and most of all, the entire Lewis family.

She cried happy tears as she embraced Martha and Marvin. "I can't tell you how happy I am to see all of you," she said. "If there was anyone I wanted to be here in that first pew, it was you." Their son Tyrone, a recent high school graduate about to begin his freshman year at U. Conn, pretended not to notice the stares of the teenage girls in attendance, while Melody, just promoted to senior, seemed transfixed by it all, probably imagining her own future wedding day.

Martha and Marvin had remained at the guest house in Green's Farms, and Martha continued her role as cook and chief housekeeper. Daphne hadn't made life as difficult for Martha as Alicia feared she might, perhaps motivated by the prospect of having to reach into her own pocket to pay the property taxes. Martha reported that it wasn't the pleasantest working environment she'd ever had, but it was bearable. But already she and Marvin had discussed moving on. Marvin had spoken to the corporate office about relocating to the Mid-Atlantic area, perhaps Delaware or Pennsylvania, after Melody finished high school next year. Melody planned to attend U. Conn with her brother Tyrone, and Martha didn't want to be too far away from them. "But it's time for Marvin and I to live in a house of our own, preferably in an area where we can see ourselves living the rest of our lives. Because of your parents' kindness to us, we're pretty well fixed."

"I'm happy for you, Martha."

While the reception went on around them with old school music and dancing, the newlyweds, who had no bridal party and skipped the traditional dais, found themselves sitting alone at their table. The other occupants, Jack's parents, Pete and Rhonda, and the Lewis family, were all dancing. Jack leaned over and said, "Where do you see us five years from now, Alicia?"

She thought for a few moments. "Five years from

now. By then you'll probably be a VP, and we would have sold the condo and bought a house. I'll probably be tired of trying to hide the fact that I don't live in my apartment anymore, so I see myself giving it up and letting the landlord charge a new tenant the market rate. I'm sure I'll still be part owner of the stenography service with Shannon. I see us driving out to visit Pete and Rhonda, wherever they decide to settle down." The Robinsons, still living in Alicia's Upper West Side studio with their small son, had begun house hunting throughout the greater metropolitan area and hoped to be moved in by the holidays.

He kissed the back of her hand. "I don't know about that part about my making VP, but I appreciate your optimism. Anything else?"

"Let's see…I want to get down here at least once a year to visit the family, maybe start a tradition of having your family up to Connecticut for Christmas. It's so beautiful there in the cold and the snow. And I want to see Martha, wherever she and Marvin end up. She's my true sister, Jack."

"I agree. Anything else?"

She looked at him, instinct telling her he was hinting at something but not knowing exactly what. "Like what?"

"Do you think there'll be more than just two of us living in that house you're so sure we'll have?"

She broke into a grin. "Of course, Jack. I think of us starting a family well before five years from now. I think it's great how Pete and Rhonda took time for themselves before starting a family, but you and I don't have that luxury. I'll be thirty-seven in December, and you'll be thirty-nine. We don't want to be too old to play with our kids."

"I'm looking forward to having fun with little Ben."

Her eyes misted. "What was that?"

"If we have a boy, I always assumed you'd want to name him Benjamin, after your father."

"I did think about it," she said, "but it seemed premature to mention it. Would you really be willing to do that for me, Jack?"

"He was your father, Alicia. He loved you as much as I do. I can be as jealous as the next guy, I guess, but not of him. I know that if it wasn't for him you and I might not be sitting here as husband and wife."

She nodded. "I think you're right, Jack."

He kissed the back of her hand. "Don't go getting morose on me. A good life awaits us, Alicia." He looked out of the window at the sunny, clear day. "I'm glad we got married in the spring. It was spring when I got that first quick glimpse of you."

"Dozens of springs, summers, falls, and winters. And I'll be with you through every one of them."

He leaned in for a quick kiss, and even with their eyes closed they saw the flash of camera bulbs going off. They broke apart and smiled wide for the cameras that captured the moment for posterity.

Alicia blinked away happy tears. She hadn't expected to see everyone at her in-law's home. She and Jack said good-bye yesterday afternoon when they left his sister Donna's house, the site of their brunch. They'd all surprised her and Jack by being there when they made their last stop before getting on the road. Alicia didn't even mind saying goodbye to everyone a second time. She would never be afraid to feel love for anyone again.

Daphne might have called her "an orphaned little nobody," but that name had no truth to it. She'd been born to parents who loved her, despite their youth and poverty. Her father worked hard for them and had been willing to fight for them. Her mother, perhaps a little frustrated and feeling life would pass her by, nonetheless died out of a wish to protect her.

Alicia might have had a miserable childhood in foster care. Instead she'd been adopted by a well-to-do couple who'd sought her out and given her every advantage. Being born was great, but being chosen was every bit as special. So what if her new father went a little overboard in his enthusiasm when a natural child was born to them three years later? He'd loved her in his own way.

And then there was her dear new mother, Caroline, who always looked out for her best interests, to the point of arguing with the husband she adored.

Alicia's eyes grew misty. She'd been more fortunate than most. Her parents were all gone now, and she had little to do with her so-called sister, but she had Martha and her longtime friends. And she had Jack…her husband.

With his help, she'd met her memories head-on, had triumphed, and now she'd became a member of a large, loving family. The children she and Jack would have would know where they came from and feel part of something. She could practically feel the love as she hugged each person goodbye.

She turned back to look at them all and wave, her

hand high as Jack drove away, one hand resting on the back of Lucky's head. The dog, his upper body resting on the center console, made a whining sound in his throat, indicating contentment.

"Attaboy, Lucky," she said. "Daphne might think it's ridiculous to bring you with us on our honeymoon, but I'd never want to drive cross country without you."

"Good thing he doesn't get car sick," Jack quipped. He took his eyes off the road for a second to smile at her. The dark eyes were covered by sunglasses, as were her own, but she knew what expression they held.

Love.

Alicia closed her eyes to enjoy the feel of the wind on her face. That orphaned little nobody had become one lucky woman. She now set off with her new husband and their dog on a cross country trip with three long weeks to see the sights. Jack had been right when he predicted that a great life awaited them.

Her parents would be so happy for her.

All four of them.

He opened the champagne with a loud pop, then poured two glasses' worth. He raised his glass to her. "Happy birthday, Alicia."

"Happy birthday, Jack."

They clicked glasses and sipped, their eyes never leaving each other's face. "Funny," she whispered. "All of a sudden I'm not hungry anymore."

"I am, but not for chocolate cake." He leaned in close, and she closed her eyes expectantly, only to be surprised when he pressed his lips to her forehead.

He pulled back, looked into her eyes, and leaned forward again, this time diverting at the last minute and kissing her chin. She held her breath as he pulled back twice more, pressing his lips to each of her cheeks. Excitement built up in her like a rapid snowfall. She wanted to scream at him to kiss her....

Every smart woman needs a plan!

DOWN AND OUT IN
FLAMINGO
Beach

National bestselling author
MARCIA KING-GAMBLE

Joya Hamilton-Abrahams's plan was simple: make a
short visit to Flamingo Beach to give her ailing granny's
failing quilt shop a makeover—then hightail it back to
L.A. and civilization. Settling down in the small town was
never on her agenda...but neither was falling for hunky
construction worker Derek Morse.

Available the first week of May wherever books are sold.

KIMANI™
ROMANCE

www.kimanipress.com   KPMKG0160507

You can't hide from desire...

A GUILTY AFFAIR

National bestselling author

Maureen Smith

Journalist Riley Kane has long suspected that the death of her fiancé—a San Antonio police officer—was not a simple accident. So she reluctantly enlists the aid of his former partner, Noah Roarke. But the sizzling desire surging between Riley and Noah fills them each with incredible longing...and unbelievable guilt.

Available the first week of May wherever books are sold.

KIMANI™
ROMANCE

www.kimanipress.com   KPMS0170507

He loved a challenge...and she danced
to the beat of a different drum.

Enchanting
MELODY

National bestselling author
ROBYN AMOS

Escaping poverty had driven Will Coleman to succeed on
Wall Street, but in his spare time he taught ballroom dancing.
Then into his dance studio walked Melody Rush, a feisty
society beauty who enjoyed the freedom of slumming.
And the enchanting dance of love began....

Available the first week of May wherever books are sold.

KIMANI™
ROMANCE

www.kimanipress.com   KPRA0180507

Sinfully delicious and hard to resist...

Can't Stop
LOVING
You

Favorite author

LISA HARRISON JACKSON

Kaycee Jordan's new neighbor, pro athlete turned café
owner Kendrick Thompson, was as irresistible as the
mouthwatering desserts she created. When he agreed to
help build her bakery business, days of work gave way
to nights of luscious pleasure...until their relationship
caused a rift between their families.

Available the first week of May wherever books are sold.

KIMANI™
ROMANCE

www.kimanipress.com   KPLHJ0190507

Celebrating life every step of the way.

YOU ONLY GET *Better*

New York Times bestselling author
CONNIE BRISCOE
and
Essence bestselling authors
LOLITA FILES
ANITA BUNKLEY

Three fortysomething women discover that life, men and
everything else get better with age in this entertaining
three-in-one anthology from three award-winning authors!

Available the first week of March wherever books are sold.

KIMANI PRESS™
www.kimanipress.com

A soul-stirring, compelling
journey of self-discovery...

journey
into My Brother's Soul

Maria D. Dowd

Bestselling author of
Journey to Empowerment

A memorable collection of essays, prose and poetry,
reflecting the varied experiences that men of color face
throughout life. Touching on every facet of living—love,
marriage, fatherhood, family—these candid personal
contributions explore the essence of what it means to
be a man today.

**"*Journey to Empowerment* will lead you on a
healing journey and will lead to a great love of self,
and a deeper understanding of the many roles we
all must play in life."—*Rawsistaz Reviewers***

Coming the first week of May
wherever books are sold.